MW00818067

PRAISE FOR *CHASING MONEY*

Winner — 2023 Best Indie Book Award — Crime Thriller

"Gritty descriptions, simmering threats, and a wry sense of humor contribute to a countdown to disaster. Exceptionally clever and compelling."
—D. Donovan, Senior Reviewer, *Midwest Book Review*

"You can't help but be impressed with Balter's fluid blending of historical facts with fiction to create a tale that maintains the suspense from start to finish. *Chasing Money* is an impressive debut novel by a gifted author."
—Awarded Five Stars; Essien Asian, Readers Favorite

"A strong voice paired with authentic dialogue …. Packed with action."
—The BookLife Prize

"A heart-pounding thriller that grabs you from the first page and won't let you get away!"
—Michael Lindley, author of the Amazon #1 *Hanna* and *Alex Low Country* mystery series

"The DaVinci Code for grownups. Balter treats his readers to a smart, tightly woven tale of greed, deception, and treachery in the worlds of art forgery and high finance. Tinged with noir and ringing with authenticity. Don't miss this impressive debut novel!"
—Warren C. Easley, author of the award-winning *Cal Claxton Mysteries*

"Readers will enjoy hunting for clues right alongside Bo and Marty, and they'll be entertained by all the dangerous, unexpected scenarios they get themselves into. A simple but satisfying crime novel that will keep readers hooked."
—Kirkus Reviews

"With crisp dialogue and tightly packed scenes, Balter tells an intense and nearly tragic tale with splashes of dark humor, an intriguing supporting cast, and a real-life art mystery."
—Steve Anderson, author of the *Kaspar Brothers* series and other novels

"Balter's acerbic wit, clear writing style, and extensive knowledge of art history make this a captivating read that you won't want to put down. Enjoy the thrilling ride of *Chasing Money*!"
—John Wemlinger, author of *The Cut*, a 2022 Michigan Notable Book

"Balter has crafted a page-turning crime novel that conjures dread as the characters are drawn deeper and deeper into danger. Each chapter takes these hapless men into a progressively more deadly game that they don't understand until the very end. It is a fantastic first novel."
—J.R.Seeger, author of the *MIKE4* series of military thrillers

"*Chasing Money* is a rollercoaster of a ride. It's wildly inventive and incredibly entertaining. A thriller with a flawed lead character. I couldn't put it down."
—Charles Cutter, author of the acclaimed *Burr Lafayette* legal thrillers

CHASING MONEY

Mission Point Press
2554 Chandler Road
Traverse City, Michigan 49696
www.MissionPointPress.com
231-421-9513

Design by Sarah Meiers

Printed in the United States of America

ISBN hardcover: 978-1-958363-95-9
ISBN softcover: 978-1-958363-96-6
Library of Congress Control Number: 2023908477

CHASING MONEY

A MARTY AND BO THRILLER

MICHAEL BALTER

MISSION POINT PRESS

To My Mother, Helga.

A woman of great character and courage

CHAPTER ONE

Monday Evening

The Pitch Meeting

THERE'S A LINE IN A COUNTRY SONG THAT GOES, "Chase after the dream, don't chase after the money."

Well, I'm here to tell you that's wrong.

Fuck the dream.

Chase the money.

Always chase the money.

It's what Bo Bishop and I have been doing, in one form or another, for several years now. Raising capital, building runway, stalking angels, bootstrapping, are all the same thing; convincing someone kind, generous, greedy, or stupid to fund your ambition to become rich. The trick here is not to find someone with money but rather to find someone with throw-away money or someone who wants to make throw-away money, also called an angel investor.

Raising capital is a trial for every entrepreneur. There are outliers who manage to bag investor money as if it were a pizza delivery because they have the genius, credentials, or connections to underwrite their venture. For most of us, however, it's an endless, soul-destroying process of begging the privileged to keep the doors open while the world works hard to keep them shut.

That's how Bo and I came to be in a shabby little wood cabin about 20 miles west of Mt. Hood, strapped to cheap chrome kitchen chairs, our hands taped behind our backs and our ankles taped to the chair legs. We were terrified and tractable. Nico, our silent partner (and the reason for everything that happened), was there as well, one of the rare times he elected to join us on a potential investor pitch. His hands and feet were taped like Bo's and mine.

The chairs sat side by side on top of a blue painter's tarp rolled out over the cabin's wood floor. It was a fishing cabin, purposely not fancy, with a slight smell of wet tent. A couple of antler mounts hung on paneled walls between a mounted shotgun and two old fishing rods, crossed like swords. A faded US flag was nailed to the stone fireplace. Much of the Sears catalog furniture had been moved about to make room for the tarp and the chairs.

A bald beefy guy with more fat than muscle stood over us. His fleshy tattooed fingers fiddled with a large roll of black Gorilla tape he'd used to strap us down. It must have been a tough job, tying our hands and feet, because he was breathing heavily through his mouth, and his face, a boxer's face with a nose that had seen more than its share of punishment, was shiny with sweat.

Another big guy, with more muscle than fat, dark oily hair, squinty eyes, and a stern face, stood a couple of feet back, waving a Beretta 9mm like a baton. Not that I knew it was a Beretta 9mm. That came later.

"Jesus Christ," Nico cried for the third time after the fat guy finished taping him to the chair.

In response to Nico, the guy holding the Beretta barked back, in a thick Irish brogue, "Shut it!" and then, "One more word and this baby goes off in the mouth that speaks!" He shook the 9mm in case we didn't understand what "this baby" referenced. He took a giant step back as he spoke, moving past what I guessed he calculated was the periphery of any potential blood spatter. I couldn't take my eyes off him or the gun.

We were in serious trouble, and none of us knew why. This disconnect, the complete detachment of the why from the what, caused our panic. Tied to that chair, I fixated on breathing evenly and squeezing my bladder. Oddly, at that moment, the possibility of being shot by a stranger in a dingy cabin for an unknown reason carried a lower priority with me than the embarrassment of possibly pissing myself.

We'd tumbled into this mess by driving to Rhododendron, a touristy village located halfway up Mt. Hood. We'd been led to believe we would meet with an interested venture capitalist from out of town. On our first and only phone call, the investor told me he was renting a cabin for the week and was looking to get some quick business done between trout fishing excursions. Bo and I figured he was a small fund manager looking for a way to write off the expense of a fly-fishing trip to Oregon. He'd been cryptic on the phone, but that was not unusual for private equity guys who get tagged regularly by scroungers like us looking for money.

The wood floor creaked as the fat guy shifted his weight and stretched out his right knee. Then, blessedly, the screen door behind us opened and slammed shut, breaking the silence with the same loud clap made by screen doors in cabins everywhere. Another guy, slim but sturdy, walked in and stood in front of us. He leaned slightly forward like he was battling a headwind. His appearance rattled me even further. His face was too immature for the rest of him. He looked like a teenager trying on his father's clothes: black cashmere sports jacket, faded clean jeans, crisp white shirt, big watch, nice shoes. He looked exactly like someone we expected to meet, expected to pitch our investor deck to, but much younger. And we wouldn't be bound to chairs.

He scanned us with dark, dead eyes and a chilling calm like he was examining a fast-food menu. I couldn't look at him directly. His mannequin-like face oozed malice, so instead, I focused on the resolute Irishman with the Beretta, watching it swing ever so slightly.

After a cruel minute of continuing the oppressive silence, the new guy took a deep breath and said, "Thank you for coming," at which point the Irishman dropped his hand to his side, aiming the 9mm at the floor.

I thought I'd pass out.

Nico gulped air and was about to expel a torrent of words, but the new guy pointed a finger at him, so Nico held his breath and said nothing.

"Let me tell you how this is gonna go," he said in a strong Russian accent, which I immediately recognized as the voice that had set up the meeting with me a couple of days earlier. "I'm sure we can talk for hours, become friends, share stories about the wife and kids." He paused. "But we're not gonna do that. You understand?"

Nico couldn't hold back. "What are you doing? You're making a terrible mistake. This is fucking crazy!" he screamed in a high-pitched fire alarm shrill, but the new guy pointed his finger at him again, and Nico went quiet.

"Screaming is not valuable at time like this," he said calmly. "It distracts me. It distracts you too." His forefinger wagged at us. "We can all scream at each other. You scream at me. I scream back at you. We never accomplish anything. What is important is that we all focus. Focus is the key to a successful talk. If we lose our focus, it never ends well. You understand?" His tone was surprisingly pleasant, almost polite, like a tour guide dispensing directions. His accent played like background music to his very understandable English.

"I don't waste my time," he continued. "The rules for not wasting time are simple. I ask questions. You answer questions. First think—then speak."

His delivery was so effortless I was convinced he was reciting from a rehearsed script.

"You tell me I make mistake." He looked at Nico with a menacing smirk. "You think maybe I'm stupid?"

Nico opened his mouth, but the Russian pointed his finger into the air, and Nico only emptied his lungs. "I don't make mistake, *mudak*. You think we all in this shithole cabin on a hunch? You think maybe you're here by accident?" He paused. I wondered if he'd practiced his lines among the pines outside the cabin while his two skeefer buddies had prepped us to be his audience.

I kept clenching my bladder.

"You know what I learned in my life?" the Russian asked soberly. "I learned that every *mudak* I'm about to end becomes a yapper. Like a barking dog when the doorbell rings." He looked down at the wood floor; his shoes were on the edge of the blue tarp. He was off script now, contemplating what to say next.

"It's fear. Adrenalin makes your mouth move. You understand?"

The "you understand" was a verbal tick for which he never expected a response.

For a moment, he stopped, his attention diverted to a small burr hanging about halfway up the sleeve of his sports jacket, probably picked up while walking through the forest. He gently picked it off and flicked it to the ground. His eyes followed its flight as the tiny pod skidded along the wooden floor and came to rest against the blue tarp. In those few seconds, he was completely absorbed, as if alone in front of a mirror. If I'd not been tied to the chair, my knees would have folded, and I'd have fallen over.

"I know you want to make an introduction with me. Have a nice talk. Like I meet you in a bar. Like a blind date. But it's not a date." His sniper-like eyes studied us.

He pushed out his forefinger. "Question." Then his middle finger. "Answer. You understand?" He paused. "Where's my friend's money?" He looked directly at Nico.

"What money?" said Bo without hesitation.

The Russian was inches from Bo's face in a second. "Now, I didn't ask you, did I? I asked Nico."

He knew Nico's name. How was that possible? This meeting was for Bo and me to pitch our company, and Nico had decided to join us at the last minute. The Russian couldn't have known Nico was coming because we didn't know he was coming. There weren't any introductions when we knocked on the cabin door and were abruptly confronted by the Irishman, pointing his Beretta at our heads and frog-marching us into the cabin where the fat man taped us to the chairs.

"But it is good. We are making progress. Yes?" The Russian stepped back but now stayed focused on Bo. "I like to make progress. 'What money?'" he mimicked. "Short, no bullshit, Bo, you understand the rules. You and I can talk."

He said Bo's name like he'd known him for years. Then he repeated, "My friend's money. You know…my friend. He paid you a lot of money. You took his money. I think maybe you stole his money. You understand? That money."

"What are you talking about?" cried Nico jutting forward a little. "Jesus Christ, we don't have any money. We came here to get money. Maybe from you, maybe not. We're just business guys looking for investors. You said you were an investor, and we came here to tell you about…"

"Stop! Stop!" the Russian barked, boosting his voice above Nico's and moving within inches of his face. "The problem here, *mudak*, your boss," he pointed at Bo, "got the rules right away, and you, you *pizda*, you didn't."

The Russian was in full shout now. "We're just business guys looking for investors," he aped. "That's bullshit! You want to fill the air with lies like confetti at Mardi Gras. I can smell the crap on you," he sniffed the air. "You stink of it. Let me tell you what the truth is. Truth is, you are a thief. You are all thieves. You think maybe it's easy to rob a rich man? You think maybe he won't miss it; just ignore it? He's so rich he forgives your theft? But you're wrong."

He scowled at Nico. "Maybe it's better I don't ask you any questions. You piss me off every time you open your word hole." He made the hand-puppet gesture. "Maybe you keep it shut."

"Oh, Jesus God!" I whimpered, conceding that my bladder would give out any second now. "I need to piss."

The Russian moved over to me and pressed his foul young face two inches from mine.

"What you say?"

I could tell he'd sucked a breath mint recently.

"I need to piss," I whispered, closing my eyes.

"Why tell me? You want me to take you to toilet? Maybe hold your dick while we gossip about these two?" He took a step back. "Stop pretending you don't know anything. I know everything already. I do my research. I read your website." He gestured with his hands like he was opening a book. "Paladin, big-time start-up... the next Amazon. I look at the team photos." He pointed at Bo, "Chairman," then at me, "President," then at Nico, "and you are," he paused, "you are Business Development Director." He smiled directly at Nico, who had gone colorless but had a look in his eyes like he was figuring something out.

"So, what is a Business Development Director? What a fancy title you have. You like fancy titles? Ok, I give me a fancy title too." He pretended to think. He was back on script, comfortable with what he wanted to say next. "I am Chief Revenue Officer. I am C-R-O. I'm responsible for the money. I bring in the money. I am here to collect the money. Now I speak your language. You understand?"

Nico started to shake his head but couldn't talk. He looked like he would vomit the moment his mouth opened, but I could see something was entering his eyes, a flicker of recognition; an idea was emerging. His fear no longer came from the unknown but from a notion forming in his brain.

"I am C-R-O. You tell me about the money," persisted the Russian, leaning forward into Bo.

Silence. The Russian let it linger. I realized then that he was purposely obscure. Dangling opaque questions in front of us amused him. He wasn't just interested in getting answers; he deliberately wanted to prolong our agony. He aimed to penetrate our psyche and scar our souls, and he'd succeeded. Then he broke the silence.

"And the painting," the Russian said softly, like it was an after-thought. He stared directly at Bo, but I looked at Nico, whose eyes widened; his burgeoning epiphany suddenly confirmed.

"Holy shit, shit, shit!" screeched Nico, chugging air. "The painting? The damn painting? Are you fucking crazy? You got the painting!" He started thrashing in his chair. The pitch of his voice climbed a full scale while fear collided with panic. He knew what was happening.

"What are you talking about?" barked Bo, all our attention on Nico now.

The Russian moved quickly, grabbing Nico's hair in a painful grip. He turned to the Irishman and jutted out his other hand, pulling Nico's head forward so the back of his chair came off the tarp.

"Give me that thing," yelled the Russian, and the Irishman transferred the Beretta with both hands. "I am sick of you. *Poshel na khuy!* I'm crazy!" He paused, breathing heavily. "You open your ugly mouth again, and I shove *moy-pushka* down your throat. You understand?" He pushed the barrel of the Beretta against Nico's blanched lips. "Tell me I'm crazy again, *mudak*. Come on! Open your corrupt mouth, you piece of shit! Say one more thing, and I will blow your ugly head off. You understand?" The Russian's rage was instant and fierce. He'd thrown away the script. He stepped away from Nico and screamed at all of us.

"You think I don't know what I'm talking about? I am idiot? Like I have nothing to do but come to fucking Oregon and deal with you assholes!" Even with his accent, he pronounced Oregon like a tourist—Ori-gone.

He wagged the 9mm. "You see this? Its name is Crazy. Say hello to Crazy." Looking at the Irishman, he waved the Beretta over his head. "You think Crazy should say a few words?"

The Irishman scowled and leveled his eyes on the raving psychopath but conveyed no fear or alarm. The fat man, on the other hand, looked as terrified as the rest of us.

Then the Russian turned abruptly and moved closer to Bo. He'd somehow decided that Bo was his target, his Huckleberry, the guy he could *talk* to.

He nodded his head at Nico. "He's a barker. He fills the air with noise, bow-wow-wow!" Then his voice abruptly calmed. "I want to talk to the man who holds his leash." He stopped and breathed. "My friend's money and painting. Stop pretending you don't know what I am talking about. Like you steal ten million all the time. Like you're a big thief selling bad paintings to rich suckers every week, and now you have to remember exactly which deal it was."

Bo's lips disappeared into a tight grimace.

"Start with the ten million. All of it. How do I get it back? Then the painting. Where it is."

We all waited for Bo to say something.

But it was Nico who spoke first. "Jesus Christ! You maniac! You have the painting. You have it! The money is gone. It's a done deal. Done months ago! It was all legit." Nico never stopped to breathe. "Someone's lying to you. Did that bitch cheat you? Did she steal the painting?"

The Russian raised the Beretta in Nico's direction.

Nico kept blasting out words like machine-gun fire. "Listen to me, goddamn it! Listen to me! It's not what you think. It's messed up. You've been lied to. The painting—"

"Shut the fu—"

The sound from the 9mm was thunderous. Much louder than I would have expected. Nico's head jolted sideways, then bounced forward and hung there like he'd fallen asleep. Blood and brain matter splattered onto the blue tarp behind him. My bladder let go. I felt the warm piss immediately. My eyes teared up. This was it.

This was how I would die.

CHAPTER TWO

Earlier That Morning

Abbie

WELL....

Although I did not, in fact, die, frankly, getting the piss scared out of me by a demented thug in a seedy cabin in the tall timbers of Mt. Hood was actually an escalation of what was already a colossally shitty day. It had started that morning when my wife Abbie surprised me as I stepped out of the shower, appearing out of nowhere to present me with a dry towel and a warning.

"This isn't working for me," were her exact words.

"What's not working for you, Hon?" I responded, patting down.

"I'm done."

"Done with what?" I was slow to pick up her tone and continued to towel off.

"All of it, Martin. Done with all of it. The company. The debt. The maxed-out credit cards. The collection calls. Negotiating with the bank. The lying, the pretending. Done. Done!"

"Can we have this talk after I put on pants?"

She narrowed her eyes at me, then turned and left.

I shaved quickly and avoided eye contact with the mirror. I knew what was coming and prepped my face to hide any guilt. My face has always been adept at hiding things. When I was a kid, it had the look of an immigrant; skinny, pallid, aquiline nose, determined denim-colored eyes, pale blond hair. Now, many years later, my face has Americanized. It is fuller, pulpy, less angular. My eyes are wearier, and my hair, now brown without a hint of grey, allows me to look ten years younger. I have a face for poker; bland is my specialty.

By the time I got downstairs, Abbie was out taking Boomer for his morning constitutional. I distracted myself by casually cleaning up the breakfast dishes left by our children, Andrew and Alison, pre-teens utterly incapable of cleaning up after themselves. I moved around the table, harvesting bacon fragments while guzzling strong coffee. The kids had already left for school, carpooling with a neighbor. Parents on our street took scheduled turns ferrying kids to and from school. God forbid they should take the bus.

Boomer is our retriever; beautiful, devoted, and courtly, his winter coat was starting to come in the color of whisky. Taking direct aim at my bacon-scented hand, he bounded toward me when he and Abbie returned.

"Hey, Boomer, buddy." He licked bacon residue from my palm.

Marching into the kitchen behind him came my wife, Abigail Elizabeth Schott, with her face radiating pique. Dressed in jogging clothes, she was always, and still is, in marvelous shape, not just because she works at it but because she gets abundant help from a benevolent genetic structure. She had the fresh smell of morning air, and I remember admiring her innate toughness and poise. Her face is naturally beautiful, fashioned by soft lines and rounded edges seemingly immune to time. Her mouth has a gentle downward arc giving her a slight sadness in keeping with her character. In direct sunlight, her grey eyes reflect a soft blue and brandish such intimidating energy that I had trouble meeting them when I first met her twenty years ago. It's still true today. She will squint them slightly when she pays you rapt attention, which is always unsettling. Her thick mahogany hair, pulled back that morning into a loose ponytail, has a brilliant and permanent sheen, which she believes is her best feature. I think she doesn't give enough credit to her eyes.

She was angry with me and had been for a long time. "Why today, Abbie? Why are you done today?" I asked.

"What?"

"It's Monday morning. I need to go to work. You had all day yesterday, Sunday, to talk about this. Why are you hitting me with this now—today?"

"Because I didn't want to spend all Sunday going round and round again. We've done this too many times. I'm just tired, and I'm telling you this morning because we don't have the time to fight over it."

"Jesus, Abbie, fight over what?"

"My credit card was declined getting gas Friday."

There it was, the last straw.

"I had to use the debit card. There'll be another overdraft notice today and another $34 penalty charge on a $56 fill-up. I didn't have the cash in my wallet. It was the damn Shell station on Boones Ferry. I know the owner. I hang out with his wife. His daughter is on Ali's soccer team."

"I'm sorry, Hon." I quickly pulled five twenties from my wallet as if at gunpoint and handed them to her. "I'll try to get an advance this morning to tide us over. We're meeting with investors all the time. We're seeing one later this afternoon near Mt Hood. More importantly, we have a big meeting Wednesday morning with a guy prepared to write a check."

"Will you get any back pay?" she asked flatly, "or just a salary check?" She referred to the fact that Bo and I always paid ourselves last, and when we ran short, we'd record it as debt on the company books. On paper, the company owed us a lot of money.

"If he invests, I'll get a paycheck, just like I've been getting the last five months since Nico put in his money." I didn't tell her that investors rarely approve the payment of back wages; they want their money to fund the company's growth, not pay back entrepreneurs who already have their equity. Any chance that I would ever recover lost wages was slim to none.

"But you didn't get paid the previous nine months, and your current salary is only about half of what you would earn in a real company." She sighed reflexively. "We're so far underwater your paychecks disappear within a day of deposit. It doesn't matter. We're just delaying the inevitable."

"What's the inevitable, Abbie?"

"We could lose everything."

I rolled my eyes. "You're ridiculous now."

"Martin! Damn it! Listen to yourself! I'm not ridiculous! I'm scared! We might lose our house. We've maxed out every credit card, including our joint card, with a $30,000 credit limit! Our kids are a few weeks away from finding out we're broke. You want to tell them, or should I? You want me to tell them we'll have to move soon, tell them to say goodbye to their friends because Dad broke the family on his way to making us rich?" Her eyes never wavered.

When we were first married, she liked to take the flat of her hand and gently slide it over my back from shoulder to shoulder. She did it unconsciously at random moments while standing together in a movie line, talking to friends in a restaurant, or reading the paper in the kitchen. Then one day, about a year ago, I realized she hadn't done it in many months. It was a subtle change, almost imperceptible, but I knew we had lost something significant between us.

"We've been here before," I said in my worn-down voice. "We've lost everything before. It's not our first time."

"No, Martin! It is our first time! We didn't lose everything before. We didn't accumulate debt so fast and so recklessly. We didn't lose our house. We didn't lose the cars. Nothing impacted the kids. They never knew. They still don't know. Our losses were paper losses. Our stock became worthless. Creditors don't hound you when your stock goes underwater. Nobody cares when you lose your stock fortune. Only you care. We didn't lose everything, Martin. We lost our possibilities; we never lost our spot."

She was right, of course. We'd been living on the rim of financial disaster for several years, and the real problem was that we'd settled there on my choice. Had I gone back to work at any good company, we wouldn't have been in this mess. Abbie's growing disappointment with my entrepreneurial endeavors had crested, and these conversations were happening more frequently.

"I need some time, Abbie. I understand your anger. It's my fault—I know that. I took the risk and stepped out onto the ledge. I knew the danger, but it's temporary. We're getting traction. I'm close."

"Martin," she sighed. "You're not close. You desperately want to be close, so you've convinced yourself you are. Stop trying to fix the company and start fixing the family." She looked directly into my eyes. "Fix us. It's not too late. We can rebuild. We'll cut more corners. If you get a real job with a real company, we can be out of this mess in a year or two. You tried something big and risky, and I admired you for it. I supported you, but it didn't work. The only thing you're close to is filing for bankruptcy."

"Paladin is a real company," I said defensively.

"It's a start-up, Martin. You take a small salary because you're living on investor money, not actual revenue. It's not a real company. It's a pretend company. It's a million dollars short of being real."

I was losing the argument. I'd been losing most of them lately.

Abbie took a deep breath. "If you stay with the company, you can't stay here."

"And there it is," I snapped back.

Her eyes softened, and she looked at me like I'd morphed into a homeless puppy. "Martin, you're right. You stepped out onto the ledge. But you can step back inside. Leave the company. Get a real job."

"I'm committed, Abbie. I can't just walk away. I have investors, employees, and Bo counting on me."

"You keep saying that, but they won't be there for you when it blows up. It's a house of cards." She paused and took a step closer to me. "Martin, you don't commit suicide by stepping onto the ledge…you commit suicide by stepping off."

////////////////////////////////////

So….

That was how that Monday started, and after my confidence was thoroughly throttled, I headed for the office, where my worst day ever continued. Jeff Spalding, our chief counsel, securities attorney, and board secretary, sat nervously on our office couch, holding a folded letter. He was resigning for the same reasons Abbie had just expressed. His new second wife had been watching their nest egg evaporate, and she had applied intense pressure on him to leave. He was tired of sleeping, as he put it, with an ice sculpture.

"I've been offered a position with my old firm," he said. "I can't turn it down. I'd be committing suicide."

There was that word again: suicide.

When top executives leave a start-up, it's always bad news, Company morale, which is continually on life support, can suddenly buckle and break. "Can we position this as a vacation for now?" I asked. "I've got to keep the troops from panicking."

"Yes, of course, whatever you want to announce is fine with me. Only the board needs to know; you and Bo are its only members. The whole thing can stay as quiet as you want it to."

"OK, I need you to leave everything in your office. Don't take out anything personal. Leave the photos and the plaques on the vanity wall. Leave it all in place. I'll tell everyone you're on a leave of absence 'cause somebody in your family died."

"Tell them it was my ex-wife." He smiled.

"I'll have to claw back your equity."

"I already assumed that. I put it all into the resignation letter. I'll keep the shares that have vested."

"Bo and I are seeing an investor this afternoon, some private equity guy, and we've got Finley coming on Wednesday for $500,000. Once that's in the bank, we'll have runway, and I can selectively leak out that you're gone."

"I can still help," he added. "I can work weekends, earn a little more equity."

My place on that ledge became even more precarious. Not telling investors that a company's top executive just resigned was potential fraud.

"Who are you seeing this afternoon?" Jeff asked.

"I don't know," I answered. "Some guy called me on Friday. Said he'd read all about us in that *Oregonian* article a month ago. I didn't think the article was that good, but if it gets us institutional interest, that's great. Said he'd checked us out and wanted to meet with Bo and me."

"Where's he from?"

"Didn't give me a company name, probably so I couldn't google him. Said he represented a private equity firm out of New York that manages a billion-two. Said he's got a hundred-million-dollar SPV to fill in the next six months, and their focus is on technology in education. Then he gave me the address, and I looked it up. It's over an hour's drive towards Mt. Hood near Rhododendron, in the middle of nowhere. He gave me directions. Said he was in Oregon on a fishing trip."

"Lots of good trout fishing around Mt. Hood this time of year. Did he give his name?"

"No. He said we'd make introductions when we got together."

"That's unusual. I'll bet the guy's trying to get his fishing trip expensed by seeing a potential client. He didn't put out his name to avoid random communications. I'll bet his interest is small. You're an expense alibi, not an investment potential."

"Well, it's even more depressing now that you put it that way. He had an accent. East European, maybe Russian."

"Careful, Marty. A lot of Russian money is trying to find a home in American companies. You know what Russia's biggest export is?"

"Oil," I answered.

"No. Dirty money."

"I'll know more when we meet up with him. If he's legit, even if he's just kicking the tires, maybe I can impress him."

In hindsight, I don't think wetting myself impressed him.

CHAPTER THREE

Monday Evening Again

The Deal

THE IRISHMAN THREW HIS ARMS INTO THE AIR like he was surrendering to an advancing army. "Jesus, shit, what you do that for?" he demanded, staring intensely at Nico's slumped head. Pivoting into the Russian's startled face, he said with deliberate emphasis, "What—the—fuck?"

The Russian looked stunned. His soft, callow face contorted as he brandished the Beretta. "I go to shoot the wall to shut him up," he shouted. "I barely touched the trigger…it went off on its own." He kept waving the Beretta, and the Irishman grabbed it from his hand. For a moment, I thought they were about to shoot each other.

"I don't believe this shit!" The Russian continued to flail his arms and holler—I think in Russian—directly at the fat guy, who looked frantic and frightened, still holding the duct tape and inching his way to the door.

"*Feckin eejit*," muttered the Irishman shaking the Beretta like it was a broken toy.

The Russian, his face tinted with a pink flush, fumed, "It's not my gun. I'm not used to it—it's junk."

Bo and I barely breathed.

"You blew out his eye." The Irishman bent over to get a closer look.

"Shut up," snapped the Russian. His teeth scraped the bottom

18

of his lip. He'd regained his composure, and I guessed from his twitching eyes that he was searching his brain for a new strategy and script. A minute, maybe two, passed.

I smelled my urine.

"You owe me ten million and a painting," he said absently.

Bo and I sat silent.

In his last panicked breath, Nico had realized what was happening and might have resolved everything—if "everything" was even resolvable. But sharing that thought would not have been helpful, and our only prayer was to stay quiet and let the psychopath figure things out.

Suddenly and brusquely, the Russian headed for the cabin door and motioned the other two to follow him. Once outside, the three talked rapidly, but I could only hear unintelligible mumbling.

"Holy Christ," whispered Bo looking past me at Nico. "We're dead. They're going to kill us."

"I don't think so," I whispered.

"They killed Nico. They'll kill us."

"Not necessarily," I insisted.

"You think they're just going to warn us not to snitch on them and send us on our way?" he scoffed. Petulance was Bo's fallback position whenever he wanted to win an argument—even this argument.

"They want money and a painting. They think we have it and can get it for them. They need us to do that," I said.

"What money? What painting? We can't get them shit."

"They don't know that," I snapped, glaring hard at him, hoping my words would register. "If they find out we know nothing, they'll kill us for sure. We're witnesses. We've got to convince them we can get them what they want."

"Are you nuts?" Bo twisted his neck to check the door. "Get them what they want? I don't have a clue what they're even talking about."

"Nico knew."

"Nico—can't—help—us!" he said like he was spelling it.

I was about to answer but stopped when the three came marching back in by order of rank—Russian; Irish; fat guy, still holding the freaking tape.

"OK, *debily*," the Russian called out. "We're done here. We lose focus, and bullshit meter will now go into red zone. With no rules, we have *krugovoy ryvok,* you understand, a circle jerk. I want the money and the painting. I don't need to hear you assholes cry you don't know what I am talking about. Hours of whining and bullshit. Barking dogs. We will do this another way. You will have three days to get me what I want. You understand?"

"A week," responded Bo in a surprisingly calm and forceful voice. Everyone, including me, stared at him. He took a deep breath and continued. "We need a week, minimum. It's not sitting in a shoe-box." I had to hand it to him. Bo sounded like he was in complete control of himself.

The psycho studied Bo's stolid stare for a second. "End of week. I get my money Friday…and painting."

"And the painting." I jumped in, oddly, as if I didn't want to be ignored. The Russian looked at me and then at my stained crotch with complete indifference, like he made grown men soil themselves all the time.

"You understand what happens if you fuck with me, right?" The Russian reached out his hand to the Irishman, who reluctantly passed back the Beretta. My bladder started to hurt again.

"You go to the cops; you tell anyone about this; you don't get us the money or the painting; I end you and everyone in your family. You understand?"

Bo and I stared back obediently. Hearing those appalling words come from such an adolescent face was as unsettling to me as the words themselves.

"I'm watching you. I'm not going away. I see something; I smell something; I end your wife first, then your kids, then your dog, then you last. You won't just piss your pants. You'll shit your pants. You understand?"

Unlike his earlier oblique ramblings about money and a painting, I understood him perfectly this time. I nodded and answered, "Yes."

Bo just nodded.

The fat guy pulled out a nasty looking flick knife and cut the tape around our wrists. He then handed us the knife to cut our ankles free—probably didn't want to strain himself bending over. We stood up and looked at Nico.

"Leave that to me," said the Russian.

I must have squinted my face at him because he yelled it again.

"Leave that fucking mess to me!"

We slowly backed out of the cabin and carefully retreated to our car, never taking our eyes off the screen door. I was sure they were lulling us into a false sense of security and would shoot us in the back as we escaped.

I've seen plenty of movies.

CHAPTER FOUR

Later Monday Evening

The Decision

BO AND I SAID NOTHING TO EACH OTHER for the first few miles as he raced the car down the dirt road heading to the highway and Portland. I don't know what went through Bo's mind. I can only tell you nothing coherent went through mine, just a torrent of distorted thoughts and images slamming into each other while rushing for the exit, as if my brain was trying to dismantle the last hour and wipe it from my memory. My heart had gone into a mild arrhythmia, and I concentrated on breathing.

Bo drove. Bo always drove. In his former life, before he lost everything, his hobby was auto racing. I know nothing about racing, hunting, rodeos, football, or the many other activities that define Bo. We are as different as two people can be.

Bo grew up a cowboy on a ranch in Eastern Oregon, while I grew up a German immigrant in the decaying suburbs of Detroit. He's athletic; I'm not. He's enterprising; I'm not. He's confident; I'm pretty sure I'm not. I could continue on this track, but in the end, the best way to illustrate how different we are is to tell you this: when Bo was rich, he raced Formula GTP cars. His career ended one day when he touched wheels with another car, careened across the track, slammed into the inside barrier and went airborne, spun three times laterally at an estimated force of 12 g's, sheared off two of his wheels, and helicoptered another three times through the infield grass. A crash so magnificent it made the ESPN highlight reel for the entire season.

When I was rich, I collected fountain pens.

I stared at the horizon and the dying light.

"You pissed yourself," said Bo.

"Couldn't help it."

"Smells."

"Don't care."

More silence.

Bo's a big man. Everything about him is oversized. Strong arms, powerful legs. Although we are the same height, he walks so quickly that sometimes I have to slow-jog to keep up with him. Bo doesn't stroll—he marches. Forward movement defines him. He is handsome, and he knows it. He uses it when he wants to charm you. He leans in, launches his generous smile, trains his clear grey eyes on you, and sooner or later, you'll blink.

We've been close friends for years. I retired from Intel Corporation in my mid-forties, having started with the company before the microprocessor was a thing. I had hitched my ride to a fast-moving train, rode out the crazy growth years of the company through the '80s and '90s, and departed rich with stock options. My wealth emancipated me. Then, in 2000 the tech bubble burst. The market value of industry titans like Intel, Microsoft, Sun, and others I was invested in collapsed, and I lost nearly everything.

During those same years, Bo built and lost several fortunes. He started buying small companies and leveraged their assets to buy larger ones. His path was quick but haphazard. He had big wins followed by bigger losses. After one substantial failure left him upside down and looking for a way to recover, he read an article about the asbestos scare going through the country. He decided to buy a small asbestos abatement company and then bought asbestos-contaminated hotels for a tiny percentage of their value, cleaned out the poisonous insulation, spruced them up with a new coat of paint, and resold them for ten times what he'd paid. He made a fortune, which he promptly pumped into a communications company just before the big communications meltdown in the late '90s, and lost everything again.

We were aware of each other during those turbulent years through the suburban family network. My daughter was, and still is, best friends with his daughter, and we'd exchange pleasantries during drop off and pick up from their frequent sleepovers. Our eventual partnership was inevitable because we both had something the other needed. I needed to make money again but couldn't bear to work for another boss. Bo needed someone to provide him with the corporate discipline and business polish he lacked.

Bo has a daring entrepreneurial ego with enough swagger to trust his instinct and ignore his doubts. He also enjoys a gift that is harder to define. He projects a casual gravitas like he's wearing a uniform. It's organic, not intentional or practiced. I was jealous of it at first but came to realize it's just something innate, and I learned to benefit from it by staying out of his shadow and forcing myself to stand a little taller in a crowd.

In many ways, we are ideal business partners. I have the corporate luster he lacks, while he has the innovative energy I do not. I am tech-savvy, while he understands balance sheets. I can organize his inventive impulses into coherent business plans and help articulate them to investors. Most importantly, we respect each other and treat each other as peers.

Finally, I have another quality that fits well with Bo: a willingness to jump off a cliff. Bo never spends time obsessing about things. He doesn't suffer analysis paralysis, and neither do I. When it comes to business, we're both fearless.

"What did you mean when you said, 'Nico knew?'" asked Bo as he rolled down the windows to blow out the stink of urine permeating the car.

Darkness was minutes away, and I studied the outside mirror for following headlights. "I saw it in his face, and he said as much just before he was shot. His eyes bugged out when the Russian psycho said, 'painting.' That was the word that triggered him, and then he started screaming about how it was all a legitimate deal, whatever the hell that meant."

"Russian psycho? You think Russian?" asked Bo.

"The shooter, the creepy looking guy, with no impulse control—yeah. He had a Russian accent for sure."

"Eastern European, maybe?"

"Really?" I said flippantly. "You want to debate this now? One guy was mute. One guy was Irish, another was Russian, Ukrainian, Slovakian—who gives a damn?"

"I give a damn," he shot back. "We have to be able to describe these animals properly to the cops."

I stared at him. Panic began to grip my bowels again. "Not the cops Bo. No! We do not go to the cops!"

Bo lifted his foot off the accelerator, and we slowed down. He turned, and his words came at me fast and loud.

"Are you out of your mind? We were just kidnapped. My hands were taped to a goddamn chair! Nico got shot in the head! His head!" He jabbed his forefinger into his temple to make his point. "We don't know why! Repeat; we don't know why! We don't know who! Trust me. We are going to the cops." He turned back to the empty highway and stepped on the gas hard.

I'll never know if Bo's impulse would have been the right decision, and looking back on everything now, I admit things might have turned out better had we followed it. Perhaps the mayhem that was about to come our way was not inevitable. But at that moment, not knowing what lay ahead, all I could think about was changing Bo's mind, which I knew was difficult to do once he started yelling. Bo doesn't yell very often, but when he does, I've always assumed it was his way of dealing with fear, which, let's face it, is better than pissing one's pants.

I kept my voice calm, determined to get him off his line of thinking.

"Bo, those assholes will go after Katherine and the girls."

"We'll go into protective custody," he shouted.

"That means uprooting your lives. You'll be in hiding, and you won't even know why. The company dies—everything dies."

"Not everything. My family doesn't die." His voice steadied. "Marty, think about it; our lives have been shredded. One minute everything is normal, the next minute, everything is fucked up. There's no explanation for it. Think of it as a car crash, sudden and unexpected." He released the steering wheel and slammed his fist into the palm of his other hand. "We can let the doctors fix things—you know, the experts—or we can try to fix things ourselves and—you know—die." He paused to breathe. "We call the cops, Marty. Let the experts do their thing; let them deal with this crap."

"You're wrong!" I said. "We've got to figure this out ourselves. It's not a car crash. It's a near miss. We've got till Friday. We can always go to the cops before the deadline if we get nowhere. Those assholes think we have what they want, and they'll leave us alone if we get it for them."

"Jesus! Are you even on this planet right now? Nico's head didn't suffer a near miss. From where I was sitting, it looked like a direct hit. Those freaks will only leave us alone if they think we've got what they want. What happens when they figure out we don't have shit? When they figure out we don't know shit, except that they killed Nico."

"Bo, how do you know they don't already have someone watching our families? How do you know there aren't more of them camped out in front of our house? Do you know where your girls are right now? Katherine? I don't know where Abbie and my kids are this second. And even if I did, tell them what?" I simulated holding a phone to my ear. "Hi honey, listen, sweetie, you've got about an hour to pack everything you'll ever want, everything important. Don't forget the jewelry box and old photos. No, don't call your mother. No, I don't know what's happening or why. Just do as you're told. And don't call or talk to anyone because we're all going into protective custody." And then I screamed into the pretend phone. "Maybe for the rest of our lives!"

We drove for about a mile in silence. Bo was stubborn, but even he didn't want to make that call.

"What's the alternative? Where do we start? What do we do?" he finally asked.

"I don't know." A kind of anxious relief washed over me, and I stared out the window. The faint horizon had gone. Everything was shadow now.

"If we don't figure this out in two days, we don't drag it out. By Wednesday, we go to the cops if we find nothing. Two days Agreed?" Bo said.

"Agreed." I nodded enthusiastically and started to count on my fingers. "Let's figure out what we know. One: Russian, Irish, and fat tattooed goons from out of state think we stole $10 million and a painting from them, and they want it back."

"No," Bo broke in. "The head psycho, the shooter, said he wanted his friend's money back. It's not his money, it's his friend's money."

"Ok. Money was stolen from a 'friend,' and the Russian and his buddies are the muscle sent to get it back." I stopped. "Wait a minute. Who does that? Who acts like that? Who uses psycho thugs to collect money?"

"Mobsters," Bo answered without hesitation. "Jesus Christ, these guys are Russian mafia. Probably East Coast. We're dead! Really dead! Screw the cops. We need to go to the FBI—immediately."

I ignored him and kept counting on my fingers. "Two: Nico freaked when the psycho said painting, and he started screaming, 'you have the painting, and the money is gone'…something like that." I tried to replay it, but it was obscure and jumbled, like trying to remember a line from a movie I'd seen a month ago. "From the start, when we first got to the cabin, Nico didn't know anything, like you and me; even when the Russian said he wanted his money back, Nico was oblivious. But then, when the psycho said painting, it was like a light switch went on, from total dark to instant light. It wasn't a slow roll. It was immediate, like a slap to his face. Bo, this is not about money. It's about a painting."

"If Nico knew what was happening, why shoot him? It doesn't make sense."

"That wasn't supposed to happen. The Irish guy was pissed about it, remember? The Russian said he was aiming for the wall, something about the gun going off early."

Bo was white-knuckling the steering wheel like he was racing. "I don't think the Irishman was pissed that Nico got shot. I think he was pissed that Nico was shot dead."

"Ok, fair enough," I said. "But it doesn't matter. Deliberate or not, neither the Russian nor the Irishman was happy. And that fat ass who taped us to the chairs looked like he'd just come in off the street and walked into a robbery."

"Yup. I'm pretty sure things didn't go as planned."

"Where was I? On two? Three. They think we're in it with Nico. Somehow, we're thieves and rob rich people or something."

Bo snorted. "They don't think we're in it with Nico. They think Nico's in it with us. There's a difference. It's the only thing that makes sense. All that creepy rubbish, 'I want to talk to the guy holding the leash'—Jesus—who talks like that?"

"I think the whole thing was scripted," I said. "The psycho thinks you're in charge. He called you boss."

Bo looked over at me. "Why the bad movie dialog?"

I shrugged and watched the road. "Maybe to leave an impression…scare us."

"I think shooting Nico in the head did that," said Bo.

"It did," I said, looking at my wet crotch.

I went back to my count. "Four. The Russian said his friend gave us money, but somehow, we stole it because we sold a 'bad painting to a rich sucker.' What the hell does that even mean? What's a bad painting, and why would anyone want it back?"

The further I counted, the less everything made sense.

"And why buy a 'bad' painting in the first place?" Bo added. "Especially for $10 million."

We stopped talking for a while, each of us struggling with our thoughts.

"I wonder if the money is even connected to the painting," I said. "Nico has never sold anything for $10 million. That's way above his class. He wouldn't know how to sell a $10 million painting if you held a gun to his head—pun intended."

Bo swerved the car almost into the opposite lane. "Not funny, Marty. What the hell is wrong with you? We're in real trouble here."

I put up my hands in surrender. Bo continued to drive in silence. The highway was empty, with no lights in front or back. It felt like we were driving through a tunnel.

"By the way, how old was that Russian freak? Fifteen? He looked like he was still in high school!" said Bo after a while.

"He's a creepy-looking bastard," I agreed. "It's like being threatened at gunpoint by my daughter's boyfriend."

"Maybe bad means over-priced."

"Or forged," I added. "But that doesn't make sense either. Nico's a little crazy. We knew that before we let him into our company. He's been a hustler most of his life, it's how he lives, but he's never been a thief. He doesn't have the skill to forge anything. He doesn't have to; he has an endless supply of his father's art."

"His father's art doesn't sell for millions." Bo's voice was tired and flat. "Nico's reckless, not stupid, and he'd never mess around with Russian mobsters. As you said, he doesn't have to. There are four Ferraris in his garage."

Bo took his right hand off the wheel and grabbed my arm, making the car swerve.

"Nico said 'she'—right? He said, 'Did she lie to you,' or 'Did she cheat you,' something like that."

"No," I answered. "Nico said, 'Did that bitch steal the painting?'"

"That's it," cried Bo like he'd just been bitten. "A woman bought a painting from Nico. We have to find a woman."

"A bitch woman," I added.

"In Nico's world, that's like looking for hay in a haystack," he mumbled.

We continued throwing hunches and suppositions at each other for the next hour, sketching a plausible scenario. Our initial and improbable synopsis was that Nico sold one of his father's paintings for a ridiculous markup of $10 million. The woman buyer hired the Russian and his buddies to get her money back. The goons, being goons, falsely concluded that Bo and I were part of the scam and decided to deal with us the same way they would deal with any other gang—violently—hence the cabin beatdown and the weirdly fabricated dialog.

But there were vast breaches of logic in our theory. Why, for example, would anyone in their right mind pay $10 million for a Benito Scava painting, and more importantly, if they did, why would they want their money back plus the painting? Why not just the money? Wouldn't they already have the artwork if they bought it? If a "she" was the buyer, why did the Russian say we'd robbed a rich man? We knew our narrative didn't make sense, but we needed to start somewhere, like piecing together a jigsaw puzzle from the center out.

///////////////////////////////////

As we got closer to the city, we stopped at a Fred Meyer store, and Bo ran in and bought me a pair of jeans and a box of baby wipes.

"If Nico tried to scam someone who had Russian mobster connections, how'd that happen?" asked Bo as he pulled out of the parking lot. "Nico doesn't know any Russians."

"Yes, actually, he does," I answered. "In fact, so do I."

I realized we were still talking about Nico like he was alive, like we could phone him, and he would answer.

As I changed in the car and momentarily relived the embarrassment of soiling myself, I shivered, processing the certainty of a singular and glaring fact. Regardless of what Bo and I had conjured up to explain what might or might not have happened, there was one undeniable truth: someone was out there—someone powerful—and they were, excuse the pun, seriously pissed.

CHAPTER FIVE

Later Monday Night

The Shangri-La

THE SHANGRI-LA'S ROAD SIGN INFORMED US "All drinks—50% off until 8 p.m." as we pulled into its parking lot with only ten minutes left to take advantage of the deal.

I'll let you in on a little-known fact not often cited in tourist pamphlets: Portland, Oregon, a city known for its self-imposed eccentricity, has also held the title of Strip Club Capital of America since the early 1960s. Yes, the Rose City proudly proclaims more strip clubs per capita than any other municipality in the US. In fact, the city boasts twice as many strip clubs as it does public bathrooms. The reason for this peculiar recreational benefit is the state's Supreme Court, which, over the years, has vigorously defended "free expression" in all forms, resulting in a kind of nirvana for strip clubs.

Dancers can practice their art completely au naturel, free from unnecessary confinement and chafing from thongs and G-strings. In a Portland strip club, dress etiquette is a pair of six-inch heels and lipstick. They're no longer called "strip clubs" since the word "strip" has become somewhat irrelevant. In Portland, "stripping" is vintage, and passé—dance club is the more accurate description.

Still amped with adrenalin, anxiety, and fear, and with no intention to go our separate ways home, Bo and I decided to swing by

Shangri-La once we started thinking about what Russians Nico might have known.

The club was Nico's favorite, or as he called it, his "home away from home," and was owned and operated by a Russian immigrant. Talking to him would satisfy our need to do something quickly.

Shangri-La was probably the city's classiest club, featuring a posh style more typical of an upscale cigar club. Deep red tablecloths, real leather chairs, discreet corner cigar booths, multiple dance stages, and a private section behind a thick purple curtain with several couches for private dances and the usual extras. The music was less raucous than in other clubs, jazzier, more Frank Sinatra than Frank Zappa. The club declared itself a "gentlemen's club" and bragged of having the city's most attractive stable of dancers. Given its tony clientele, I was sure they had no difficulties recruiting the best.

The owner was Alexander Danilenko, a stocky Russian whose loud, boisterous hospitality masked his instinctive distrust and skepticism of anyone entering his club. He was quick to greet you with a hearty guffaw and backslap, but it always felt a little like he was patting you down to find the shiv.

Nico had introduced me to Alex a few months earlier, after becoming a partner in our company. Bo and I knew about Nico's addiction to clubbing—how could we not? Nico was openly proud that his first wife had been a Shangri-La dancer and his second wife a Shangri-La bartender until he'd diverted them into domesticity. The club was Nico's favorite hangout, and while Bo had never joined us, I followed Nico willingly and frequently, justifying it as a "professional vice."

We paid our cover charge and meandered through the mostly empty club. Alex saw us immediately from behind the bar, recognized me, and looked around for Nico. He'd never seen me without him.

"Martin—Marty—it's you, Marty? Yes? Of course, Marty," he trumpeted, coming around the bar to welcome us. "Are you looking for Nico? He's not here unless maybe he snuck in when I wasn't looking and is now seeking indulgence behind the curtain." He flashed a broad smile and slapped his hand across my shoulder. He wore a white short-sleeved shirt open to the third button, black slacks, no belt, black shoes, a gold necklace, gold bracelet, gold pinky ring, and diamond studs in both ears. He was hairless. Nico once told me he shaved his head and every other body part. "It's a sexual thing," Nico had whispered.

Alex matched Bo in size and muscle, and he had a tattoo of an ornate cross on his right forearm and an even more ornate knife tattooed on his left. I was told his chest had a heart tattoo, as detailed as if it'd been copied from a medical journal.

"Yes, I'm looking for Nico," I said. "Say hello to a friend of mine, Bo Bishop."

They shook hands, and Alex leaned in with his typical curiosity. "Welcome to my place. You are Nico's other business partner in his big new adventure, yes?"

Bo smiled awkwardly, and Alex shuffled us to a cigar booth for more privacy. He signaled for a waitress in very high heels wearing only a threadlike thong to come over and take our drink order. She was beautiful, with closely cropped red-dyed hair and a tattoo sleeve of cherub angels entwined with climbing roses on her left arm. The base of the rose cane emanated from her left breast, and I remember thinking, she'll regret that after she turns fifty.

"Angel-Rose, meet Bo Bishop," Alex said, raising his eyebrows. "An angel and a bishop together in Shangri-La…God smiles on me today." Alex enjoyed his cheap wit. His Russian accent unnervingly matched the psycho from the cabin. "Sweetheart, you remember Marty, Marty Schott, Nico's friend. One Glenlivet, when you get the chance." He turned to me. "You're a Glenlivet man, I remember." Then he looked at Bo, "And you, Bo, you are a what? Also, Glenlivet?"

"On rocks," said Bo, looking discreetly at Angel-Rose's left breast.

"Two Glenlivets it is." Alex aimed his eyes directly at her and said,

"Let's see if we can convince Mr. Bishop to become a Shangri-La regular."

She then smiled widely at Bo. Her smile was the smile of a supermodel, dazzling and empty.

"We have a policy here, Bo; new customers must leave desperate to come back." As he spoke, Alex's hand slid down Angel-Rose's back and settled on her naked ass cheek, which he slapped lightly.

"Alex," I interrupted, "Bo and I want to talk to you about Nico if you have a minute."

"You're catching me at a bad time," he said, looking over a nearly empty room. "This is when we start to get busy," but he slipped into the booth opposite us as Angel-Rose sashayed away to get drinks.

"Has anyone asked you about Nico recently, like how to find him?" Bo asked.

Alex squinted and again surveyed his club. "You mean anyone other than Charley?" He laughed. "You know Charley?" he asked Bo, who explained he'd met Nico's wife several times since Nico had become a business partner.

Alex said, "Yes, yes, I know. You and Marty have made an honest businessman of him." He laughed at his cleverness.

"Wasn't he an honest businessman before?" I asked.

"Honesty, my friend, is a relative word. Yes?"

"I don't understand."

"Well, Marty, I am an honest businessman. I own Shangri-La. This club is the best in all of Portland. Maybe the best in all of country. But it is a dance club with naked women, so many people think I am naturally dishonest. I am judged very unfairly, yes?"

We bantered through three scotches at twenty dollars apiece. Bo and I entertained Alex with carefully chosen stories about Nico. We're excellent storytellers because it's a required skill when chasing money. We collect anecdotes like souvenirs, condense them into pocket-sized memoirs, and deploy them as cocktail chatter to carry us through awkward introductions and tedious investor pitches.

We'd briefly lose his attention whenever someone exited or entered the club. Then, as if it had just occurred to him, he asked why Nico wasn't with us and why we were looking for him.

"He owes you money?"

"Why would Nico owe us money?" I asked.

He laughed. "You're partnered with him, but you don't know him? Nico always owes money. It is his nature. He told me once, 'there is great power in pretending poverty' and, truthfully, he lives what he preaches."

"Nico drives a hundred-thousand-dollar Ferrari. He's not a poor man," said Bo.

"Ha! Nico has never paid for anything in his life. Nico doesn't pay. He barters. Nico is American, but he has the heart of a Russian."

He then said something in Russian, something I couldn't possibly understand. "It is a Russian expression," he explained. "It means a tit for tat, a favor for you, a favor for me. It is how Russia works, how the country stays alive. I grew up in Russia. I left with my father in '86, when Gorbachev brought in glasnost, and for most of my life, we bartered for everything—food, clothes, medicine. In Russia, you trade to survive. My mother died of stomach cancer. Very painful. We ran out of things to trade for medicine, especially morphine. After the furniture, there was nothing of value left. We welcomed her death because it ended the dying." He stopped for a minute and scanned the room. His voice conveyed no sadness. His mother's death had become just another anecdote, not unlike many of my own.

"So, I am open to bartering and will always take a good trade." His eyes moved to a new customer finding a seat at the bar. "I know Nico well. He is perhaps a friend, but for sure my best customer, and maybe that's why I let him steal my best girls and marry them."

Alex waved at Angel-Rose for another round. "Many of my girls barter as well. They mouth-barter for money, rent, car payments, and sometimes even for husbands. You understand?"

Bo and I lifted our glasses in accord.

"I will tell you a story about Nico and his bartering." He leaned forward. "In the old days, Nico had a routine when he came in. He would go to bar and get a hundred ones from bartender. We keep stacks of ones in small safe under the bar for customers to make it rain for the ladies. But Nico doesn't like to throw money—not classy—with him, it's all show. He puts his stack of one-dollar bills on his table, nice and neat. You know how big is a stack of one hundred, one-dollar bills?" He held his hand about two inches above the table. "It's a magnet for the girls. They all circle his table. They all try to get as much of the stack as possible. When the stack is gone, he gets another one. All of it goes on his tab. I have his credit card on file."

"He's efficient," I acknowledged.

"One time, Nico's card got declined," he laughed again and pointed. "You see that sculpture on the bar?"

Halfway up the liquor wall, in the middle of the shelf between all the bottles, stood a massive bronze sculpture, almost five feet long, of cowboys guiding a stagecoach over mountain terrain. It was one of my favorite pieces from Benito Scava's western works, it was so striking it was featured in his bio brochures and the home page of his website. The edition was limited to four, but I always suspected Nico had secretly expanded it.

"It is even better than edition number one. It is the artist's proof," he said proudly.

Bo and I smiled knowingly and raised our eyebrows in unison to show we were impressed.

"A couple of years ago," Alex continued, "when Nico was neck deep into Charley, he came in every night, working her with hundred-dollar tips. He just handed her an entire stack with the rubber band still wrapped around it every time he got a new drink. It was a short journey for the money, from my safe to his hand to Charley's hand in seconds. We made a joke out of it and called it the Charley Express." He winked.

"One night, Nico worked up a big tab. Bigger than usual. About three thousand or something. I don't remember exactly. I ran his card that night after he left with Charley hanging on his arm, and it was declined. But I didn't panic. I knew he'd come back. Sure enough, the next night, he came in with Charley. They'd spent the night together. I smelled the sex on her." He tapped the side of his nose. "I have excellent nose. If my girls have sex, I know it. It is a good nose to have in my business, yes?"

He nursed his drink—judging from its light shade, Angel-Rose had ensured it was mostly water—and continued. "I pulled him aside and told him to fix his tab and maybe pay cash because his card was not working. Instead, he made me an offer. He said if I let him run up the tab to fifty thousand, he'd give me a hundred thousand dollars of sculptures and paintings to help decorate the club. I know he's got it. I know his father's famous artist, so I thought about it for a minute and told him he could run up his tab to forty thousand, but he'd still be on hook for a hundred K. We shook on it, and he ran his tab for two months. Then one day, some guy drove over in truck and unloaded two sculptures and a painting. I got a hundred thou of art for a few bottles of whiskey and many stacks of one-dollar bills which kept my ladies happy, and I got half back anyway."

"Nice," said Bo.

"Yeah, I got two sculptures, and I give one away as a gift to my mother."

I played with my glass. "I thought you said your mother died."

"She did. I give gift to my stepmother."

"Where's the painting?"

"Hanging over my fireplace in house."

The idea that Nico ran short of money was as unsettling to me as learning he'd spent forty thousand dollars in a dance club in two months. Apparently, we didn't know him as well as we thought.

From Bo's solemn expression, I assumed he was as puzzled as I was. Nico had invested a half-million dollars in Paladin a few months earlier. It was a significant investment and the first half of a full million-dollar commitment. The money had kept us alive.

I knew about Nico's bartering, but I always thought it was a side-line, an amusement he enjoyed but never depended on. It was just part of his pretense, his pose, and he always came out the winner. Alex Danilenko thought he had bargained a great deal, but the truth was Nico cleaned up on the transaction. The sculptures probably came from the warehouse, and the painting came off one of Benito's walls. Benito, most likely, was too addled to notice the space it left. The deal may have cost Alex little, but it cost Nico nothing.

Alex's phone rang, and he stepped away. Angel-Rose strutted over with another round of Glenlivet. The club was fuller, with over a dozen men spread out near several dance stages. Naked women undulated around the center brass pole on each stage, gyrating to Frank Sinatra singing "Luck Be A Lady."

Alex was on the phone for a while, and when he returned, he stood at our table looking at us with remorseful eyes as if he wanted to apologize for something. "Ok, guys, we have nice visit, but I go back to work, yes?"

Bo and I just nodded.

Thinking back on it now, I should have paid more attention to that rueful look. Something had happened, and I should have noticed.

"Christ…" I said, watching Alex walk back to the bar, "his voice is deeper, and he doesn't look like a preteen, but if I close my eyes, his accent sounds like that freaking psychopath. It creeps me out."

I finished my scotch.

"Let's get out of here," said Bo.

I knew he was uncomfortable watching the girls on stage. Bo isn't a bluenose about strippers, but I understood his discomfort. He has three daughters, and years earlier, he'd promised his wife, Katherine, never to do anything that would shame him in the eyes of his girls. He took his pledge seriously. Dance clubs are not a natural habitat for him, and as the place began to fill, he became increasingly nervous he'd be seen by someone he knew. I flagged Angel-Rose for the tab.

"Nico just put a half million in the company, Bo," I noted while staring at an attractive naked Latina on her back on a small circular stage, slowly scissoring her legs open and shut. She wore Christian Louboutin knockoffs, black stilettos with villainous red soles.

"Out of a total million," said Bo. "I don't want to sound ghoulish, but we'll never see that other half million."

"Maybe that half-million was part of the ten million we're supposed to find."

"I'm forcing myself not to think about that. It would make my idea to go to the cops even stronger, and my gut can't take any more grief."

"Give it a couple of days. Tomorrow we start to figure things out."

"We already found out one important thing," said Bo as he finished his scotch and pushed himself out of the booth. "Nico spends more in a month on strippers than I spend to live—wife and kids included."

"Spent," I said.

"What?"

"He spent—past tense."

"You missed my point completely."

We drove in silence to the office, where I'd left my car. Exhausted, talked out, and our anxiety diluted by scotch, we split up for the night. We agreed to secrecy, but I worried Bo might tell Katherine anyway. Bo was not a man to keep secrets from his wife.

I kept secrets from Abbie all the time.

For the rest of the night, we were on our own.

CHAPTER SIX

Sidebar
The Scava's

FOR THIS STORY TO MAKE ANY SENSE TO YOU, it's time for me to explain a few things about Nico Scava, his father, Benito, and his brother, Dante, and what they were doing in our orbit.

I could describe Nico as a charismatic, shrewd, amoral narcissist, but he's dead, and I don't want to pile on. I liked him in a patronizing way because I realized early on he was just a sleazier version of me. We were different only because he was rarely bound by shame or conscience, which freed him to enjoy his indulgences far more than I ever would or could.

On the other hand, Bo always kept Nico at a stiffened arm's length. His ethical compass has always been less pliable than mine. He believes character is like wet paint; it'll rub off on you if you're not careful.

Suffice it to say, Bo and I were disingenuous friends pretending a false camaraderie with Nico because we wanted—no—*needed* his money.

Inevitably Bo and I stumbled onto the Scava family because the money pond in Portland is small. We targeted the same one-percenters but for different reasons. Bo and I were entrepreneurs raising capital from people with accredited deep pockets while the Scavas sold appealing but unremarkable art at swollen prices to those very same pockets.

Nico was not a natural fit for us, and I would never have predicted our partnership, but, to our surprise, he showed up in our Lake Oswego office one day and persuaded us otherwise.

More about that later.

Nico's father, Benito Scava, sat on top of the family organizational chart like a proud potentate. A six-foot-two, three-hundred-pound enormity in the fullest sense of the word. He's an artist of reputation and talent but without the judgment or wisdom to properly manage his endowment. He had the skill and creativity to market himself into national recognition but was too stubborn and egotistical to rise above mediocrity.

At 81, Benito consumed every day angrily. He raged about losing his mind to paranoia and creeping dementia. I was never sure if I should acknowledge his mental deterioration or ignore it. Occasionally I wondered what he must have been like as a young man. His bio photos showed him to be a handsome, vigorous naval cadet. After the war, he became a hunting and fishing guide in Alaska, and then he moved to Oregon, determined to make a living painting and sculpting the creatures he'd been killing the previous twenty years.

His character, if you could call it that, was, and still is, so vigorously contemptible that I believed it to be contrived and manufactured as part of his self-promotion—the eccentricities of his minor celebrity.

Over the years, Benito had self-promoted his way into the B-list of artists. He had a recognizable following that collected his works, primarily his sculptures. While he'd never received A-list recognition or A-list pricing for his work, he'd made up for it in volume.

The art world is a winner-take-all business, where revenues and profits are distributed unequally and often unfairly. The market is broken into three separate tiers: the first tier is the low-end market, where ninety percent of all art is sold for less than $50,000; the second tier, or middle market, is where prices range from $50,000 to $1 million; and finally in the third tier, the high-end market, prices begin at a million and go to infinity.

Less than ten percent of the world's artists make it into the second tier and less than one percent into the coveted third tier. The crucial point here is that Benito managed to clamber his way into that second tier and consequently enjoy the spoils of the privileged few.

The true genius behind Benito's success was not his artistic skill but rather his marketing. Benito bypassed the traditional art galleries that generally set the value for an artist's work and went instead for marquee value. His strategy was to donate his art to anyone famous, pose with them for a photo, and then promptly provide the said photo to local newspapers and glossy art magazines. With the public affirmation of an iconic patron, he could charge thousands of dollars for the rest of the edition. Benito figured out early in his career that the conventional rich emulate the celebrated rich and will pay for the privilege.

His most famous work, which pulled him into the middle tier, was a forty-four-inch bronze of an American eagle taking flight from a treetop, accepted by Ronald Reagan at a campaign fundraiser when he was a presidential candidate. When Reagan moved into the White House, he brought the sculpture with him, and it became part of the permanent White House collection of American sculptures, alongside Remington, Borglum, Alston, and the rest. This propelled Benito out of obscurity, and he followed it up with another famous collector, Pope John Paul II. His Holiness received a four-foot bronze depicting a gladiatorial Joan of Arc on horseback as part of a multimillion-dollar donation to the church by a wealthy Catholic dying of cancer. The generous gift bought the dying philanthropist an audience with the Pope. As a bonus, he took Benito with him to present the bronze effigy to the pontiff, who was kind enough to pose with Benito for the all-important photo.

To be fair, Benito's work was easily gifted to the famous because it was highly competent, even if uninspired. A critic once wrote, "Each masterpiece evokes a distinguished style that reflects the integrity of creation." So, let's give credit where credit is due.

While Nico took after his father, looking very much like the handsome young Benito, his four-year-younger brother Dante looked like he'd been adopted. He was three inches shorter, quiet, unimpressive, and dull in every respect, but with one crucial exception. While Nico possessed all the charm and social dexterity in the family, Dante was gifted the true genius. Without question, he's the finest artist I have ever met; a savant, dwarfing his father, especially with a brush.

Both boys were raised on adrenalin, and by the time Bo and I met Nico, he was in his mid-thirties and an expert hustler. Without any personal talent but awash in his father's and brother's, Nico recognized early that he could live a very indulgent and decadent life by exploiting them.

The fact that his father's art never achieved stratospheric third-tier market status played perfectly into Nico's enterprise. When an artist is at that rare altitude, and their paintings or sculptures sell in the millions of dollars, the art world tends to pay attention to the number of pieces in circulation. But when an artist's work sells at second-tier pricing, few art critics and elite buyers ever notice. Suppose, for example, an original Benito sculpture, with the edition size of one, sat on a plinth by the Pope's private bedroom door in Casa Gandolfo, the Pope's summer residence. In that case, the art's value is determined by the artist's reputation, its location, its ownership, and its edition size. But who would notice if that limited edition of one was expanded quietly to four or even five? Then each of those pieces, imbued with the whole Vatican story and accompanied by the Pope's photos, could be sold to private collectors for prices in the six figures.

Nico didn't just sell his father's art, he used it as currency, trading it for equally valuable merchandise. Although I'd never seen him do it, he often bragged how he would wander into a luxury sports car dealership, find a car he liked, and offer to exchange an original Benito sculpture for the vehicle. He'd show the owner a photo of Mario Andretti, Richard Petty, or Paul Newman holding a Benito sculpture and explain that the artwork was worth $80,000 and he possessed the original artist's proof, the AP, which was even more valuable than the piece owned by the celebrity, because the AP is cast from the artist's original mold, so it's like number zero of the edition.

More often than not, the owner took the deal and displayed the art in the middle of his showroom next to a beautifully framed photo of his favorite superstar with the same sculpture. Nico, then, drove his latest Porsche, or Ferrari, off the lot, conveniently failing to mention that he had several more APs locked away in storage.

Nico's appetite for bling and expensive toys was ravenous and insatiable. At any one time, he owned multiple sports cars, gold and diamond Rolexes, cigarette boats, and a running tab at every dance club in the greater Portland metro area.

Dance clubs were Nico's version of a dating app. He liked his women thin, beautiful, sexually compliant, and financially depen dent. Dance clubs were fertile ground.

Now, where was I?

CHAPTER SEVEN

Tuesday Morning

The Company

I SMELLED THE RAIN AND HEARD FAINT VOICES drift through the air ducts. The satisfying scent of petrichor wafted into the bedroom through the open window, and I pressed my eyes shut as if anticipating an explosion.

Not yet, my mind droned. Not yet, a minute more.

I thought about anything but the obvious; *October rain cleans away summer dust; the roads will be slick today; which closet has my old Burberry—I'm watching you; I will end your wife first.*

"Dammit!"

I stayed in bed and paid attention to the morning pulse, waiting for Abbie, Andrew, and Alison to exit for school. Tuesday was Abbie's turn to drive, and I'd avoided them all the night before and intended to avoid them again that morning. I was still too fragile, too transparent, and I knew my resolve to keep the previous day's horror a secret was as frail as a soap bubble and might disintegrate the moment any of them engaged me in conversation.

I detected the brood moving. Someone was looking for shoes, and closet doors were opening and shutting.

"Let's go, guys!" Abbie commanded in a high pitch.

"Boomer stole my shoes again," Alison hollered outside our

bedroom door, and my eyes snapped open as if I'd been poked in the ribs.

Don't come in, sweetheart. Don't come in here.

"Wear boots!" Abbie yelled back. There was more scuffling. "We're going to be late!" Abbie's patience was fraying, and I sensed Ali's resistance.

Finally, the back door leading to the garage, nearly at the opposite extreme of the house, slammed twice; a minute passed, then a third. The house shivered slightly as if it was happy to be rid of them. They are only three, but they live like six.

I stood up slowly. My head felt like it was wrapped in gauze, and I waited for vertigo to pass. The bedside clock said 7:09, and I struggled through the simple calculation that I'd slept for only two hours.

By the time I got home Monday night, after Shangri-La, the kids were in bed, and Abbie was horizontal on the couch, buried in a book. The argument we'd had that morning about ledges and suicide felt trivial to me by then, but it had provided me a reason to skulk into the TV room without greeting her. I sat in the dark, bathed in the dim light of my laptop, and got lost in a kind of post-traumatic delusion.

My mind crafted alternative scenarios for the cabin where I wrestled the Beretta-wielding Irishman to the ground saving everyone. I whispered imaginary threats to the invisible Russian psycho as he shrank into a corner and begged for mercy. I conjured scenes where I kicked ass like James Bond and never soiled myself.

The night was half over when I finally got to bed, and Abbie softly snored. I lay on top of the covers like a corpse in an open casket, fully dressed—clothes were my armor against my feeling of vulnerability—staring at a black ceiling, my fingers intertwined on my chest as I fought back a swelling hysteria. My frantic brain bounced between morbid speculation ... would I die before or after Bo?... and macabre reality ... what happened to Nico's body?

///////////////////////////////////

On my way to the bathroom, I opened the double doors to the hall-way, where Boomer waited.

"Where are Alison's shoes?" I grumbled, then continued to the bathroom. Boomer followed, his head cowed, cautious; he could smell my mood. His nature is so tempered that he enters every room with solemn trepidation.

I studied myself in the mirror, my clothes wrinkled and pasted to my body. I wondered if Abbie even noticed. My panting friend stared up at me with what I speculated was too much understanding. *He knows*, I thought.

"How much money you got?" I asked him. "How about paintings? You know anything about art?" Clearly, I'd lost my mind. His tail thumped the door frame, and he moved to a pile of clothes discarded by Abbie. He buried his nose in the mound, looking for the usual. Boomer steals shoes; it's what he does. He hides them behind couches, chairs, and curtains, under stairs, and for one month in Alison's closet behind a long-abandoned pink Barbie house.

I showered, dressed, ignored even the idea of breakfast, and drove through the morning drizzle to the office. I took the narrow roads that hem the lake to see if anyone followed me.

About ten miles southwest of Portland, Lake Oswego is a small private lake, and its houses—mansions squeezed onto lots meant for homes half their size—are jammed together so tightly that the amount of space between them is a measure of wealth and status. Ours isn't among them. We aspire to a house on the lake someday, but for now, the bank would determine if we could even stay in the neighborhood.

Muscle memory guided my steering, as my mind was obsessed with gloomy apprehensions.

Our company, Paladin, occupied most of the ground floor of the only multi-story office building located directly on Lake Oswego.

Bo and I shared a sizable room we called the glass cage. Its entire exterior wall was a floor-to-ceiling window facing the lake. The building was set back only five feet from the shoreline, so looking out from our office was no different than standing on a lakefront lawn staring at the water's edge. The view was spectacular. The other walls were floor-to-ceiling glass as well, hence the "glass cage" moniker. The company occupied additional office space down the hall, but those windows looked out over the parking garage.

Bo knew the building's owner, and we'd talked him into leasing us space at half its usual cost for our first two years in exchange for company equity. We then filled the glass cage with worn but stylish leather furniture that Bo had collected from his previous businesses, and when Nico joined us, he brought sculptures and paintings from his private inventory. The result was a workplace resembling a lakeside art gallery and one of the plushest locations for a Portland start-up.

When I arrived at the office, I saw Bo pacing in large circles, his thick hands choking a mug of black coffee. We'd agreed the night before to stay as close to our routine as possible. Any sudden change in our daily activities could spook our employees, so while our lives had plunged into chaos, maintaining a perception of normalcy could help quell our anxiety. The office was our sanctuary, and our routine was like an atheist's prayer.

For Bo and me, winning over investors was an all-consuming priority; everyone around us knew our focus. Regardless of what you've heard or thought you knew about raising capital, it is not the plucky game Hollywood makes it out to be. There are no cinematic moments of intense financial parley or surprising windfalls from a little old lady you rescued from an oncoming bus. Generally, it's a relentless rummage through a paucity of characters whose only appeal is that they have more money than you. Every person you meet becomes a potential wallet to breach and depending on your level of desperation, you can fall into a cringing sycophancy that steals any self-esteem you might have had. You learn to sell the future with unrepentant confidence.

I said hello to the people wandering around beginning their workday. I spoke to Christine, our administrative assistant, who Bo and I often called "Chief," and reviewed my calendar for the day. Fortunately, it was empty, which was on purpose because I had reserved the day to prepare the pitch deck for tomorrow's investor presentation to Chester Finley, better known as Fin.

"I heard the investor meeting yesterday in Rhododendron didn't go well." Christine's voice relayed disappointment, and I avoided her eyes, watching Bo pacing in the office instead.

"Yeah, complete waste of time," I said, heading for the cage.

"My head is about to explode," said Bo as soon as the glass door closed. "My brain was on fire all night."

"Me too. I kept wishing it was all a con, like that TV show—like we got 'Punked.'"

"Come with me," he said abruptly.

He walked me out to the parking garage and opened the trunk of his black Mercedes Benz, which he'd bought in better times and meticulously maintained. It was loaded with weaponry. Bo was a hunter, and he'd emptied his locker. He said he'd never get caught defenseless again and then guided me through his arsenal.

Two AR-15s with four twenty-round magazines each; two Mossberg 12-gauge pump-action shotguns with high-velocity three-quarter shell double aught buckshot; a Browning bolt-action .223 Varmint rifle with attached sound suppressor; two Glock 9mm's; one .357 Magnum; one snub-nosed .38, and countless boxes of ammunition. Deeper in the trunk lay a camouflaged compound bow with a dozen razor-sharp broadhead arrows.

"Jesus, Bo! No hand grenades?"

"You think we need some? I know where we can pick up a few," he said flatly, then stuck the .38 into the pocket of his sport coat. "I'll never get tied to a chair again without somebody losing a hand.

Which one do you want?" He waved his arm over the inventory like it was an invitation to sample the buffet. "I recommend one of the Glocks; the Magnum has a bitch of a kick."

"No thanks, Bo, I'll just hurt myself. I haven't fired a gun since basic training almost thirty years ago. I aced the marksmanship test but haven't shot a rifle since."

"But you went to Vietnam."

"I was an air traffic controller. We had M-14s in the barracks next to our bunks. I never took mine out of the locker."

"You never got shot at?"

"I never left the base. The only danger was from satchel runners."

"Satchel runners?"

"Yeah, insurgents. The Viet Cong cut through the fence to infiltrate the base. They'd be loaded with grenades and satchel charges to blow up everything they could before getting shot down. Charlie's version of a kamikaze run. But you already know this; it's my standard war story."

"So, no gun."

"Not for now, Rambo. I'll stand directly behind you as you mow them down."

"At least take the Browning and put it in your trunk. Then if anyone messes with you, it's a rifle; you'll know what to do."

I did as I was told, and as we walked back into the office, I felt better knowing Bo was packing heat.

////////////////////////////////////

I named our start-up "Paladin" after the Knights of Charlemagne, known for their chivalry, loyalty, and good works. It was a lofty name for a lofty intent. A business model that was both profitable and philanthropic. An online retail company for a very niche market. The idea was Bo's, and it came to him while attending another school fundraiser for one of his daughters. He told the story as part of our investor pitch.

He'd been seated at a cramped table with too many other parents, drinking heavily, heavy drinking being his survival strategy—that always got a laugh with the investors—and watched his wife Katherine raise her paddle continuously, determined to win the highly coveted Lake Oswego boat ride proffered every year by the Stuarts—champagne, and hors d'oeuvres included. The bidding accelerated through the $500 reserve as if the auction was for a luxury cruise, which I assure you the Stuart boat ride was not, and Bo pondered two things simultaneously.

First, how could he stop attending these lame fundraisers—another intentional ad-lib that got a laugh—and second, what if every school had an online retail operation that made money for them? What if every grade school, or for that matter, high school, church, or charity in the country had a mini-Amazon working exclusively for it? And why not? Every university has a crowded and busy school store. Why were there no stores in K–12 schools? Or, for that matter, other nonprofits, also known as 501c3's.

In his narration, Bo described how he barely noticed that Katherine finally outbid everyone else for the boating extravaganza at the hammer price of $900 because he was deep in thought about academic retail models. The truth was, Katherine never won the bid but claiming the win made for a better story.

Bo explained how the internet solved most of the problems a school store might present. There was no need for physical space, security, management, or labor—everything could be outsourced. He felt that adrenalin rush that always came at the beginning of a big idea.

As our investor deck explained, if schools or nonprofits opened an online store, then the store operator—Paladin—would get a cut of the profits. Our "value proposition" (that's investor speak for why our idea was good enough to invest in) was that shoppers would flock to the store if they knew that profits would support the organization that owned it. Our business model leveraged patron loyalty, which was already hardwired. The formula for success was simple: we delivered the store, and the nonprofits delivered the customers.

That was the dream Bo and I launched with no money except what angel investors could provide. The business model required a couple of million to start, and we took our investor pitch to the venture capitalist (VC) community. Many thought it showed promise, but we were too early. They wanted us to return after we had several hundred sites up, and they could assess how much traffic every site could capture. If the numbers added up, the VCs would jump in, and our money problems would evaporate.

But our starting costs were substantial. Paladin could not be bootstrapped. We had to chase money—unsophisticated money, angel money.

That's where Nico came in.

//////////////////////////////////////

Neither Bo nor I could sit; our energy levels were fueled by fear and anxiety. We marched around the office furniture in a kind of zombie dance, chewing our way through endless theories and possibilities. If anyone had watched us, they would have thought we were working on a business strategy to capture the Entrepreneur of the Year award.

We turned off our phones to keep the world at bay and continued our frantic speculating through a second pot of coffee. Perhaps we thought we could brainstorm our way out of the madness like it was a business problem. We made a list of people who might know something; we reviewed everything we thought we knew about Nico; we googled news articles on multi-million-dollar art sales; we even researched "Russian Mafia in Portland."

The only thing we didn't do was diagram the problem on a whiteboard. Not because we weren't tempted; we just couldn't figure out how to properly disguise our actions. How do you maintain secrecy when you work in a glass office?

After a while, I turned my phone back on, and it rang almost immediately, bringing us both to silence. The phone screen said, "Unknown."

I looked at Bo.

"Does the Russian know my number?" I asked.

"Jesus, Marty, it's on our website. Just answer the damn thing."

"Hello?"

CHAPTER EIGHT

Tuesday Midday

Charley

"HAVE YOU SEEN NICO?"

"Hello?" I repeated.

"Marty? Marty Schott?"

"Yes," my body slackened. It was a woman.

"It's Charley."

Nico's wife.

"Have you seen him? He didn't come home last night."

"Uhm…no…" I didn't know what to say. My stomach clenched.

Bo and I had been jawing all morning without ever confronting the reality of Nico's death. Locked in our office, our safe space, we shunned not just other people but also the specter of our dead partner. We'd talked about him and around him as if he was late to the meeting and might walk in at any moment when we could scold him for the mess he'd gotten us into. We'd purposely avoided the truth or how to manage its consequences. What do we tell people? How will it affect the company? Will his body be found? What did they do with him?

Nico's fate could easily have been ours. Talking about him explicitly meant returning to the cabin in our minds and reviving horrible images, mental photos of Nico's head slumped forward, blood, brain, and bone seeping down his face and neck, saturating his shirt collar.

"I've been calling you all morning!"

"I had my phone off. Sorry, Charley."

"Nico left yesterday at noon for work. I haven't heard from him since. I've called a dozen times, texted all night." Her voice accelerated with concern. "Nothing. Not one word. I thought at first his phone went dead, but he has charging cables everywhere, in his car, trunk, office. He never lets his phone die. He always calls, even if it's just to prove he's not picking up whores."

I was still rummaging through my head to find a response when her voice suddenly went cold and angry.

"I know he's hunting whores. I'm going to cut his dick off."

"Charley, I'm sure that's not it."

"I know he's off somewhere with a new bitch he picked up at Shangri-La, or Pink Runway, or some other dive. His phone is buried in his pants pocket, which are probably around his goddamn ankles."

Her voice reached through the phone and grabbed me by the throat. "I'll call the cops. They'll find that son-of-a-bitch."

I coughed. "Charley, before you do that, I'll come over. We'll talk."

Bo shook his head and waved his arms in the air as if he was trying to stop traffic.

"Talk about what? Just tell me where he's at and the name of the whore he's fucking."

"Stay calm. I'm on my way." I hung up, afraid of her. Afraid of what her wrath might compel me to confess.

"We've got to go see Charley," I said as Bo quickly refilled his coffee mug again, injecting even more caffeine.

"Not a chance. No way. She's crazy."

"She's minutes from calling the cops," I warned.

"So what?" he shrugged. "Nothing's on us. We didn't call the cops. The Russian said not to call the cops; we haven't. We can't stop her from calling anyone she wants. If the psycho doesn't like it, he can talk to her, like he did to us. The cops are going to get involved sooner or later."

I threw on my jacket.

"What if they come to his house while we're there?" he said, trying to dissuade me.

"They won't. Cops don't show for about three days on a missing person report unless it's a child."

"How the hell do you know?"

"Too much television, but we need to go there anyway; look for clues."

"Look for clues? Really? Like in the bedroom with Colonel Mustard. Jesus, Marty, listen to yourself!"

"I'm looking for answers, asshole!" I returned fire. "Why are you fighting me here? Yes! I'm looking for clues in the house of the murder victim. You know—the—murder—victim. That would be the poor bastard who got shot in the face. The same poor bastard who probably knew everything we don't." I was overreacting but couldn't help myself. "What is your problem, Bo? You want us to stay here for the next five days warming the furniture and talking ourselves to death?" My nerves were frayed; no sleep, adrenalin, caffeine, and dread made for a toxic brew.

"Yeah, and Nico has a $10 million painting under his bed," said Bo, attempting to decompress.

"Knowing Nico, he'd hang the damn thing where everyone could see it." I took a deep breath and pretended to see something interesting in the middle of the lake.

"I'll take that bet," said Bo as he headed out the door.

///////////////////////////////////////

Bo drove like he was competing for best pole position, downshifting through turns and slipstreaming any car in front of him. The morning rain had ended, and the roads were beginning to dry. Nico lived just north of Portland, across the state line, in the town of Vancouver, Washington, atop an isolated hilltop. We got there in a little over forty-five minutes. Charley met us as we drove up, her front door open, running to our car, phone in hand, her hair in a loose bun, sweatpants flapping, an old U of O sweatshirt hiding all contours, no makeup, and even with all that she was gorgeous.

"Oh my God!" she exclaimed, looking at Bo. "What happened? What happened to Nico?" She had expected to see only me and assumed we were the casualty notification team when she saw both of us.

"No, no, Charley," said Bo climbing out of the car, his arms outstretched. "Marty and I were together when you called, and we're worried about Nico, like you."

She calmed immediately, and anger replaced her distress. "That son of a bitch. I'm done with his shit! I'm divorcing his ass. He's with a new girl, I know it. It's not the first time." She turned and walked back into the house. We followed at a safe distance.

We'd decided in the car that Bo would keep her occupied while I snooped. Charley didn't know Bo very well. He'd managed to dodge her whenever she visited the office, so we'd calculated his appeal would be higher than mine. Bo was the unknown, hence good partner, while I was her husband's booze-swilling, cigar-smoking confederate on his odious club runs. Her familiarity with me bred contempt.

We stood in the mahogany foyer, which was ridiculously large and echoey. Nico lived well. His house sat at the summit of a small mountain, most of which was designated a public park. His property was the only residence for several miles in any direction. It was an impressive estate with a gated entry and a long driveway that ended in a circular courtyard with a massive bronze monument of a bucking stallion. A main house, a guest house, and a renovated barn were spread over the property.

I didn't know it then but would come to learn that Nico was probably the wealthiest poor man I'd ever known. It's not that he was poor; it's that he was never rich. He churned money like he was a casino.

A case in point was the estate. I always thought it was his. He certainly talked about it like it was. But several months after Nico's disappearance, after the press died down and the bodies were buried, Charley told me he never owned the place. She'd called me to help get her husband declared legally dead, which, ironically, even though I knew the truth, was grotesquely premature. She went into great detail about how Nico had leased the property from a guy who was a direct descendant of the Weyerhaeuser lumber family. The house had sat empty for several years because the owner preferred living in his penthouse in New York City overlooking central park. The owner was a collector of Benito's work, which was how Nico knew him, and when he lamented to Nico about his empty mansion in Washington State, just north of Portland, Nico jumped. He negotiated a deal to pay for all renovations to the place if he could get a ten-year lease for a mere $1,000 a month plus an endless supply of art to furnish the owner's other homes in New York, the Bahamas, and France. It was a win-win. The owner was happy to have someone maintain the sprawling residence, and Nico got to live in a princely manor for less than it would cost to rent an apartment in a bad neighborhood.

For Bo and me, our ignorance was convenient. We were never too curious, and we never pried. We wanted Nico to be wealthy, and so he was. We disregarded any indicators telling us otherwise. We didn't just believe he owned the estate; we *needed* to believe he owned the estate.

Charley looked into my eyes and said, "Did Nico come to the office yesterday?"

"No, Charley, we never saw him," I responded, never breaking her gaze.

Bo and I had agreed earlier that we'd claim we'd had no contact with Nico since the previous Friday to avoid awkward questions. We'd been lucky in that regard. Nico had called me Monday as we peeled out of the office garage on our way to the cabin in the woods, and I told him where we were going, and he'd asked to join us. I said sure, and we picked him up at a Starbucks about four miles east of the office in the direction we were headed. Nico left his Mercedes convertible in the strip mall parking lot, where we intended to drop him back off and where I assumed it was still parked. I didn't think anyone had seen him get into our car, so no one could place the three of us together for that day.

Nico had the habit of turning off his phone when he didn't want to be bothered by his wife or father, which he did with great fanfare when he got into our backseat. "Leave me the fuck alone, crazy old man," he shouted at the phone as he deactivated it and stuck it in his pocket.

Charley began complaining to an uncomfortable Bo about Nico's addiction to dance clubs, and I took the opportunity to wander cautiously about the house. Oddly, I had never seen the inside before because Nico had always intercepted me in the courtyard to guide me to the barn whenever I visited. I thought it peculiar but assumed the reason to be Charley, who didn't like me.

I wandered through the rooms, staring at the crowded walls like a tourist. The damn house was a gallery. Paintings and sculptures everywhere. Some of the canvases as big as tapestries, Benito's masterworks, somehow confiscated by his son. Other images I recognized as Picasso, Pollock, Degas, and Warhol.

It surprised me, but I wasn't alarmed. Anyone with four bartered Ferraris in his garage could probably trade some Benito originals for minor works from major artists. And, regardless of what I heard the night before from Alex Danilenko, I was still convinced that Nico was loaded. So, I strolled through the rooms enjoying the artwork like a pilgrim in a museum, without ever wondering how it was possible.

"There you are," Bo said, startling me a little.

"This house is unbelievable!" I declared.

"Why did you leave me alone with her?" Bo didn't care about the art. He was on a different track. "I just got a year's worth of Nico's stripper history."

"Must have been riveting," I answered. "Where is she now?"

"Phone call. She's been calling dance clubs all morning; they're reporting back. She's got a regular search and rescue operation going."

"Bo, this house is filled to the rafters with paintings. Mostly Benito, maybe some Dante, and big-time artists like Warhol, Picasso, Pollock, I think a Chagall."

"You think maybe a $10 million painting is hanging here?"

"They could all be worth that much. I don't recognize them, just the artists' style. But a Picasso or Warhol sells for many millions."

"You think they belong to Nico? Or do they belong to Benito, and he hides them here?"

"Or Nico stole them from Benito. I don't think the old guy knows when things go missing."

"Bo, Marty," said Charley coming into the room, sounding irritated. "I just got a call from Alex Danilenko. You were in Shangri-La last night looking for Nico—you never told me that!"

Shit.

"We weren't looking for Nico directly," said Bo. "We haven't seen him since last week. We were in the neighborhood and pulled in to see if he might be there, to maybe have a drink with him."

"That's typical!" She clapped once, slapping her palms together with such force it made me lean back a little. "If you're looking for my husband, you can always find him in a dance club. Most men can be found at work, or a sports bar, or even a Starbucks, but not Nico. No one sits on your lap at Starbucks or gives you a blow job."

"Well, he doesn't drink coffee," I said, immediately regretting it.

"Fuck you, Marty," she responded.

"Charley, there's some serious art here. Do you know if Nico was selling any of it?" asked Bo, rescuing me from her fierce glare.

"I don't know shit about art. Don't laugh; I get the joke. I married a Scava and don't know art from furniture, and I never pay attention. He brings this stuff in all the time. Whenever I turn around, he's hanging another painting or placing a sculpture."

"Any chance we could go to the barn and look in Nico's office?" continued Bo before I could say anything and possibly get into more trouble.

She eyed him suspiciously. "Why? He's not hiding there. I already looked."

"No, we want to pick up something in his office while we're here," I said.

"What?"

"Just something we need for a brochure write-up."

"The key is above the door along the jamb. Just feel around for it. I can come with you if you want."

"Not necessary. Just keep working the phones," I said, faking concern to keep her occupied and out of our way.

"I'm going to call the cops now."

I was about to tell her it was too soon when her phone rang again. It was her mother, and she turned immediately and walked back to the kitchen, denouncing her husband as a lowlife and arranging to move back home with mom and dad.

Bo and I trekked to the barn.

"God, she's a handful," said Bo as soon as we were out of earshot.

Watching Nico's misadventures from the bleachers was always entertaining, and one of our vices was gossiping about Nico's life and its diverting anarchy. We reveled in watching it from a safe distance—but now that distance had shrunk considerably.

Nico had been a curiosity from the first time he entered our office uninvited about half a year ago and made his proposal. "How would you guys like to raise money faster and easier?" he had asked. He slumped into one of our chairs and looked out over the lake. "What a view! You got binoculars?"

I gave him field glasses and a Coke, and the three of us chatted casually, trading names and gossiping about rich people we knew; potential investors for us, potential buyers for him.

"What if," he said after a while, "you can protect investors from the risk of investing in Paladin by underwriting their investment with an equal value in art? You guys are still too new and too small for institutional money, and the VCs won't touch you until you prove you can make money, so you're left shaking the private investor tree. Angel hunting—unreliable and painful, right?"

Bo and I nodded.

"But you know," he smiled and paused, ensuring we were all ears. "I can take away the risk of investing in your company. I can match any investment with something of equal value and liquid enough to satisfy any risk-averse investor."

"And why would you do that?" asked Bo.

"Paladin could be huge, as big as Amazon—or more likely, get bought by Amazon—and I want to be a partner. I make good money selling the old man's art and can afford a good life, but I just collect commissions. What I want is to make serious money." He stood an inch from the window and stared at the lake like it held his fortune.

"I've got forty-three galleries carrying Benito's work. The right locations and playgrounds for the rich and famous: Boca, Palm Beach, Malibu, Carmel, Dubai, Shanghai—the Chinese love my father's stuff. They love western art, cowboys, and Indians. Everybody collects Benito Scava: the king of Spain, Prince Phillip, the Pope—imagine that! The goddamn Pope! Reagan, Bush, all the conservative politicians, even a few liberals, the ones that hunt, anyway. Celebrities; Meat Loaf, Michael Jackson! I just shipped a monument-sized eagle and flag to the lobby of the Hoover building. The damn thing is eight feet tall, two eagles circling a waving flag. Weighs over a ton and cost them a Wilson."

"Wilson?" I asked.

"Woodrow Wilson, twenty-eighth president, on the hundred-thousand-dollar bill."

Nico was an excellent salesman, animated, generating energy as he pitched. He strutted around our office like he was claiming conquered territory, waving his arms, slapping his palms, and never losing eye contact. He wore a tight T-shirt showing his muscular torso, taunting my middle-aged paunch. A snakeskin belt with a silver buckle held up his jeans, and his black crocodile cowboy boots were freshly polished.

"This is only possible with art," he continued. "Take Picasso, for example. It sells for millions, right? But how much did it cost him to paint it? Maybe fifty bucks. Same for a Rodin sculpture or a Remington. Casting a sculpture costs a few hundred bucks, a few thousand if it's big or complicated. What other product in the world is like that? What else has a profit-to-cost ratio like that?" He shrugged his shoulders. "But even with all that profit, I still have a problem. Art is singular. Every piece is a limited edition, and then when dear old daddy dies, the cupboard goes bare."

He lifted the binoculars to his eyes, thinking he'd spied someone he knew wander out on their lake-view balcony. "And it's slow," he continued. "Art isn't a volume business. Believe me; I've tried for years to create volume, and I'm tired of it and shifting to a higher gear. I want equity. I want to build something big. I want to be part of an IPO. I want big money."

In my mind, I'd already reached my conclusion, and looking at Bo, I could see he had arrived there as well, but we let Nico continue to talk.

"So, my idea is that the investor gets their stock equity for every hundred thousand dollars invested in Paladin, and we give them a couple of sculptures at equivalent value. Benito's sculptures typically retail for around $50,000. Combined, they'd be worth as much as the investment, give or take. Some start-ups give their investors a mug, a hat, a bottle of wine, well... screw that; we give them art worth as much as their entire investment. Think about it! We raise capital much faster because we mitigate the risk. If the company fails—which it won't—the investor doesn't lose their money. They only lose their equity in the company, which is a write-off, and they still have a hundred thou of art. They can even sell it if they want. It's a win-win."

"Is it legal?" I asked, noting he already sounded like a partner.

"I don't know why not. We totally protect the investor's downside."

I checked for flaws, "What are the tax consequences of giving away high-value art?"

"I never worry about taxes, mine or theirs; I leave that to their accountants. Not my problem."

"You have enough art?" asked Bo. "If a specific piece is valued at $50,000, give or take, you'd need to deliver 20 or more for every million invested in the company. Five million, and you're up to a hundred pieces."

"I can do that without breaking a sweat," said Nico. "The trick is bronze, not canvas. You can't get volume out of paintings. Sculptures are Benito's brand. Edition sizes are generally limited to three or four. But there are tricks. For example, every original bronze has an AP—that stands for artist proof—and it's generally not counted as part of the edition.

"It's a critical loophole in the art world. Artist proofs are not limited in quantity. That's because the AP is supposed to be the first sculpture cast, but who's to say how many proofs the artist needs. The general rule is to keep the APs down to one or two, but there's no legal requirement. The artist can cast as many APs as they want. So, we cast a few extra, like four per piece. We also increase the edition size just enough to keep its value. So now, you said we need a hundred sculptures to raise five million bucks. But if the foundry casts ten pieces from every newly created mold—an edition size of six, plus four APs—then we only need ten original works. A sculpture's value depends on the edition size, not the AP count.

"How do we value the sculptures?" asked Bo. "Investors won't just take our word for it."

"Bo! You think I sell sculptures in my galleries without justifying their price? Every piece Benito creates is examined and valued by a third-party appraiser. I use IAI, International Appraisal Institute; they're out of London. You think people buy serious art from a gallery without an appraisal? Every buyer gets a leather-bound portfolio with a letter of authenticity, an appraisal from IAI, a color glossy of Benito, his bio, a list of his collectors, and other cool stuff."

And so it went for the rest of the day. We knew the idea was unique and untested, but it would help us raise capital.

Nico agreed to pay all production costs and get a dollar-for-dollar exchange in equity. If we raised $5 million in seed capital using this program, he would get five million shares in the company, making him about a million shares shy of what Bo and I had. Nico also agreed to buy an additional million shares in two tranches at a dollar a share. The first half-million came wired from an account in Panama. As I said earlier, it had been our most significant investment to date and temporarily took us off life-support.

We would never receive the second half million.

⁄⁄⁄⁄⁄⁄⁄⁄⁄⁄⁄⁄⁄⁄⁄⁄⁄⁄⁄⁄⁄⁄⁄⁄⁄⁄

Bo unlocked the door, and we stepped into Nico's barn and turned on the lights. Immediately we were transported to what looked like a bar at Disney World—a twenty-foot raftered ceiling covered in a colorful tableau of country and corporate flags. The northern wall lit up like a band pavilion with a floor-to-ceiling mirrored bar framed by fluted mahogany columns and a dozen shelves inhabited by perfectly aligned bottles of the finest scotch, cognac, rum, gin, bourbon, vodka, tequila, whisky, sake, and liqueurs. Bottles, lined shoulder to shoulder, like colorful soldiers, waiting to be pulled away from their brethren to fill a glass or be fondled by an ardent fan. I did that once with the 21-year GlenDronach.

A green marble counter topped the mahogany bar, belted by a polished brass footrail. A dozen leather stools awaited occupancy. I loved that bar. It was lavish, extravagant, and pretentious. It *was* Nico.

An entire row of pinball and slot machines occupied the west wall, accompanied by a poker and pool table. The south wall was the garage door, which opened into the center barn, where, parked with perfect precision, were four buffed and beaming Ferraris; a red Daytona, a yellow 360 GTB, a silver 456, and a red 288 GTO.

The grey-painted walls were decorated with vintage advertising signs. The clincher, however, was the O-scale model train that chugged its way through the entire barn on a specially constructed shelf, mounted about ten feet off the ground, circling the complete interior of the barn. Triggered by the light switch, the train with lit passenger and cargo cars clacked and whistled through hand-crafted tunnels and craggy mountains, including the bar's middle shelf, which had a transparent tunnel splitting the bar in half. The liquor above the tracks was more expensive and required a sliding ladder to retrieve. Nico's running joke for all newcomers was asking them from where they wanted their liquor—the right or wrong side of the tracks.

Bo surveyed the scene in wonderment, like I had when I first saw it months earlier, and then we climbed the stairs to Nico's office in the loft above the bar. We dug through his desk drawers and rifled through his PC, which was not password-protected. While I opened files, Bo drifted to the vanity wall covered with photos of collectors and selfies of Benito presenting sculptures to recognizable and iconic figures—Hugh Hefner, Mario Andretti, Robin Williams, Paul Newman, Duchess something-or-other, Richard Nixon.

Having seen them in Benito's brochures, Bo was already familiar with most of the photos, but one was new to him. He'd never seen it in marketing materials and could not recall Nico mentioning it. The picture was of an unknown man, very distinguished looking in a suit and tie, sitting behind an expansive desk. His round, handsome face, with a tightly trimmed beard and expensive haircut, looked directly into the camera. Behind him sat a collection of framed photos on a wood credenza, angled so the camera could not pick up their images. In the middle of the credenza, surrounded by the photos, stood a striking Joan of Arc bronze sculpture, a shield in one hand and a drawn sword in the other. Bo recognized the bronze immediately as the same piece presented to Pope John Paul II. We'd been told it was an exclusive edition, yet the pontiff's photo accepting the Joan of Arc hung directly next to the picture of the mystery man with his own Joan of Arc.

It was a posed shot, probably meant for publication in a magazine or newspaper. But what made it different was that Benito was not in it. The photo was not meant to promote the art but rather to promote the man. Unlike every other picture where the art was the central focus, it was just a prop in this one. Curious, Bo pulled it off the wall and opened its frame.

"Who the hell is this guy?" he asked as he pulled out a magazine cut-out. "And what's he doing with the Pope's sculpture?" He brought it over to me, assuming I might know.

"Never seen it before." I narrowed in on the tiny photo credit at the bottom of the paper. "Dmitry Chernyshevsky, overseeing his empire," I read aloud.

"A Russian collector," said Bo. "He's never mentioned him. Ever!"

I quickly typed the name into Google and then clicked on the first listing: Wikipedia.

"Dmitry Chernyshevsky," I recited. "Russian. Born July 1955. A Russian-Ukrainian billionaire businessman, investor, philanthropist, and art patron."

"Jesus!" exclaimed Bo.

I continued, "Chernyshevsky is the primary owner of the private investment company Lopukhov LLC. He is known outside Russia as the owner of an Australian football club, a stable of racehorses, and a Russian F1 racing team. According to Forbes, Chernyshevsky's net worth is US $12.3 billion making him the 5th richest person in Russia and the 48th richest person globally. Dmitry is celebrated for his philanthropy, having donated more money to charities than any other living Russian."

"Is this real?" Bo was incredulous.

I skipped over a bunch of irrelevant material. "Blah, blah, here we go; Chernyshevsky built his business empire after Boris Yeltsin was elected President of Russia in 1991. The former Soviet Republics struggled for nearly a decade transforming from a command economy to a uniquely Russian hybrid model, so unfailingly corrupt that economists labeled it 'bandit capitalism.'"

I scrolled further. "The entrepreneurial nature of Russia's Organized Crime, and its willingness to use exceptional violence, gave it a vital role in those early years. Thousands of businessmen were victimized by criminal gangs and were forced to turn their business over to the corporate raiders. This 'criminalization' of the Russian economy resulted in establishing *Nomenklatura Capitalism*, a corrupt economic system where the political party elite operate in tandem with oligarchs to ensure the success of their business."

"What about the billionaire?" said Bo testily.

I scrolled some more. "Dmitry Chernyshevsky started his career working for the KGB, the Soviet Union's security service. After the KGB dissolved, Chernyshevsky used his network of criminal friends and political elites to buy companies. He diversified into everything from tractor repair to pig farming, acquiring over 100 companies."

I skipped over more details. "He's considered the originator of the corporate raider movement, becoming the most powerful and dangerous businessman in Russia, but his greater fortune came when he began selling oil from Noyabrsk, located in the middle of the Western Siberian oil fields. He was awarded those government contracts after Vladimir Putin became President on his personal recommendation to Boris Yeltsin."

"You've got to be kidding me," muttered Bo looking over my shoulder.

"Chernyshevsky knew Putin from his days in the KGB, and rumor is that he helped Putin get elected by bribing the appropriate people. Putin rewarded him by granting him the exclusive carrier rights for the Western Siberian oil fields."

"Are you guys still here?" Charley called from downstairs.

I turned off the PC and ran downstairs to stop her from coming up. Bo put the photo back into the frame and brought it with him.

"I called the cops," she informed us.

"I'm sure Nico will come home soon," I said calmly.

She looked at the photo, "Found what you were looking for?"

"Yes, thanks," said Bo. She showed no curiosity, and we didn't want to spike her interest by asking her about it.

Her phone rang.

"It's Alex again. God, he's calling me every hour. He's worried about his Ferrari," she said, irritated.

"Ferrari?" I asked.

"Yup. According to him, one of them is his now. I don't know why—he just told me. My asshole husband never tells me anything. Alex wants me to find the title like I got nothing else to worry about. He probably fixed Nico up with a new Shangri-La whore."

We exchanged more worried words about Nico's erratic behavior, locked the barn, said our goodbyes, confirmed we'd call if we heard anything, and then fled.

A house that a few days earlier had reliably given me a dissolute thrill to visit had turned into a doomed place, cursed forever by Nico's oppressive shadow.

CHAPTER NINE

Tuesday Afternoon

The Phone Call

I SAT ON MY HANDS IN THE CAR TO STOP THEM FROM SHAKING. Contrary to my expectations, things were not falling into place.

"Does this rich Russian mean anything?" I wondered aloud.

"You mean, is he a *clue*?" Cynicism dripped from Bo's lips. I could tell Bo regretted letting me talk him out of running to the cops. "I don't know. Looks like Nico found the photo in a magazine, maybe by blind luck. He can't promote it without answering embarrassing questions, like how a Russian billionaire got a copy of a single edition Vatican sculpture."

"You think Nico could sell a painting to a Russian oligarch?" I asked. "Like one of the paintings hanging in his house?"

"Do I think it's possible? Yes. Do I think it's probable? No." Bo paused, working his jaw. He had a habit of grinding his teeth when he was anxious. "Shit, Marty, nothing about this smells right. A $10 million-dollar art sale invites the press. Paintings don't sell for that kind of money without an army of parasites—advisors, appraisers, authenticators, experts—all with their hands out. A $10 million deal is big enough to pull in a lot of bloodsuckers and moochers. Somebody would know something, but all we've got is crickets."

Again, he drove with his usual fury, like he was between a green and checkered flag, trailing by a lap.

How the hell does he still have a license?

"And then there's the whole security thing," Bo continued, leaning into his words. "Why would Nico have millions of dollars of paintings in his house without proper security? He's got a gate to his driveway, but I only saw a little ADT panel on the wall in his house. Are you kidding me? He couldn't get insurance for those paintings without better security. Nothing makes sense. It feels unreal, like a dream where things are always a little off balance."

"We're back in the same circular logic we were in this morning," I grumbled.

"What if we level with the Russian?" Bo mused. "We tell him we don't know what he's talking about and convince him we need to work together. He tells us what he knows, which might be enough to put us on the right track."

"It's a big risk," I replied. "Why would he believe us? The truth is not very persuasive, and he might think we're just stalling."

"Stalling for what?"

"Getting our families to safety; hiring our own goons; could be anything. And if that freak *does* believe us, if we convince him we know nothing, then we become expendable. We're just unfinished business—loose ends."

"I'll shoot the motherfucker," he said calmly. "If I ever get close to that bastard again, I'll kill him."

"If Nico's half-million investment in Paladin was part of the ten million, he'll never believe we weren't involved."

"I think it might have been." Bo winced. "The money was wired in from Banco Alaido in Panama. At the time, I thought it was weird, but—you know—it's Nico." He shrugged. "I figured he had an account to handle international sales and avoid taxes. I asked him about it at the time. He told me he had a small timeshare in Playa Bonita and went there several times a year. He bragged about the beautiful women. According to him, they're all thin and half-naked. He said he kept an account in Panama because he didn't trust the

US government. The IRS once put a lien on his Wells Fargo account for back taxes. Said it cost him nearly a million. He bitched about how some collectors paid in cash. It's a tricky business, and the IRS was always on his ass because art is used to launder money."

"Why'd you never tell me this?" It wasn't like Bo to keep things from me.

"I didn't think it was important. I never figured Nico to be a money launderer. I've taken investor money my entire career. Sometimes wired from a European bank, sometimes an American bank, sometimes a handwritten check, and even once it was cash, in a goddamn plastic Ziplock like it came out of a freezer. I didn't care how Nico's money came in. Our bank processed it, and we made payroll. We paid down a lot of debt, and then we took Nico out for drinks at McCormick's. Remember? We drank those sweet Irish whiskies all afternoon and talked about how big Paladin would become. I never gave it another thought."

Bo and I stopped at McDonald's and ate burgers in the car. I left my phone on, and it had vibrated all morning while Bo turned his off completely. I checked my messages. Most of them were from employees, needing one thing or another, concern for the company in their voices. I should have responded, but talking to anyone then was impossible, like conversing with a stranger immediately after a terminal cancer diagnosis.

"So, Alex Danilenko owns one of the Ferraris," I said. "He bartered it for something, and I'll bet it was for more than just a naked girl."

"I don't care; it's not my car," said Bo, clearly distracted.

By the time we returned to the office, well over half the day was gone. Bo slumped onto the couch. He looked as tired as I felt. "Where to now? Where do we find another one of those—what do you call them—*clues*?"

"Benito's," I answered. "And you're being an asshole."

"Because it's messed up, Marty. We're acting like we're in a buddy cop movie, and if we survive the hijinks, it'll all end well. Fact is, I'm scared for our families."

"We agreed to give it a couple of days. We're exploring the most logical places."

"But what if we're wasting our time? What if the FBI can solve this mess? They catch these guys and throw them in a dark hole. Why are we so convinced it'll end in witness protection? Maybe we wouldn't even qualify for it."

"Maybe. But those goons told us they were working for a friend. Who's the friend? Another mob guy? Whoever hired those assholes is still out $10 million and a painting. We saw the Russian murder Nico, which puts him in prison for life, and he'll do what's necessary to stop that from happening."

We were repeating the loop we were in that morning as if repetition was a refuge from wandering too far into the unknown. "Let's find out more about the Russian oligarch."

"He's just a photo on a wall, Marty. He means nothing. You're chasing a fantasy." Bo's earlier interest had faded. "You honestly think this is all connected to a goddamn oligarch? Nico Scava of Portland, killed by a billionaire in Moscow? Jesus!"

I ignored him and searched the internet for the magazine article containing the photo we had of Dmitry Chernyschevsky.

Bo stared out at the lake.

My search didn't take long. I found the photo as part of an old *ARTNews Magazine* article entitled "Eastern European Art Collectors," which dealt with the emerging influence of post-Soviet oligarchs on the global art market. I scanned the article until I found something interesting and read it aloud.

"Chernyshevsky inherited his love for art from his father, the leader of a trophy brigade. Trophy brigades were groups of Red Army soldiers dispatched by Stalin in 1945 to travel throughout defeated Germany to pillage cultural valuables that could be appropriated as compensation for Soviet war losses. His father would return home with Nazi-looted paintings, antiques, and cultural treasures, which ultimately fueled Dmitry's love for art and a fascination with Nazi artifacts."

I looked at Bo. "What a charmer," I said, not knowing if he was listening. "He collects Nazi loot."

"Everyone's got a hobby," said Bo, still staring at the lake.

I went back to reading the article. "Chernyshevsky owns a significant art collection including Gauguin, Rodin, Modigliani, Picasso, and many other important 19th- and 20th-century artists. He has allegedly used offshore companies to hide art from his wife, who he is divorcing, a charge he denies."

I closed the PC and sighed. "You're right, Bo. This guy is out of our league. Ten million is chump change to him. He hangs paintings in his garage that are more valuable. Let's go see Benito."

It was late afternoon by then. We were near the end of our first day and had nothing to show for it.

My phone vibrated again. I stared at its screen. Once more, it said unknown, and I expelled a loud sigh. My phone, the one gadget I could never live without, the widget that unceasingly got my attention, had become a tiresome nuisance.

I looked at Bo. "It's probably Charley." I answered it on speakerphone with an annoyed "yes."

"I think I will end your wife first."

That unmistakable voice made every muscle in my body tighten. Bo instinctively pulled the snub-nosed .38 out of his pocket and immediately stood up. Neither of us spoke.

"You hear me? You recognize me?"

"Yes," I said.

"I'm on speaker, yes?"

"Yes."

"Bo?" he asked.

"Yes," said Bo.

"I told you no cops."

"We didn't call the cops," said Bo.

"You went to Nico's house, you talked to Nico's wife, and she called the cops. You think I'm stupid? You think I can't add that up?"

"There was nothing we could do," I answered immediately. "She's freaked out about her missing husband, so she called the cops. We weren't even with her when she did it."

"You were at the house. Does she have the painting?"

"No," I answered, even though I didn't know.

"Why'd you go then?"

"To get some information," I said quickly. Bo looked at me, puzzled.

"You are a liar, Marty. You are like Nico. You went to pick up a photo. Why you need to pick up a photo?"

His comment was like a kick in my sternum; I coughed, ejecting the air in my lungs.

How did he know that?

"It was an excuse," said Bo quickly, seeing I couldn't speak. "We needed to get into Nico's office to get some information, and we didn't want her to go with us. She called the cops while we were in Nico's office."

"You have the money?"

"No. Not yet. You gave us four days," said Bo, the .38 swinging slowly at the end of his arm.

"I don't trust you. I think maybe you are plotting against me. You understand?"

"We're not plotting anything…it's complicated," I said. No one said anything for half a minute.

"If cops get involved, I hurt you. Don't think I joke about this. You understand?" Silence. Then he continued. "I end Marty's wife first. I find her easily. Maybe she walks to her car in a parking lot, maybe with groceries in her arms. I drive by slowly, wave to her. Maybe I ask for directions. I smile like I know her, and then, while she's thinking, 'who is that handsome guy smiling at me'—bang—right through her smiling face, she never knows what hit her. You understand this, yes?"

I nodded, temporarily dazed.

"I don't hear you."

"Yes," I said.

He hung up.

I collapsed, shell-shocked, into the leather chair and stared out over the grey lake.

Bo knew not to speak first.

"Maybe you're right," I conceded. "Maybe we go to the cops and get everyone under protection. But before that, I want to shoot this dirtbag myself. This piece of shit needs to die—slowly—and I want to watch it."

CHAPTER TEN

Tuesday Late Afternoon

Benito

BENITO SCAVA HAD A SMALL FARM IN CANBY. Our drive there was quiet. We were both talked out. I'd changed my position about going to the authorities. The Russian's call had cowed me into a docile surrender, and my feelings were now aligned with Bo's.

I will admit to being embarrassed about my capitulation. Running to the cops now felt like throwing a punch after the fight—defiance soaked in impotence. It took only one terrifying phone call to expose my bravado as the thin veneer it always was.

"If we get nothing from Benito, we wait till it's dark, load everyone into cars, and caravan to the cops," I said, staring absently out the window.

"I don't think we go to the cops," said Bo. "I think we go to the FBI. The cops are too disorganized and will ask too many questions we can't answer. They might even arrest us for not reporting the murder and send our families home. We should take Jeff Spalding with us."

"Jeff is a securities attorney. He can't help us. We don't have an attorney for this kind of trouble."

We shelved the discussion as we neared Benito's dirt driveway. Enclosed by a decaying split-rail fence, his property was seven acres of high grass, wild shrubs, and groves of fir trees. On the opposite side of the street was a multi-acre flower farm preparing for the upcoming pumpkin festival. Half a dozen teenagers hung banners and piled hay bales around pumpkin patches. Clouds hung low and ominous, but the kids were undeterred.

Benito lived alone except for his caretaker, who worked for Nico. Always a young female, often an art student from one of the colleges around town. Nico would convince them that being an apprentice to a great artist would be a positive resume item.

"God, I hope he's on his meds," moaned Bo as we pulled up to the house, a sprawling and neglected white brick ranch with a portico entrance.

Melina, a comely young woman with a brown and pink ponytail and a coiled snake tattoo on her right shoulder, met us in a paint-stained tank top and denim overalls at the door. I had met her several times before but had never taken the time to get to know her. I hated visiting Benito and treated everyone in his house as a wretch, deserving or not. Her smile, which would have been prettier without the lip piercing, welcomed us into the oversized wainscoted foyer. The open hall was lined with a dozen plinths about three feet apart, each holding up a Benito sculpture.

"Benito is in his studio," said Melina in a lyrical voice.

"My two least favorite people," called out Benito. His deep baritone rolled down the hallway, greeting us well before his hulking presence. "Are you here to steal my latest masterpiece?"

Bo and I reviewed the row of sculptures and locked onto a large bronze American eagle in flight, grasping an undulating Declaration of Independence in its claws. We shuffled closer to the sculpture, studying its detail.

"It's beautiful," said Bo.

"Beautiful?" Benito thundered, coming up behind us. "It's brilliant! It's magnificent!" His sallow face, long ago handsome, now just rutted and truculent, was covered in sweat. Odd colors streaked his thin, oily hair like he'd run paint-stained fingers through it. His eyes were suspicious and indignant as usual, while the rest of him was just a stooped fleshy heap. No one shook hands.

"How are you, Benito?" I asked, putting my hands in my pocket to avoid touching him.

"Why do you care? You don't visit me. You don't worry about me. You don't give a tinker's damn about me. I am just the slave whose back you break to make money. I'm your art mule."

His voice had no banter or mockery, and he didn't breathe between sentences. Benito blathered. He needed the rhythm of his voice to steady himself, to anchor his reality. He'd talk to whoever was within hearing range, and when alone, he'd talk to himself. He'd adjust his chatter from group to solo, from friend to foe, with just a slight drop in volume and a single missed beat like a palpitating heart.

"You are here to steal from me as you do every day. Today you want my *Deliverance*—I'm calling it—*Deliverance*. I sent a photo…."

The trick to communicating with Benito was to talk past him like you're on an international call with a delay.

"It's fantastic, Benito," said Bo.

"…to our dumb-ass senator, and he wants to put it in the Library of the Justice Department…."

"In Washington," I contributed.

"…in Washington DC. The Robert F. Kennedy building. Imagine they named a goddamn building after that crook. The whole family crooked. Just thieves and communists. I told him…."

"That's a great location for it," injected Bo.

"…I want lots of photos from the dedication. I can't go, I'm too old to fly anymore, but Nico can attend. Where is Nico?"

"How big is the edition?"

"I haven't seen my bastard son for days…five and the AP. I'll put number one in the Justice Library. Then I got a dozen collectors willing to fight over the rest. It's an easy half million, and I already told Nico it's not for your stupid little company."

Benito was casually aware of our deal with Nico, and to keep him happy, we'd given him a few thousand shares of Paladin.

"Have you seen Nico recently? We're trying to find him," I asked.

Bo and I had agreed that we would ask everyone if they'd seen Nico because, knowing the cops were now looking for him, we wanted to leave a trail indicating we were doing the same thing.

"Nico is never around when I need him," he said, turning to shuffle back down the hall from where he'd come. His paint-stained poncho shirt looked like a loose shawl about to fall. "He owes me money."

Bo and I trailed after him. Melina had disappeared. The house felt like the inside of a desk drawer, with odd things lying everywhere and walls covered in sketches, doodles, and graffiti. Benito kept talking, pointing to various drawings as he lumbered forward, but I stayed far enough behind not to hear him. I let Bo pretend to care about his grievances, which he did by grunting strategically.

A long hallway papered with drawings spilled into his studio, a cavernous room he'd created by tearing down three interior walls and cutting half a dozen skylights into the peaked ceiling. The giant space was a mare's nest—a turbulent mess of metal tables, wood stools, clay maquettes, unfinished canvases, discarded palettes, broken brushes, paint splatter, mangled tubes of acrylic, and an impossible number of half-empty water bottles. There was a rumpled beauty to it all, a pell-mell of colors and plunder that reminded me of my young daughter's room after an all-day birthday party.

Benito walked directly to his latest project, which looked, from a distance, like a massive portrait of a stout gnome. The outsized canvas rested on an easel in the center of the studio.

"I'm waiting for Nico to bless me with his appearance today, but so far, nothing. He's supposed to bring me a check, or I don't go on with the work," he lamented, glaring at the canvas. Staring back was the light charcoal sketch of a familiar-looking man in full royal uniform, sash and all. I recognized the sash before I recognized the man.

"Is that Von Baltruschat?" I asked, leaning in to study the facial lines more closely. More sketches and partial outlines lay on a table near the easel.

"It's the baron," chortled Benito. "You know he wants to be called Baron. Pretentious bastard is what he should be called." He started organizing brushes into jars, his lips always moving. "Damn Nazi owes me $25,000, and Nico promised me a check today. I think it was today. I don't remember. But I remember I don't work for free." He looked at me and tilted his head towards the canvas. "You know that Nazi?"

"Not well, Benito. Bo and I talked to him a few years back about financing a project, but it didn't work out."

"Well, he's got money now, loaded with it. Came to me a while back and said he wanted a portrait. Something big to hang over his fireplace. Something grand, like portraits from the old days, life-size like the ones in castles. Vain son-of-a-bitch. Said he'd pay the first half when I outlined it for him. Said he'd give the check to Nico."

I did the math in my head. Benito charges about $25 per square inch, and the painting looked to be about forty by fifty inches. Then add a nice frame, and you get to $50,000 quickly.

"I didn't think Albert had that kind of money," I said. "I mean, to spend on a vanity project."

"Have you seen Nico? I need to talk to him. He's supposed to deposit the check today." Benito clucked his tongue as if he knew he was repeating himself. "Nico said the guy had come into big money recently—probably sold something. You ever seen his house? Like a museum. He came to pose a long time ago, can't remember when." He mumbled something under his breath. "His family was big with the Nazis…German nobility…Euro-trash. Damn Germans, the only thing they did right was solve the Jew problem. You're a Jew, right?" He looked directly at me.

"Only my father, Benito," I responded flatly.

"Then you're not a Jew. Has to be the mother—fathers don't count. Consider yourself lucky."

"I do, Benito, I do," I said, looking at Bo, who was about to start laughing.

"I never fought the Nazis," he declared. "I was in the Pacific."

"Lucky for the Nazis," said Bo, rolling his eyes.

After a short while, Melina appeared in the studio carrying a large bucket of Kentucky Fried Chicken and a brown bag filled with the "fixins."

"It's about time," bellowed Benito. "I'm starving. Set it up for me, will you, sweetheart?"

Melina smiled curtly and cleared an area on one of the crowded tables by throwing the contents haphazardly into a large plastic storage bin, then used the napkins in the bag to wipe clean a spot for paper plates onto which she started to dump chicken pieces.

"Not for them, sweety," Benito said. "I'm not a restaurant."

Melina picked up several pieces and plopped them back into the bucket. She looked at me and blinked repeatedly. "Sorry," she mouthed.

Benito stuck a drumstick into the mashed potatoes, scooped a large dollop, and stuffed the entire load into his gaping maw as we watched. He ate like a buccaneer, famished from pillaging a village. I thought about how he would soon learn of his son's disappearance, and I promised myself to be as far away and unreachable as possible. While Benito was unusually lucid that day, his fragile hold on sanity would likely rupture beyond repair.

"Benito, do you own any valuable paintings?" I asked.

"What a stupid question," he responded indignantly. "Every damn thing I do is valuable."

"That's not what I meant. Let me rephrase the question. Do you own valuable paintings from other artists? Famous artists, like I saw hanging in Nico's house earlier today, Picasso, Warhol, works like that?"

"Warhol isn't art. It's garbage posing as art. You saw Nico? At his house?"

"No, he wasn't there, but several masterpieces hang in his house."

"The only masterpieces he has are mine. My paintings are masterpieces; everything else is garbage. You know, he steals from me, and he steals from his brother, Dante."

"Benito, you ever sell a painting for $10 million?" Bo asked, changing the subject to something more productive. Benito stared at him for a full minute. Mashed potato dripped off the drumstick in his hand and made a tiny *splat* sound when it hit the filthy floor. His suspicious brain was trying to understand the underlying meaning of the question; was Bo looking to know something, or was he looking to propose something?

"No," he finally said. "But I can. I've never been properly managed by Nico. He turns my work into a commodity. He wants volume. To him, I am just a factory. He increases my edition numbers all the time. He thinks I don't know."

"You think Nico ever sold a painting for $10 million?"

Benito's mind, always on the brink of paranoia, now fell headlong into it. "He better not, that bastard. I have a contract, and if that shit represents another artist, I will castrate him. He robs me every day." He took another bite and chewed furiously while his eyes flew between us. Melina stood stock still.

We stayed through another drumstick, listening to how Nico mismanaged Benito's art and talent while slowly inching out of the studio. I could tell Benito's erratic mind was shutting down for the night, like a shabby convenience store dimming its lights to announce its closing.

I was eager to leave and get our families to the FBI. It was past dusk, and the FBI building was near the airport. There was still a lot of explaining to do, but we could get there by midnight. I thought about the conversation I needed to have with Abbie. I hoped Bo would help me, two voices being better than one.

Melina, silent all this time, saw us edging our way out and said, "If you guys are heading out, I'll take you."

"No, they know their way out, sweetheart. Stay with me; help me get through this chicken. You can wash the grease from my lips after I'm done."

I shuddered and started walking faster.

"I need a cigarette, Benito," she said. "I'll go with them."

Outside, Melina sprinted to our car and stood before the driver's door like she wanted to block our exit. "I know something about Nico and that baron guy," she said. "But I want money before I tell you."

"Don't you get paid working here, Melina?" I asked.

"This place is a freak show. Benito is demented and a lech; it's creepy as hell. I told Nico I needed to get out of here, and he begged me to stay a few more weeks so he could find someone else."

"OK, Benito's a douchebag, but what do you know that's worth money?" I asked.

"Maybe it's worth money, maybe not, but I need money. Benito doesn't pay me. Nico pays me, and I haven't seen Nico in a week. I've got to pay bills just like you."

The cold evening air gave me goosebumps, and I shoved my hands into my pockets. "Nico pays you?"

"Yes, he pays everything. All the bills go to Nico. I collect the mail, sort out the bills and give them to him. He gives me cash every week. A few months ago, I made him put me on a week-to-week retainer cause I'm not sure I'm willing to do it anymore. If I didn't have student loans, I'd already be gone. I get $200 a day, six days a week, under the table, no taxes. It's good money, but I can't do it anymore. Benito needs to be in a home, assisted living."

Bo was already pulling his wallet out and counting his money, and I did the same. We had $287 between us and offered all of it to her. She pocketed the cash and lit a cigarette.

"Long time ago, maybe six months, I was new, and that baron guy came to pose for his portrait. I never talked to him. Benito let him in, so I never met him. I just did my daily routine cleaning up Benito's mess in the studio. Benito had him sit on a high stool while he gabbed away at him, posing him in different directions. It's funny how Benito calls the baron guy a Nazi cause when he was here, Benito kissed his ass and talked about how great German culture was. For all his drivel, Benito will suck up as much as anyone to make a sale." She took a deep pull on the cigarette and blew the smoke out her nose.

"Anyway, I was cleaning up, trying to organize tubes of paint and crap near the backbenches, where sculptures go to die." She chuckled. "I don't think he knew I was in the studio because I was behind him."

"Benito?" I asked.

"No, the baron guy, but now that you ask, maybe Benito didn't know I was there either. I was sitting on the floor in the middle of boxes, crap all around me. Point is no one was paying attention to me. Then Benito announced he had to take a shit and disappeared." She shook her head and drew in another lung of smoke.

"Who in hell tells you they have to take a shit? A pee, ok, but Jesus, he's so frigging crass. One of these days, he's not going to announce anything. He'll just pull his pants down and take a dump right where he stands—Jesus!" She shook her head. "Anyway, he left, and the baron guy sat on the stool for a while, got bored, took his phone out, and called Nico. I knew it was Nico because he said his name. He told him he was posing for his portrait and then said he'd been thinking about the $10 million, and he didn't think it was enough. He wanted Nico to get more. He said something about trying to get $12 million. Have you ever heard him talk? Like he's got a stick up his butt. He said…'not satisfactory'…like he was telling the sommelier the wine was no good. Ten million is *not satisfactory*," she parodied, throwing a limp hand into the air.

My knees wanted to buckle, and I desperately needed to sit down, but I locked them in place and stayed upright.

"I couldn't hear what Nico said, but the baron guy was insistent. At one point, he said, 'Tell her I won't settle for anything less'… something like that."

"Her? He said, tell her?" asked Bo.

"Think so. I'm pretty sure he said, 'tell her.'"

"What else? Did he say any names?" I asked.

"No, just Nico's name at the beginning of the call. Then I guess I made some noise, and he swung around and saw me working on the floor. He didn't stop talking, but he whispered."

"Anything else?"

"Well, Benito returned, and the baron dude hung up."

"What happened when Benito came back?" asked Bo.

"Nothing. Just more poses. But one thing stood out in my head, making me remember everything. When Benito came back, and the baron hung up, Benito asked him if he was talking to Nico, and the baron said no. He said it was his wife, and he told this elaborate lie about what he said to her. I guess he didn't realize I'd heard everything. That's why I remember it." She took another drag and leaned back against the car.

"You sure about what you heard? You said it's been half a year." I said.

"Yeah, I told you I remembered because it was so obvious the baron was working with Nico on something worth millions, and he was lying about it to Benito. That's when I figured Nico was probably scamming his father, and I remember thinking about that."

"You think Nico is scamming Benito?"

"Yeah." She coughed. "Every day."

"Six months ago, and the baron portrait is still just an outline?" Bo said, looking at me as if I had an answer.

"It's a long story," she said, lowering her eyes as she flicked ash to the gravel. "Benito's not what he used to be. I think it's fair to say he isn't himself anymore. Working here is like working in a zoo.

Benito's the monkey." She took a long breath. "Nico better show up soon. I've got to get out of here."

"Listen, Melina. I wouldn't count on Nico if I were you. Maybe you should just quit regardless," I said.

"Then what happens to the monkey? He can walk and talk and look like he's all together, like today. Today was a good day. But I swear, sometimes he's barely coherent. He's not stable. He needs to go into a home or something. But that won't happen because Nico needs him to put out more 'masterpieces.'" She used air quotes. "Or make it *look* like he's putting out more masterpieces. The poor old bastard isn't productive anymore. He can't remember what he's working on from one day to the next."

"He just finished the *Deliverance* sculpture. It's great."

Her grin indicated more to that story than she was willing to tell.

"Why doesn't Nico start to use his brother more? From what I've seen, Dante's as good as Benito," said Bo.

"He's better. Dante's a freak of nature—a genius. I would sell my soul for his talent. He's like Mozart, he sees the work in his head, and his hands create it without effort or thought. I asked him to sketch me one time. A little portrait for fun, and he asked me in what style. At first, I didn't know what he meant, and I said just standard portrait style, and he said, 'no, whose style,' so I said Malevich; I thought that would throw him off balance, and in twenty minutes, no lie, twenty minutes, he gave me a pastel sketch of myself I would swear was by Kazimir Malevich."

"Never heard of him, but you're still making my point," I said.

"Dante is gifted, but he's also lazy and a pothead. He'll binge for days. He's completely unreliable."

"Maybe money would change Dante's attitude," said Bo.

"Maybe. But in the end, Dante is still Dante, not Benito. Benito has a reputation, he's a brand. He has the collectors. Dante would have to build up his reputation, and he has no interest. Just cause you're the son of a big artist doesn't mean collectors are willing to buy your work. In the art world, heredity doesn't translate into success."

The door to the house opened behind us, and Benito's silhouette threw out an elongated shadow. I remember thinking *God, even his shadow wants to escape.*

"You done with that cigarette yet?" he barked.

She dropped the cigarette into the gravel and ground it to pieces alongside a dozen other butts. Apparently, we'd parked in her designated smoking area. "I can't leave without a replacement," she whispered. "I need Nico to find someone else. When you see him, please tell him to call me."

I looked at her, hiding my pity, and Bo didn't look at her at all. We thanked her and climbed into the car.

As soon as we were on the road, Bo slapped the steering wheel and said, "The baron was selling something worth $10 million bucks. Want to bet it's a painting?"

"And it looks like the buyer was a she," I added.

CHAPTER ELEVEN

Tuesday Night

Walk In the Woods

PARKED IN OUR EMPTY OFFICE LOT, WE SPENT AN HOUR chewing on Melina's comments. Although just fragments of conversation overheard surreptitiously, her information shot needed adrenalin into our veins. New confidence replaced relentless dread. Fleeing to the questionable safety of the FBI was no longer our primary option. We'd stumbled onto a new target. A giant metaphoric X on a pretend pirate map, with the cartoonish name, "The Portland Baron."

"Nico was the go-between, the negotiator, for the baron's painting," said Bo.

"Again, why Nico? If Von Baltruschat had Nico sell a valuable painting for him, and $10 million or $12 million is a holy-shit valuable painting, why him? As I said before, Nico's never sold anything at that altitude. It's completely over his head. Why not call up Sotheby's or Christie's or any big auction house or go to a reputable gallery? Portland is crammed with good galleries."

"That doesn't make sense to me either." Bo stared out the car window into the dark lot, trying to divine the answer from his translucent reflection, while I redialed the baron's number. "Maybe it's because Nico had a buyer already in his pocket."

"That would be the mysterious she," I said, shaking my phone. "Why doesn't Von Baltruschat answer? Maybe he changed his number. I haven't dialed him in a few years; I'm surprised I still have him in my contacts list."

"It's possible the baron couldn't go through regular channels. Remember, the Russian psycho accused us of selling 'bad paintings to rich suckers.' We thought 'bad' meant forged or overpriced. But maybe it meant stolen."

"Jesus, Bo, you think Nico was dealing in stolen art?"

"It'd explain a lot. What if Nico sold a stolen painting to this mysterious 'she,' and something went wrong? Then she hired the Russian maniac to fix the wrong. Nico's our business partner, so we're guilty by association, and we get our heads kicked in. It makes sense."

"Yes, and no," I said, turning things over in my head. "If Nico fenced stolen art from the baron, then the baron is an art thief by extension, and that's not possible. We've met the baron, been to his house, had drinks with him; he's an eccentric cartoon, not an art thief."

"You don't know for sure, Marty. We all have secret lives. Look at us. We're being stalked by a murderous goon who'll kill us if we don't deliver $10 million and a painting in three days."

He had a point.

"Fact is, we know nothing about Albert Von Baltruschat other than he's a weird guy who inherited a useless title and turned his house into a shrine to German pride. For all we know, he could be an art thief, a closet Nazi, or a serial rapist."

"Okay." I nodded. "So why didn't the Russian psycho go after him? Why stick a gun in our face when he could easily have aimed it at Von Baltruschat?"

"That's the $10 million question. It's all we got, Marty. We've gone through one of the two days we agreed on. We run with it, or we don't. If not, we go directly to the FBI tonight."

As he was talking, Bo received a phone text commanding him home.

I didn't hesitate. "I think we run with it." It was the easier deci-sion because telling Abbie and the kids would have been hard and irrevocable, and going to the FBI had a finality I didn't want to confront, at least not yet.

Bo nodded, a dubious look in his eyes.

"You told Katherine already, didn't you?" I offered.

"No, I haven't, and you're a jerk for asking." I could tell from his tone I'd angered him.

I shrugged. "Not trying to be a jerk. It's just we have different marriages, Bo."

"I know. And believe me, I thought about it. I was up all last night, going back and forth. I figured I could tell Katherine and the girls and send them to East Oregon to my mother. I could even follow them for a while in my car to see if anyone tailed them. I mapped out the route in my head with plenty of sudden turns to watch the traffic behind them. But in the end, I didn't. You know why? Because Katherine would call Abbie, and I can't stop that, and neither of us can stop Abbie from calling the cops."

"Maybe calling the cops would be better," I thought aloud.

"Jesus Christ! Marty! Stop it! You're like one of those happy flappy tube balloons on a used-car lot," he waved his arms to and fro. "No cops—maybe cops—no cops—yes cops—it's driving me nuts, and it's too damn late now. You're the one who talked me into this. We're up to our eyebrows. We've gone over 24 hours not reporting a murder, and I don't know how many other felonies we've committed."

"Other felonies?"

"Yes, goddamn it. We've delayed the investigation, lied to Nico's wife, lied to Nico's father, and rifled through Nico's files. I'm not a lawyer, but since those actions are attached to a murder, we're probably accessories after the fact. And let's not forget aiding and abetting."

"Don't try to scare me with the drama-queen crap, Bo," I

retaliated. "I get it; we're at the bottom of the well looking up. But our lives are being threatened. Our families are under threat of death. No cop would ever charge us."

"Don't call me a drama queen. And you're right. The only thing keeping me upright and still walking normal is that I agree with you. We have a damn good reason for our actions, and like in the movies, innocent guys who commit minor crimes to protect their families generally get to have a happy ending."

"Well, that's Hollywood; it's all make-believe." I forced a fake smile.

He shook his head as I climbed out of his car. "Keep calling Von Baltruschat," he said, "we'll head over there in the morning."

"Oh shit, Bo!" I suddenly remembered the investor pitch we had scheduled for the following day. "We've got Fin at 10 a.m."

"Let's deal with it tomorrow. I'm exhausted. I'll meet you here at 8. Take the rifle out of your trunk. It can't protect you there. Sleep with it under your bed."

"Or under the couch," I mumbled, but Bo was already driving away.

///////////////////////////////////

Like most nights, the kids were in their rooms; Andrew playing Counter-Strike, and Alison on her phone. Abbie lay on the couch reading a book in her customary evening position, and she didn't move when I entered the room.

Since the kids hit their early teens, I've lived in a quiet house. Abbie makes the kids do their homework at the kitchen table under her watchful eye, and after they're done, they sprint to their rooms, chasing teenage privacy. Abbie's routine is to open a Chardonnay, find a book, and plant herself on the couch with Boomer taking up the foot end, always looking like he wants her to read to him.

She's a good mom: warm, kind, and more stubborn than the

typical twelve and fourteen-year-old. Both kids know better than to pick a fight with her. There is no doubt about who manages the family. Abbie and I never suffered through power struggles because I came to our marriage already wrapped affably in a white flag. Abbie is the decision-maker. The only thing we spar over is what I do for a living.

I'm attracted to strong, confident women. I realized early in life that abdicating power also meant renouncing accountability, which allows me certain perverse liberties. Truth be told, I put a lot more effort into my work than into my family.

"Anything new?" I called to Abbie while digging for cheese and beef sticks in the refrigerator. I hadn't eaten since lunch and wasn't hungry—I was on the "life-threatened-by-Russian-mobster" diet.

"I have an appointment with the bank tomorrow to negotiate a payment schedule," she said flatly. When I took no salary, our mortgage payments stopped, the bank became belligerent, and Abbie took it personally.

"I'm feeling good about our morning meeting with an investor," I said. "He's got the money, and he wants the art. I'm sure he'll write a check, and we can continue to count on my salary for a while."

"I told you yesterday, we're so far behind, if we get money on Friday, we're back in trouble by Monday. Didn't you have a pitch meeting near Mt. Hood yesterday? You got home late."

"The guy wasn't interested. He liked the concept, but we're too early for him. He said he'd be more interested in the B round."

When did lying become so effortless for me?

"I'm taking Boomer for a walk," I said, and Boomer's tail flogged the couch pillow at the word "walk."

"I'm also meeting with Tom Barnes tomorrow," said Abbie indifferently. Tom was a friend and, more specifically, a family law attorney.

I kept my voice calm. "You have to bring our friends into this?"

"Yes, I do, Martin, because our friends are free. If we had money like we once did, and if you'd stop playing a game you're not good at, I could afford an attorney who isn't also a friend." She kept her face hidden behind the book.

"But, you wouldn't need an attorney then, would you?"

"That's true."

"Are you seriously looking to get a divorce?"

"I never said I wanted a divorce. I said I want you to leave the company and get a real job. Maybe a little time living alone will push you to think about that. I want to talk to Tom to understand what a separation might look like. Like, can I force you to move out so the kids can keep going to school here?"

"And kicking me out will improve things?"

"I don't want to, Martin, but I don't know how else to get you to stop chasing a dream that's devouring our lives."

Abbie's words should have made me panic, but I felt oddly serene. Maybe because twenty-nine hours earlier, I thought my life was over, and just six hours earlier, her life was waved in front of me by the Russian psycho like it was dirty laundry. The threat of a separation felt insignificant. I had bigger problems. She lowered the book and placed a finger where she'd stopped reading—a habit I always found endearing.

"I can't predict the future, Martin, and I can only fight one battle at a time. We're barely surviving now, and your salary depends on angel investors. Our family will be destroyed if I can't convince you to do something about that. On the other hand, if we fix things, and you still come out resentful and angry, the family will also be destroyed. But maybe not. Maybe you'll watch the train wreck from a distance, and you'll know you got off the train just in time, and we high-five ourselves for saving our lives."

I avoided eye contact with her.

"Maybe you'll like making money again," she continued. "Maybe you'll look at the people you left behind and their broken lives and be thankful you pulled out when you still had the chance. I don't know the answer, Martin. I know something has to change because we're on the wrong trajectory." She raised the book back to hide her face.

Trajectory—what an odd word.

Boomer was sitting by the front door, waiting.

I will readily admit, had I known then what I know now, I might have made different decisions—better decisions—and maybe avoided some of the horrors to come.

As an air traffic controller in Vietnam, I sometimes worked Precision Approach Radar to land planes. I navigated their arrival on a glidepath. *"Approaching glidepath, begin descent…on course… on glidepath…slightly below glidepath…slightly right of glidepath. Turn left heading one seven three…turn right heading one seven zero…on glidepath…on course…check wheels down, clear to land."*

If the glidepath on the radar scope had been off by just a few degrees, I would have guided the aircraft directly into the ground. The crash would've killed everyone on board.

That was my marriage. On course to crash unless I recalibrated the glidepath—changed its trajectory.

//////////////////////////////////////

We live across the street from a small, thickly wooded park with many foot-worn paths and graveled trails. It's Boomer's domain to explore and race around. I got him as a puppy and never trained him. I never had to. He just knew what I wanted. I brag the most about Boomer never needing a leash. He lollops a few feet before me but never runs away, regardless of other dogs or distractions. He learned this in his puppy years when I would take him into the woods, and he would scamper far enough away to be out of sight, and as soon as he was out of range, I would jump into the bushes and hide. He'd return along the path a few minutes later, sniffing, whining, and looking for me. He was always upset until I jumped out of the bushes and showed myself.

As he grew older, he became wise to the trick and solved it to his satisfaction by sauntering ahead but never out of sight. Every time he got about twenty feet ahead, he'd get nervous and turn around to assure himself that I was still there. Our neighbors and friends comment on how well-behaved and trained he is. He isn't. He's just afraid of being left behind, like all of us.

That night Boomer and I navigated our path by flashlight. There was no moonlight. I redialed the baron, but no one answered—no voicemail—it just rang forever.

"What if he's not answering because he's as dead as Nico," I said to Boomer. I talk to Boomer frequently; unlike my wife and children, he listens to me.

Bo and I had met Baron Albert Von Baltruschat a few years earlier. He was an odd man; eccentric, flamboyant, and ostentatious to the core, abundantly evident by the fact that "Baron" was not a nickname but a genuine appellation he insisted on being called.

"Baron—Freiherr—Your Majesty—My Lord—My Liege—what a pretentious jagoff," I said acidly to Boomer, who sat in the path waiting for me to catch up. I could hear his panting before my flashlight settled on him, and as I got close, he ambled further into the darkness.

I resumed our one-sided conversation, projecting my words into the night's brisk air so he could hear me. "How pathetic does your life have to be to want to call yourself "Baron?" How small does your dick need to be?"

As always, Boomer just listened and let me draw my own conclusions.

I'd been introduced to the baron by Nico at Portland's annual Charity Ball. Abbie and I attend the grand event every year as a token reminder that the Schotts were once conspicuous members of the city's haut monde. Our attendance, well after our money had evaporated, was a tacit validation of what I like to call Marty's axiom: the halo of wealth never fades.

A truism I exploit frequently.

I'd been socializing my way past Nico's table when he grabbed my arm and pulled me towards him. He was just a casual acquaintance back then, and I often saw him at charity events looking to connect with potential buyers for his father's art.

He was sitting next to a fleshy fellow with a crown of thick ginger hair and alert, ardent eyes, wearing a double-breasted tuxedo with a marvelous green sash adorned with medals draped across his sizeable chest. When Nico introduced me to Baron Von Baltruschat, he emphasized his "baron" title so I wouldn't mistake it for his first name. I remember thinking seconds before I said it. "What's a baron doing in Portland, Oregon?"

"It's a long story," he said without hesitation, probably having been asked that question a thousand times.

One thing led to another, and after a short conversation, we exchanged business cards, and I continued to mingle. Back then, before Paladin, Bo and I had a small private equity firm that raised capital and invested in other start-ups. A few weeks after the charity fundraiser, I received a call from the baron, and—long story short—Bo and I visited his home the following day.

He lived in a three-story Tudor mansion in the pricy neighborhood of Dunthorpe. Although I didn't know it then, I discovered later that he didn't own the residence but leased it for nearly nothing from a local church that had received it from a wealthy donor. The church planned to turn the three-story building into a rest home for its older members but could not afford the upkeep. So, as the story goes, Albert Von Baltruschat came along just in the nick of time and negotiated a deal to maintain the place if he could live in it. He told the church he would convert the house into a museum honoring his noble family.

Yes, I know, there's a symmetry between the baron's living condition and Nico's, and I'm telling you this now because it matters later.

As Bo and I walked up to the manor's giant porch, the baron flung open the door and welcomed us with outstretched arms in a fake theatrical manner that annoyed me and amused Bo. He was shorter and wider than I remembered. He came at us in full preppy attire; khaki slacks, blue shirt, and navy sports jacket, but the discordant pageantry of his jewelry dazed me for a moment. Around his neck, he wore a large gold medallion, a lustrous malachite pendant, and a St. Christopher medal. The malachite hung low enough to skip buoyantly on the shelf of his belly.

He thrust a beefy right hand with polished signet rings on the third and fourth fingers. His left hand sported a large jade ring and a diamond pinky ring. A gold Audemars Piquet with a mesh band wrapped his left wrist, and multiple gold bracelets coiled his right. They jangled faintly as we shook hands.

I remember thinking he was either a fan of pretentious bling or a man attempting to impress us by cleaning out the jewelry box. Either way, he'd succeeded in making a poor first impression on Bo, who had no use for jewelry on men. Bo's entire cache of jewelry consisted of a single Rolex, which I had given him for his birthday years ago when I still had money.

"Thank you, sirs, for coming to my home," he chirped, "please, please, come in, come in, let me give you a tour."

We stepped into the house, and our eyes adjusted to the low light. I say house, but in reality, it was a reservoir for the Von Baltruschat family tree, which traced its roots back centuries, ladened with long branches of European nobility. Every wall on the main level was crowded ceiling to floor with paintings, tapestries, flags, medals, pistols, armor, and swords—The Baltruschat Collection, he called it. Faded Persian rugs decked the floors. Baroque furniture filled every room, alongside glass cases stuffed with porcelain vases, plates, and tea sets. Photo frames and candlesticks rested on embroidered doilies. Leather-bound books were stacked on the floor. In some rooms, larger paintings, suspended on chains, covered the windows blocking the natural light.

The baron steered us through the maze of historical clutter with such courtly geniality that I started to think of him as a practiced guide I needed to tip heavily at the end of the tour. He spoke about himself, his lineage, his ties to the House of Habsburg, and his German castles. He waxed eloquent about how he came to own Mahatma Gandhi's letter opener, how members of his ancestral family built famous European edifices, and how the King of Spain came to his mother's bedside during his birth in a Chicago hospital to place a mound of earth on the floor beneath her bed so it could be said he was born atop European soil.

The baron was a compelling storyteller, gracious and friendly, with a sort of synthetic modesty about his aristocracy that was oddly appealing. His wildly implausible stories gushed with legendary names and historical events. I felt the pull of his charm and the seductive allure of consorting with someone drenched in the luster of nobility. We were the hoi polloi, mingling with a patrician, and what mattered was not that it was inconsequential but that it felt momentarily…momentous.

But there was something not quite right, and it nagged at me. As the tour rolled on, I gradually recognized that while the entertaining yarns were beguiling and delivered flawlessly, the accompanying trinkets and finery looked more and more like standard junk found in the neighborhood antique barn, absent the discreet price sticker. What was impressive for the first twenty minutes due to its sheer volume grew into just a giant compilation of curios, like my grandmother's collection of souvenir spoons.

"Ever had these things appraised?" asked Bo on cue with my thoughts.

The baron looked annoyed and said, "My godfather is Otto von Habsburg, from the House of Habsburg, which created the European Union. My godfather would have been Holy Roman Emperor if history had been different. My family has been around for a long, long time. My heritage is the appraisal."

I remember turning to Bo at that moment, and we both smiled at each other because we'd realized in unison that the baron was just a steamer trunk of pompous pretensions.

He wanted to hire us to help him raise money, on contingency, of course. He needed a large sum to pay the legal costs for a nasty intra-family brawl regarding Schloss Baltruschat, a castle in Mecklenburg, Germany. He lamented how he'd already tried other venues with no success. Even auctioning some of the "Baltruschat Collection" failed.

"Why's that?" I asked, already knowing the answer.

"The company I hired to manage the auction failed to generate enthusiasm. They told me my things were either overvalued or too damaged. How stupid! This treasure has been through two world wars; my bloodline has existed for centuries."

After an hour of polite conversation, accompanied by dwindling enthusiasm, we shook hands, promised to keep in touch, and never spoke to him again.

///////////////////////////////////////

What was that?

I stopped. The night forest moved gently like a dense crowd of shadows.

Voices?

I heard voices. I thought I heard voices.

"Hello," I called out. "Boomer, here, buddy, come here." I swept the flashlight beam over the inky thicket around me. I pushed my head forward, listening with my eyes.

"Hello. Anyone out there?" I yelled as Boomer came panting into my limited view.

Nothing.

"Kids?" I whispered to Boomer. "You think kids? Or Russians?" I stayed motionless, bolted in place. The voices had stopped, but I felt motion—something near me—my skin, even buried under my jacket, sensed it. Branches moved.

Wind?

Russians?

I turned off the flashlight and grabbed Boomer's collar. I knelt and put my arms around him as he panted in my face. "Why won't they answer me?" I hissed. "And why aren't you barking?"

I hoped he wouldn't run towards the sound. He doesn't run away, but he is a dog and is easily persuaded. My heart was beating much too fast, and it affected my breathing.

"Hello. Is anyone out there? I have a dog," I shouted.

I have a dog—well, that will scare the shit out of a homicidal maniac.

I stayed dead still. I held my breath.

Then I heard murmuring.

God damn it—murmuring!

Or was it just my eardrums rumbling in fear? Why the hell wasn't Boomer paying more attention?

Can't you hear it?

I turned on the light and pointed it in the direction my ears advised me. Motion? More motion?

Boomer was alert now, looking sharply toward my light beam. The blackness felt like a straitjacket.

What the hell am I doing? Why am I out in the woods at night when hired killers threaten my life? What the fuck am I thinking?

I grabbed Boomer by the collar and started running back along the path. I frantically tried to calculate time and distance. How long had I been reminiscing about the baron? How far had I walked into the woods? How deep in the darkness was I? Ten minutes? Fifteen?

Running bent over to hold Boomer's collar was more difficult than I thought. The flashlight beam jumped and jerked, and I lost all visibility. Within a minute of running, I hit an exposed tree root and flew into the air, letting Boomer go and landing face-first on the rough trail. Boomer immediately turned and bounded back along the pitch-black path we'd followed. Half my face was covered with trail pulp and mud, which hurt when I tried to scrape it off. I shone the flashlight beam on my hand, and the pulp had mixed with blood.

"Shit! Boomer! Boomer!" I yelled, pointing the light back in the direction he ran. "Boomer, get back here." I waited, breathing heavily. "Boomer, get back here now." I held the flashlight like a pointed sword while I pulled out my phone, punched 911, and held my thumb above the dial button. I spoke as loud as possible without shouting.

"If you can hear me, I will kill you if you hurt my dog. I have a rifle and will use it to kill you." I waited, standing rigidly, listening for any sound. Boomer came walking into my light a minute later, panting and looking like he'd been on a happy stroll. I patted my hands over his fur and looked for blood. After finding nothing, I started jogging back to the house, keeping the flashlight on the trail and letting Boomer sprint ahead.

I'm watching you. I'm not going away. I see something, I smell something, I end your wife first, then your kids, then your dog, then you last. You won't just piss your pants; you'll shit your pants. You understand?

When I got home, I took the rifle out of the trunk and hid it between the washing machine and the wall in the laundry room. Abbie hates guns, and our house is a gun-free zone, so I couldn't just take it to bed with me, which was my immediate preference. It wasn't helpful in the trunk, but in hindsight, it wasn't helpful behind the washing machine either, unless, of course, while being tortured by the Russian assassin, I could explain that I needed a moment to switch some laundry from the washer to the dryer.

Yup, that would do it.

CHAPTER TWELVE

Wednesday Morning

Harry Callahan

"BOOMER IS GONE!"

"Wha?" Abbie woke me from a fitful sleep, and I was disoriented.

"Boomer is missing." She yanked the sheets off me.

I sat up and held my head in my hands. I'd been out for a couple of hours, and morning sun was now streaming into the bedroom.

"He's somewhere. Have you looked by his shoe stash?" I managed to rasp.

"Yes, of course. I haven't seen him all morning. I think he slipped out an open door. I called him. I even bribed him with bacon I made for the kid's breakfast. I held the entire frying pan out the door, so he could smell it."

Panic shot through me like a bullet. Boomer doesn't pass up bacon—ever. Even if he accidentally got locked in another room. Once he smells bacon, he starts barking his head off if he can't clear-cut his way to the kitchen. I replayed last night in my head: soft, sinister sounds boiling up from the cauldron of swaying, pitchy underbrush. Was it my imagination?

I end your wife, then your kids, then your dog.

The psychopath had successfully set up camp in my head, his voice as clear as my own, down to the accent. I googled it during my nightly bout with insomnia, and it's called an auditory hallucination.

I smile like I know him, and then, while he's thinking, who is that man with the doggie snack—bang—right through his panting mouth, he never knows what hit him. You understand this—yes?

Every molecule of my body screamed alarm, but I had to stay calm. I had to move with steady assurance. Honesty was not the best policy for that morning, nor for that matter, any time soon. I had slept in my sweats, still unable to sleep without clothes. I did not run down the stairs even though I wanted to. Andrew and Alison ate breakfast at the kitchen table, and I stayed clear of them.

Abbie followed me into the laundry room, and I asked her, "how'd he get out?"

"The deck door was open. I never checked it. It could have been open all night."

I gave her my evil eye. Abbie's worst habit was not locking doors, and she once told me she disliked thinking about evil possibilities before bedtime. She'd grown up in Charlevoix, a small resort town in northern Michigan with more boats than people and where, even today, locked doors were not an imperative.

Years ago, I'd flown home on a redeye after being gone all week on business and found our front door fully ajar at four o'clock in the morning. The door had just swung open, probably from a slight wind gust, and Abbie and both kids were asleep. At that precise moment, I decided to get a dog, a vicious man-eating beast that required a pronged choke collar, a pit bull, a Doberman, or a German Shepard.

We settled on Boomer.

"I don't remember seeing him since last night," she said.

"I don't either. We both went upstairs to clean my bleeding head." I thought momentarily, then added, "I don't remember him coming to lie by the bed."

I counted the shoes lying haphazardly by the garage door, and none were missing, another bad sign. I reminded myself there was a Browning .223 behind the washing machine and went outside.

I breathed deeply, pushing out any remnants of sleep nesting in my bones. There are days in October when the weather in Oregon is near perfect. The air is so clean and crisp it feels like it's been exhaled directly from God's lungs. It was one of those mornings. I walked the streets anxiously, calling Boomer's name. I covered a good portion of the neighborhood before Abbie pulled up in her Jeep to let me know she would take over as soon as she returned from taking the kids to school. Andrew and Alison pouted that they couldn't stay home and join the search. I jogged home grudgingly and got ready for work.

///

We wanted the office to buzz whenever an investor was scheduled to visit. Office attire was mandatory, and everyone needed to be prepared for an impromptu conversation with the potential investor, which was always, in reality, a short interview. Christine had emailed everyone to come to the office and work in their cubicle instead of at home. As soon as I walked into the office, I felt a higher-than-usual energy.

The right side of my face stung from my fall, and I fingered it tenderly. Abbie had treated the sizable laceration the night before with antibiotic cream and left it unbandaged, believing it would heal faster if left exposed and allowed to scab.

"Jesus...Marty, that's a nasty scrape," said Bo as I entered the glass cage. "Did Abbie take a frying pan to your head?"

"Boomer's missing," I said, ignoring everything else.

"What do you mean missing?"

"Missing, goddamn it! What don't you understand about the word missing?"

I was close to hyperventilating. Bo handed me a bottle of water, and I could see the weight of the snub-nosed .38 tug on his sports jacket.

"You think you need a gun to pitch the company?" I asked, pointing to the pocket bulge.

"I sleep with it," said Bo. "Did you get the baron on the phone?"

"No. But I googled him, and he's moved."

"No voicemail?"

"No. It's weird. But then, he's weird, so I don't know. It could be he's not answering, or he's changed his number, or he's dead."

Bo puckered his lips in concern. Then I told him about the night before and the purring forest and how I took a header into the thicket.

"Bo, that murderous freak said he'd kill my dog," I said anxiously.

"Marty, you're tripping on adrenalin." He paused while I traded the water for coffee. "Boomer's OK. Besides, he'd have barked if anyone came at him."

"No, he wouldn't. Offer him a snack, and his whole body wags. He's not a guard dog; he's a family pet. He thinks everything with two legs loves him—shit—since my wife started hating me, he's been my goddamn best friend!"

"OK, well, now you've hurt my feelings," said Bo leaning into me. I knew what he was trying to do, but it didn't work. My entire body was stricken with the same distress I felt in the cabin.

"We need to get ready for Finley. You want me to take it today?" he asked.

We had a routine with investors. I would do the pitch because I was more articulate and talked sequentially. Bo would get distracted and divert from key points, so he was assigned to jump in at critical times to emphasize or clarify a specific subject.

"No, I got it. I need a break from thinking about how terrible my life is."

///

Fin, whose full name was Chester Finley, was a former neurosurgeon who had started a clinic to treat people plagued with chronic pain and then sold it for millions of dollars when he retired. He was rich and loved entrepreneurs because he'd been one himself, and his success had persuaded him to take a run at making even more money. He was the classic example of what I described earlier: someone with money who wants to make throw-away money, the perfect angel investor. He also loved Benito's art, which was how he came to our attention.

He'd visited Nico's gallery in the Portland Pearl District, interested in buying some of Benito's sculptures for his ski cabin and home office. Nico had explained how he could provide the art for free if Fin would take an equity position in an exciting start-up, a "twofer," as he described it.

The deal we expected to strike with Fin was for an investment of $500,000; he would receive half a million shares in the company and eight sculptures of his choice from Benito's inventory. All the images had been appraised between $45,000 and $65,000. It was a no-lose proposition. Fin didn't need eight sculptures, but with the investment, they were free, and, as he pointed out sardonically, he'd force himself to find places for them in his three homes.

Fin showed up on time, and Christine led him into the glass cage where Bo and I had our investor deck loaded onto the 50-inch flat-screen hanging on the inside wall. He came dressed in clean jeans, a cashmere sweatshirt with the requisite Polo logo, white and blue Air Jordans that had never seen a minute of exercise, no socks (of course), and a well-worn Breitling Navitimer. His grey hair was uncombed, and he hadn't shaved for a few days. I smiled broadly, shaking his hand, guessing he'd spent some time that morning in front of a mirror getting his affluent preppy look just right, dressing down to show his esprit de corps with the proletarians trying to get his money.

"What an amazing view," he said as he watched a fat smallmouth bass jump half out of the water to snag a bug. It was a common observation, gushed by virtually every new visitor to our office, and we used it, like always, to generate small talk and make him feel comfortable. I even pulled out a pair of binoculars for him to scan the lake and its surrounding mansions. I gave him a brief bio and pulled out some of my better anecdotes before turning it over to Bo, who did the same. Then I started on the presentation.

I was about halfway through the power-point slides, focusing on Fin, when I was distracted by movement in the corner of my right eye. Something was happening in the outer room around Christine's cubicle. When I looked, I stopped cold. My heart accelerated, and I locked my knees and planted my right hand squarely on our small conference table.

Loping into the office, panting feverishly, Boomer pulled on a leash held tightly by the Russian psychopath. Bo spun around, and his jaw dropped. He rose immediately and shoved his hand into his jacket pocket. I saw what he was doing and thrust out my hand to signal him to stop. He lowered the .38 back into his pocket before anyone had seen it and kept his hand there.

Christine opened the glass door. "Look who's here," she said merrily. Boomer pulled on the leash to get around her and get to me. He whined in frustration, and I knelt to get my arms around his neck.

"I found him wandering," announced the Russian in the same merry voice as Christine. "I think he was looking for his home, but he is a boy dog, so he's not good at asking for directions. You understand?"

I unclasped the leash from his collar, and he jumped forward, pushing me over onto my back.

"Maybe you two get a room," laughed the Russian. He turned to Fin and reached out his hand. "Hi...who are you?"

Fin stood. "Chester Finley, but call me Fin. And you are?"

"Harry. Harry Callahan," he said dryly, offering us Clint Eastwood's name from the classic film "Dirty Harry."

All three of us stared at him for a full beat, and then he grimaced and said, "I know; you think it's funny, yes?"

"Your parents had a good sense of humor," Fin said, sitting back down, and I got back on my feet.

The Russian looked intently at Bo, whose right hand was still wrapped around the .38 inside his sports jacket.

"What's in your pocket, Bo? You have gift for me?" He winked tartly, and I realized things could easily spin out of control.

"Fin, Harry lives on my street," I injected quickly. "Thanks, Harry, for bringing Boomer. He must've gotten out this morning. We were looking for him."

"Marty, you have a big sore on your head. Did you get in another bar fight?" The psychopath grinned and then, without waiting for an answer, pivoted back to Fin and said, "Mister Fin, you are investor, yes?"

"Ha!" Fin laughed. "Well, I'm considering becoming *an* investor, but I'm not yet committed."

I could see the color drain out of Bo's face. His conflict was clear. He could pull the .38 out of his pocket and shoot the Russian intruder between the eyes, seriously discouraging Fin from becoming *an* investor, not to mention going to prison for second-degree murder, or do nothing and somehow manage the situation. He chose the latter.

"Thank you for finding Boomer, Harry," he said uneasily, releasing his grip on the .38 and pulling his hand out of his pocket. "Marty was worried, and we're in an important meeting right now—"

The Russian cut him short. "I think maybe this is an investor meeting, yes? I am an investor too. I think maybe I join you." The maniac fell into the leather chair opposite Fin. He looked like he hadn't changed clothes since Monday, except for his white shirt, which was pressed and clean and buttoned at the top, probably his notion of proper business attire.

"Harry," I said anxiously. "That's not a good idea. Fin may not want to share investment decisions with a stranger." Sweat started pooling around my collar and armpits.

"No, I'm good. Harry, join us," said Fin. "You can answer questions for me. One investor to another."

Bo and I looked at each other as if another business partner had just been shot in his head. After so many years of working together, we could communicate without speaking. In a matter of three seconds, we shared the following silent conversation.

Bo: "What the fuck!"

Me: "No, really…what the fuck?"

Bo: "We can't blow this."

Me: "We really, really can't blow this."

Bo: "Keep going. I'll kill the asshole later."

Me: "Keep going. Just keep going."

"OK, Harry," I said. "I'll keep going from where I left off."

"Martin, you are a poor host. I need some water, yes?" The psycho quickly and casually established control. "And maybe some more for Mister Fin."

I smiled, opened the door, shuffled Boomer out to Christine's cubicle, and asked her to bring Pellegrino for everyone.

"When did you invest in Paladin, Harry?" asked Fin as I was about to continue with the presentation.

"A few days ago."

"Did you take the art option?"

The Russian's eyes popped at Fin, and he snickered. "Oh, yes, I take the art option. I am still owed the art, and I wait for my painting."

"Painting? I've never been a fan of Benito's painting. I think his three-dimensional work, especially the wildlife and western images, is brilliant." He paused and looked around. "Where is Nico anyway? He told me last week he would be here."

I stared at the Russian, who stared back at me with dull, inert eyes. "We don't know. We haven't seen him for days," I said solemnly.

We were falling deeper into the rabbit hole. A murderous maniac who shot Nico Scava a day and a half ago was now sitting casually in our office discussing investor strategy. I wanted to flush my brain—clean it out and start over. I don't remember how, but I finished presenting the slides left in our deck.

"If I may ask, Harry, how much did you put in?" asked Fin when I came to my summary slide.

"It is a sensitive question, you understand, but I am committed to ten million."

Fin practically came out of his chair. "Ten million!" He turned to me. "I am thrilled to hear that, Marty. I was concerned you guys were undercapitalized, and my contribution would just get eaten before the company failed, and I'd lose my money. I was waiting to tell you after you were done with the pitch. It's a good presentation, guys, and I love the art option, but I thought you were on fumes. But ten million from Harry!" He smiled excitedly. "I assume it's a line of credit, so you don't swallow up all the equity, right? You're not undercapitalized at all. I feel terrific about this, especially now that I know you have enough runway to get to BEP." (That's investor-speak for "enough money to get the company to its break-even-point.")

I smiled, but Bo had put his hand back in his pocket. We had to be careful. Raising money has many rules that carry liability. We could never acknowledge that what the Russian just said was true because if Fin's decision to invest in the company was based on a lie, he could sue us into oblivion.

"Your accent is Russian, right? Is Harry your English name?" asked Fin. "You're a young man to make such a large investment."

Fin's curiosity annoyed me, and I sought a reason to end the meeting.

"I manage my family's money," he answered.

"What do they do? If I can ask."

"Many things, but biggest family business is drugs."

"Pharmaceuticals. Well, that explains why you have a lot of money. What company?"

"We don't manufacture. We are big in distribution—wholesaler—not a company name you'd recognize."

This conversation had to end. "Harry, thanks very much, but Bo and I must get Fin to sign some important paperwork. How about if we talk to you again later?" I interrupted.

"OK, I understand. You want me to leave." He stood and shook Fin's hand. Bo stood but stepped backward like he needed the distance in case he wanted to pull out the gun.

"Mister Fin," said the Russian, looking directly into Finley's eyes. "I like meeting you, and I think maybe you should watch your money. Make sure the art is good."

Fin laughed. "It's just Fin, Harry, no mister, and I love the art."

"I just look out for my new friend," said Harry, smiling.

After he left, I had to grapple with a whole new reality. Harry Callahan, Dirty Harry, psychopath, killer—just helped us close a critical investment. To describe it as surreal did not do it justice. I don't think the Russian meant to be helpful, but he was, and I noticed a slight smugness in his departure. His stunt with Boomer was heinous, but his stunt with Fin was catalytic.

Angel investors are often motivated by greed and the fear of missing out on the next big deal. Fin understood that we wouldn't need his money if we were well-capitalized, and he could lose the opportunity and the art. He began to pitch us why his money was necessary and how he could help us manage our success. We went from begging him for money to him begging us to take his money.

Over the next hour, Bo and I finished the contracts and agreements with him. Fin would send money immediately before we changed our minds. After he left, I sat with Bo staring out at the lake. Neither one of us had the energy to speak. It felt the same as when we'd driven away from the cabin, an ugly kind of exhilaration, like a POW enduring a pause in his interrogation.

"We can't take the money," said Bo.

"We never acknowledged we had $10 million in the company," I responded.

"Jesus, Marty! You think Fin's not going to find out? One look at the cap table."

"Let's get out of this shitstorm first. We'll talk to Fin after, and if he wants his money back, we'll return it."

My phone buzzed. It was Abbie.

"Christine called me. You have Boomer?"

"Yes, you should come and pick him up. I'm slammed all day."

"Who brought him to your office? Why bring him to your work and not home?" She was winding up, and I needed to contain things.

"Let's talk about it later. I'm right in the middle of a meeting. We got our money. Can you pick Boomer up? Maybe between visiting the bank and your attorney friend." I couldn't resist the jab. I knew Christine would tell Abbie about Harry Callahan, inviting more questions, and the first domino would fall. I hung up, and Bo checked his watch.

"Let's try the baron's number again. Maybe we'll get lucky," said Bo. I read it to him from my phone, and he punched it on speaker. The baron picked up on the first ring, and I rolled my eyes.

"Baron Von Baltruschat, it's Bo Bishop and Martin Schott. Do you remember us?" There was a short pause.

"Yes, I do. It's been a while, but I remember you."

"We would like to come and visit you," said Bo.

"What about?"

"I'd rather wait to tell you in person."

"I don't like impromptu meetings. Perhaps we can schedule this another time."

"I'm sorry for the short notice, Baron, but we tried to call you last night."

"I never answer the phone after six. It's not civilized."

Bo's voice shifted from polite to stern. "Baron, civilized or not, we need to talk to you. It concerns Nico Scava."

The next pause was awkwardly long. "No, I don't think so. I'll talk to Nico, and perhaps we can have a joint meeting."

"No, that won't happen," I jumped in. "Look, Baron, it's not a request. We must see you today. It's critical."

"I don't care what it is. You can't just demand a visit. There's a protocol."

Bo's face began to glow red. "Screw protocol, Baron! We're coming over now, not later, not tomorrow, but right now, and if you don't answer the door and talk to us, I will call the cops. Am I clear?"

"What in holy hell are you talking about?"

"Nico's in serious trouble, and we know you had something to do with it."

"Is Nico with you right now?" he asked.

"No," I said.

"I will call Nico now."

"You can call Nico all you want," I said. "But I don't think he'll answer."

Bo leaned into the speaker, dropping his baritone another octave. "Albert, we're coming over, and if you don't open the door, I will hunt you down. I will break into your house. I will take a hammer to your windows. I am not playing around. It's life and death. More specifically, my life, your death."

CHAPTER THIRTEEN

Wednesday Afternoon

The Baron

THE BARON HAD MOVED.

I'd learned this the night before after Abbie cleaned my head abrasion and went to bed. I lay next to her, on top of the covers, laptop on my chest, searching the internet, keeping the night terrors at bay. I'd found a small article in the *Willamette Weekly*, published almost a year earlier, detailing the Portland baron's troubles with his manor house.

As Bo drove to Von Baltruschat's new address, I told him what I had read, describing that the local diocese, which owned the mansion we'd visited two years ago, sued him, and he'd been forced to move out.

"I knew he was bad news," said Bo weaving through traffic.

"No, actually, you didn't," I corrected him. "You thought he was pompous, not perverse."

"Tomayto—Tomahto."

"The *Willamette Weekly* article said that although the baron's credentials were all in order, his, and I quote now, 'regal roots read like a soap opera script.' Apparently, Albert was born in Chicago, an average kid who grew up and became a high school history teacher. Then at the ripe old age of thirty-eight, he was legally adopted by his great aunt, a Countess Helene Von Baltruschat." Then I did a short drum roll on the dash for effect. "He went from *Boring* Albert to *Baron* Albert in one swallow."

"Seriously?"

"I can't make this up, Bo."

We pulled up to the baron's new digs, a single-story grey brick ranch with dark blue shutters tucked neatly into the end of a cul-de-sac just outside Lake Oswego on Indian River Court. He'd taken quite a plunge from baronial swank to suburban simple. When we knocked, he yelled out immediately, "Go away."

It took some verbal scuffling before he finally opened the door. He did not offer us a tour this time. Instead, we scowled at each other for a few blinks, and then he slumped his shoulders and invited us in for tea.

He hadn't changed much—still portly, if anything, a little more so, and his ginger hair had receded. He wore khaki dockers, a white shirt with a blue blazer, like the last time, sans the bling, except for a garish gold cross on a thick chain that swung back and forth in a tight arc as he walked.

I imagined the transition from the manor house to this cookie-cutter, three-bedroom bungalow must have been painful and taken profound logistical skills—like trying to shove the entire Portland Art Museum into my basement. What had looked crowded in a three-store mansion now looked like an overstuffed secondhand furniture store. For a minute I felt claustrophobic in the cloying, stale air. It stank of diminished grandeur.

"Please excuse the mess," he said with a hint of shame. "I was forced to squeeze my entire life into this tiny place, and I had to put much in storage. But I will be moving back soon."

"Back?" asked Bo.

"Yes, I am negotiating with the owners of the house we used to occupy. The Church is very accommodating. It was a good home in a perfect neighborhood, and the lieutenant governor was our neighbor."

"I'm surprised," I said. "I read in *Willamette Weekly* that your relationship with the diocese did not end well."

"Nonsense. Just negative news to sell papers. I have a good relationship with the Church. I was forced to move a year ago because of the lawyers. They make everything impossible. But we have recovered now. We have agreed on a price, and it's no longer a lease. I will buy back my home."

"You have the money to buy that mansion, Baron? Several years ago, when we spoke, you were not as…financially secure," said Bo carefully.

We single-filed our way down a furniture-lined hall and shoe-horned ourselves into his overcrowded living room. Bo moved quickly to the open leather armchair and left me with the only other available seat, an indented cushion on an old couch next to a packing box labeled "Living Room."

Albert then shuffled off to the kitchen.

"More nonsense, Mr. Bishop," he called out amidst dish clatter. "I have never been, as you would say, financially insecure. We talked about raising money for a protracted lawsuit. I was not looking for bread money. I told you I have a very long and noble ancestry. Members of my family are directly responsible for the West's civilized history. I am not a parasite."

I looked at Bo, put my finger in my mouth, and pretended to vomit.

"I think you are insulting," the baron continued. "You threatened me on the phone. You have no right to speak to me in that tone." A minute later, he appeared carrying a tray with an old-fashioned English teapot and several teacups. "You may call me *Freiherr* if you wish," he continued. "Baron is just the English translation of my German position."

Was it my imagination, or had the baron become more of an arrogant ass?

"No, Baron is fine with me," answered Bo.

I looked closely at the baron's damp fleshy face, his eyes avoiding mine. He was either nervous or scared, and then it struck me: he wasn't an ass at all. He was attempting to distance himself from us through his contrived social rank. He thought he could avoid our invasive questions by ineptly reminding us he was an aristocrat while we were not. It was a defense tactic, and I felt a little sorry for him.

"Why did you threaten me with life and death? Were you referring to Nico? You said he was in trouble?"

"Have you seen him recently?" asked Bo.

"No, but then why would I?"

"We heard you had business with him."

He sipped tea and purposely remained standing so we would have to look up at him. His hand shook slightly, and the cup rattled on its saucer. I grinned.

You should avoid delicate teacups when you're nervous, Albert.

"I have never done business with Nico. He is only a friend," he said firmly.

It was a response meant for a deposition, not a chat over tea. Both Bo and I said nothing but stared knowingly at him. His head and neck grew pink, and he said, "I am a German citizen, you know—I have diplomatic immunity."

It was such an odd non-sequitur it answered my earlier suspicion. He wasn't nervous; he was scared and quickly losing control over his ability to conceal it. I recognized the panic in his eyes and thought I must have looked like that to the Russian in the cabin just before I wet my pants. I recalled the cold, callous stare from the Russian's opaque eyes, and a surge of empathy washed over me. I signaled to Bo with a slight wag of my finger to slow down and go in a different direction to bring the baron back from the edge.

"I read that you were adopted, Albert," I said. "I didn't know that. How'd that all come about?"

His body relaxed. "It is a complicated story, but I am happy to tell it if you want to hear it." The flush in his face subsided, and he was back on familiar ground.

The baron then removed a large box resting on the only other comfortable chair in the room, sat down, put his teacup on the fully laden cocktail table, and launched into his family history. Bo and I sipped Earl Grey, stayed alert, and hoped we would find a thread we could pull to get to the information that might save our lives somewhere in his bizarre biography.

///

Freiherr Albert Von Baltruschat Zu Warendorf was born Albert Paul Fuller in Chicago, Illinois, with a birth certificate listing his parents as Sarah and Frank Fuller. He was the middle child between two sisters and the only child with ginger hair. He skipped over his childhood entirely, making me think it was unremarkable. I supposed being bestowed a noble pedigree later in life made any ordinary youth seem trivial. Like Mark Twain's *The Prince and the Pauper*—if you're *the* grimy pauper and *the* long-lost heir to the kingdom, why spend time recounting a prosaic adolescence?

So, how does an inauspicious middle son of a middle-class family from middle America become part of the European gentry?

How does red blood turn blue?

Depending on what you want to believe, the quick and easy answer is a little incestuous depravity.

Albert spoke uninterrupted for almost an hour. His verbal skills were prodigious, and he defused scrutiny with an avalanche of chatter. Eventually, however, I assembled a few truths.

His great-aunt Helene Fuller, his paternal grandfather's sister, adopted him. She wasn't German, nor was she born a countess. She was a beautiful American woman who married into an aristocratic German family in the 1930s.

The particular branch of the monarchial tree that the countess married into was the Baltruschat branch, a noble tribe whose lineage had begun with a knight in the early 1200s. I could bore you, as the baron did, with different accounts of the illustrious ancestors of the Baltruschat clan—their propitious comminglings, their castles and hunting lodges, their crests and their jewels, their intersecting marriages, resulting in many offshoots and errant limbs, and finally their unique (according to the baron), fascinating personal histories.

But I won't.

Suffice it to say, over the centuries, Europe's patrician tree grew into such an unwieldy, colossal genealogical chart that every new twig could rightfully claim a relationship with every other part of the tree. Hence, in Lake Oswego, just outside Portland, Oregon, a pompous middle-aged man could realistically claim—and did—a family connection with kings and queens, present and past, and, without embarrassment, even a link to Charlemagne, Emperor of the Holy Roman Empire.

"My mother, Countess Helene," he said, "was never accepted by the family, and they treated her unkindly. They would not share any of the family's possessions."

"What the hell is all this then?" I asked, waving my arms around.

"The family did not welcome my mother. I only have what she was able to 'appropriate.'" He used air quotes.

"Appropriate!" exclaimed Bo. "What did she use, a U-Haul?"

"The countess was an amazing woman. Beautiful, intelligent, resourceful…"

"Old," I injected.

"Excuse me?"

"The article I read said she adopted you when she was 85. You were—what—38?"

"Martin, you make it sound odious. You should stop reading gossip papers. They are in business to make a profit, so they make things sound scurrilous. They leave out everything decent, everything human. I was cared for by the countess during my life as if I were her biological son. I believe I have two mothers. The countess was my German mother, and my American mother is my birth mother.

My father most certainly was Count Konstantin Joseph Albert Von Baltruschat."

He told us how his life was changed in the early 1960s when Helene and her husband, Konstantin, visited the Fullers in their modest Chicago home on a visit to America. The count and countess planned a trip to California to see Disneyland and took the young Albert with them.

Yes, I said Disneyland.

Unbelievably, while at "the happiest place on earth," the count admitted to Albert that he was his biological father. How suspiciously convenient to be told by a German count that you were his illegitimate son while enjoying an ice cream cone at the world's most famous land of make-believe.

"If I'm following you, Baron, your great aunt, Helene, the countess, went to her nephew's wife, your mother, and asked her to let her husband Konstantin fuck her, so he could have an heir." I was purposely rude to stress the decadency of his story.

"That is a distasteful thing to say. It didn't happen that way at all."

"OK, then perhaps a different angle; your biological father, Count Konstantin, old enough to be a grandfather, banged his wife's brother's son's wife, his niece-in-law, your mother. And your mother's husband, Frank—that would be the guy you called Dad until you went to Disneyland—either knew or didn't know he was just a caretaker for the old man's progeny."

"This is none of your business and improper for us to discuss. My mother told me that it was an accepted arrangement. Old families, like ours, with a long lineage to protect, do what is necessary to preserve the family line."

"Which mother?" asked Bo. "Which mother told you it was an acceptable arrangement. Your German mother, the countess, or your American mother, the commoner?"

"Both of them," he said as he lifted his bulk from the chair, picked up the teapot, and strutted to the kitchen.

"Then they are both very agreeable women," sighed Bo, knowing the baron was out of earshot.

"They weren't preserving the family tree," I whispered. "They were preserving their inheritance."

"All this junk?" asked Bo, looking around.

"One man's treasure..." I said wistfully.

Bo's eyebrows arched, and I could tell he was losing patience. So far, there'd been no thread to pull, only salacious and voyeuristic tripe, which would have been fun to pursue if our lives were not in danger. I looked at my watch. We'd spent an hour and a half amassing farcical anecdotes about a frivolous man, which, no doubt, we would deploy as future party fodder if we ever managed to escape our mess. But that wasn't our mission.

"We need to push him. Give me some room, Marty, don't wave me off," Bo whispered as Albert returned with more tea, which he poured attentively for all of us.

"I have a silver tea set that belonged to Marie Antoinette," he said.

"That's nice, Albert, but now I want to talk about you and Nico and what you sold," said Bo.

"Once again, I had no business with Nico. He will confirm what I am telling you."

"We don't have the time anymore, Albert." Bo stood up, and although he was already a large man, he appeared to grow even more menacing. "You sold a painting for $10 million or more, and so help me, you're gonna tell us all about it, or I will rip your aristocratic, *freiherr*, holier-than-thou heart out."

In college, Bo played cornerback, probably the most demanding defensive position on any football team. He can lower his shoulders, lean into you, and look like he will break your spinal column. Albert took three steps back.

We already knew the baron was a bit of a nutter, and the stories that spilled from his mouth were well-practiced and tedious half-truths, embellishments, and blatant lies. He was not, however, as adept at improvising immediate deceits. At his core, the baron was craven; but try as he might, he could not hold the hauteur. Bo continued to press him, and his veneer began to crack—like a hard–boiled egg being rolled back and forth over a countertop.

He backed into the main hallway, every inch of wall space lined with furniture, and started working his way up and down the narrow floor, pacing with such speed that I thought for a minute he might faint. His face reddened, the heavy cross around his neck swung like a pendulum, his hands gripped the back of a chair wedged between two dressers, and he rattled it as he shouted. "Get out! I don't have to talk to you! You are not the police! You have no right! I have diplomatic immunity!"

"I don't care if you have a presidential pardon," growled Bo, following him into the cramped hallway. "Call the cops! Go ahead! You won't call them because whatever you sold wasn't legal, and that's why you're scared."

"Yes, I am scared. But I'm scared of you! Where is Nico? What have you done to him?"

"We didn't do anything. But somebody else did. They shot him."

"I don't believe you. You are insane."

"I don't care what you think."

The baron swallowed hard and looked at me, avoiding Bo's threatening hulk. The only sound was a tall grandfather clock ticking further down the hallway.

"I asked him to sell one of my paintings," he murmured.

"What painting?" I asked.

"I cannot tell you."

"For the love of God, are you fucking serious!" It was my turn to yell.

"I will tell you what Nico did for me. I don't have to tell you anything more."

He walked past us back to the living room, and we followed. We all sat back down in our respective places. I wished I'd let Bo go at him when we first arrived.

"Who bought this mystery painting?" Bo asked.

"I don't know. I never met her. I know her name was Natalya. Nico didn't even give me her last name. He kept everyone in separate boxes, afraid I would go around him if I knew too much."

Bo and I believed him. It was how we did business. You don't reveal your sources because clients have a bad habit of going around you to avoid paying the fee. The baron was probably telling us the truth.

"Did the sale go through with this Natalya woman?" I asked.

"Of course it did. Nico knew Natalya was representing someone else, although she always claimed to be the buyer herself."

"Did Nico know who she represented?"

"I think so, but he never told me."

"All this secrecy about a stupid painting. Was it stolen?" asked Bo.

The baron stopped breathing for a moment. The tip of his tongue slid over his upper lip. I could tell he was looking for a way not to answer the question. "It was…" he paused, "appropriated…but not by me."

"Baron! Albert! Stop it!" I yelled. "You don't want to play word games now. Tell us everything."

He stood up and folded his arms across his chest. He was trying to stop himself from shaking. "I cannot tell you more. It will put me in danger. Don't you understand? Nico and I sold a painting that should not have been sold. Nico received a substantial commission. He told me very little, to protect me, but maybe more to protect himself. I never met or spoke to Natalya. Nico would not allow it. I know she inspected the painting to confirm its authenticity. I was not allowed to be there. I don't think Natalya knew about me. I don't know how Nico managed to get around the provenance without telling her about me, but he did. The whole thing took many months. I gave up the painting in December last year and got paid three months later. The stress nearly killed me. That's it. I have told you as much as I can. Now please leave!"

"We can't do that. We need to find the painting, and we need to find the money," said Bo.

"What are you talking about? The painting is sold. I will not return the money. The sale was legitimate."

"Albert, listen to me carefully now," Bo stood up and moved closer to him. "Nico said the same thing just before he was shot in his head. He said it was a 'legitimate' deal. But nothing about this deal is 'legitimate.' You and Nico don't know the meaning of that word."

I nodded in agreement, and Bo showed me his open hand, signaling me to stay quiet.

He continued. "We think the painting never got to the true buyer because a Russian mafia goon and his Irish buddy took us hostage Monday night and demanded we deliver $10 million and the painting to them by the end of this week or they will kill our families and us. They put a bullet in Nico's face to make their point. You don't want to meet these guys, Albert. One of them is a total psychopath. He'll cut your heart out and whistle while doing it. Since Monday night Marty and I have been running around trying to make sense of it all. The psychopath watches us. He drops in on us to let us know he can hurt us anytime. It's a game for him. We're insects in a jar." He slowed his cadence.

"You will give us all the money, so Marty and I can return it to the psycho. And you will tell us about the painting. I don't give a rat's ass about it. I don't care if it's the *Mona Lisa* or dogs playing poker. I want the damn thing only so I can give it back to the freak threatening to kill us. The only reason that bastard and his posse didn't come for you is that he probably doesn't know about you. He only knew Nico because Natalya—whoever the hell that is—knew only Nico, and to our misfortune, Nico was our business partner. That's how we got dragged into this holy mess."

He paused to be sure Albert was tracking him. "You will get us out of it, Albert…you. Or I will introduce them to you, and you can sip tea with them and tell them about your thousand-year-old family and how your seventy-year-old aristocratic father fucked your thirty-year-old bourgeois mother so he could have a little baron all his own."

The only sound was the rhythmic pulse of the tall clock in the hallway.

The baron's facial muscles slackened until his cheekbones protruded, and his mouth hung open. "Stop threatening me. You have no right," he cried.

"It's not a threat, Albert," I said, keeping my voice as calm as Bo's. "Nico was shot in the head next to me. I still smell it. I pissed myself. It was not my proudest moment. If we can't get what we need from you, we're going to the FBI."

"You cannot do that," he said with a slight burst of new energy like he'd bounced from an old panic to a new one.

"Yes, we can, Albert. It's the only way to save our lives."

"By saving yours, you will destroy mine." He dropped his arms and looked defeated. For a moment, I thought he would cry, and I felt a rush of pity for him.

"You can come with us, and we'll all go to the FBI together," I said consolingly.

"No, I can't. Nico and I broke too many laws. International laws. US laws. German laws. Polish laws. Laws in just about every civilized country in the world."

"What are you talking about?" My impatience returned. "You and Nico just sold a goddamn painting."

"Not just a painting, Martin. We sold *this* painting."

CHAPTER FOURTEEN

Later Wednesday Afternoon

This painting

I WISH I COULD TELL YOU AN INSPIRING STORY about *this* painting. A painting celebrated more for its stubborn elusiveness than its historical significance—a painting known more for its fate than its destiny. But sadly, the true history of this masterwork of the Renaissance, this slippery yeti of the art world, is mostly a chronicle of theft, greed, luck, and spite.

"What is *this* painting?" Bo asked placidly, coaxing the answer like a social worker talking to an abused child.

"One of the most valuable paintings in the world." Albert's shoulders had collapsed, his body had shrunk, and his pretension and pride deflated like a day-old party balloon.

"$10 million wouldn't make it one of the most valuable paintings in the world, Albert," I said casually, taking my vocal cues from Bo.

"Try $100 million—maybe $200 million. Its true value is just conjecture, a fantasy appraisal, a projection. Because to the world, it doesn't exist...it's a ghost."

"What—fucking—painting?" I leaned into him as his emptied eyes stared past me into what I imagined was now just a future of faded ambition.

"Raphael's *Portrait of a Young Man*. Some scholars call it Portrait of a Youth, but I prefer *Portrait of a Young Man*."

"Never heard of it," I said.

"You wouldn't have. It's been lost for too many years. Since before you were born."

"Lost?"

"The world believes it to be lost, stolen, or destroyed. But it's none of those things. It's just…" He paused, and the corners of his lips turned up. "…been detained."

"We're going to need scotch," I said. The smell of thrift-store decay permeating the house was beginning to give me a headache, and I hoped to rinse my nostrils with the whiff of scotch.

Hanging his head and walking like the last man in a funeral procession, Albert shuffled to a Biedermeier cabinet in the hallway and pulled out three dusty glasses and a bottle of Dewar's.

Blended scotch—another reason why we would never become friends.

Seeking elbow room, I picked up the packing box with which I'd been sharing the couch and placed it on the floor. Albert clutched the heavy cross draped around his neck, pulled it over his head, wrapped it in a handkerchief, and tucked it into his jacket pocket. I supposed he didn't want God to hear this part of the story.

Bo poured the Dewar's, and Albert began to pontificate, recovering some of his formal demeanor.

"*Portrait of a Young Man* was painted around 1513 by the Italian Renaissance master Raffaello Sanzio, better known as Raphael. His self-portrait is considered the most valuable painting to have gone missing during World War II. It was stolen by the Nazis from the Czartoryski family estate in Poland shortly after the Germans invaded."

While he spoke, Albert set up a MacBook in the center of the already crowded cocktail table, and then next to it, he laid a thick anthology called *The Complete Works of Raphael*, which he'd retrieved from one of the book stacks under the table. He opened the picture book to a page he'd marked with a yellow sticky note while the laptop booted up, and then he opened a file labeled photos. Like art students studying for finals, we examined the laptop photos and compared them with the glossy images in the anthology.

Raphael's self-portrait is an oil painting on wood showing a young man with delicate, almost feminine features seated at a table in front of a blank wall with an open window. Not yet quite a man, the boy is dressed lavishly in a voluminous shirt tightened at the wrists by cords and a large, attention-grabbing fur cloak casually draped over his shoulders. The shirt is so ample and billowy that I thought, at first glance, he was wearing a bedsheet. The young man's right elbow rests on the table, and his right hand casually hangs over its edge while his left arm is wrapped covetously around the fur stole, serenely stroking its luxury.

The youth's dark hair, parted in the middle, drapes to his shoulders in long curls and is capped by a black beret the size of a small pillow. His face is at odds with his attire. He looks too young to wear such extravagant clothing. His effete lips and languid eyes give him a look of melancholy and conceit. A delicate pattern of dense cracks—Albert called it crackling—spread across the entire portrait like uneven brickwork. A thin fracture ran the whole length of the painting, missing the youth's face but cutting through his right arm, left hand, and down to his lap. The paint had begun to flake and bubble along the break, causing tiny concentric fissures to extend into the upper torso.

We followed Albert's finger on the laptop screen as he traced the thin crack.

"That was done when my mother hid the painting between two mattresses. She told me an American soldier sat on her bed while he talked her into letting him rape her. She always said American soldiers were much more polite about their war crimes. Unlike the Russians, who just struck, they would first offer chocolate or cigarettes for what they wanted.

"She did her best to repair the damage but is not an expert. The masterpiece will need to be restored. It's easy to fix, and I'm sure the new buyer will do his best."

The photos on the MacBook showed the painting's damage and age, while in the anthology, the portrait looked clean and fresh, as if new. Albert clicked through the photo file to reveal the back of the painting.

"Twenty-nine and a half by twenty-three inches, to be exact.

Quite large for a wood panel painting for that time. Half an inch shorter and two inches wider than the *Mona Lisa*."

From the back, the painting looked its full 500 years. The entire panel was sheathed in a pattern of interlacing wood slats—Albert called it a "cradle"—fashioned by the countess to protect it from warping and additional fractures. I could see bits and pieces of the medieval poplar, pitted and rough, through the cradle. I could read the faded letters LRR along the top flax-colored edge, and next to it, what looked like a name written in a buoyant cursive but no longer legible. In the upper-middle, between the cradle's slats, right on the cracked seam, was a small, gray wax seal, fossilized and unreadable.

"The painting was entrusted to Samuel Woodburn, London's principal art dealer in the 1840's and I believe that's his seal," said the baron.

"There were very few photos taken of the painting before the war, mostly monochrome, and no photos at all of its reverse side. All the images today, like in this anthology, are colored reproductions of black and white images. No one alive today has seen the original masterpiece except me, Nico, Natalya—I suppose the buyer—and now you."

I didn't feel fortunate or privileged. I felt only hostility. I looked at Raffaello Sanzio, the young man in the painting as if he were my enemy. This pretty boy of the Renaissance had seriously fucked up my life, and if I could have laid my hands on the original at that moment, I would gladly have thrown the entire panel into an open fire and watched the flames melt his face.

///

Albert explained how Raphael, together with Michelangelo and Leonardo da Vinci, formed the trinity of great masters of the Renaissance—that period in European history when the continent started to awaken from nearly a thousand years of cultural blight known as the Dark Ages. Born in 1483, Raphael lived only thirty-seven years but achieved immortality in his short life. He was heavily influenced by Leonardo and Michelangelo, who, in turn, despised him for his youth and genius. Pope Julius II commissioned him to paint murals on the Pope's private library walls when he was just twenty-five. At the same time, just down the hall, so to speak, Michelangelo worked on the ceiling of the Sistine Chapel.

"Imagine such a thing," Albert said. "Two of the greatest artists to have ever lived painting different rooms in the Vatican Palace. It would be like having Gauguin and Van Gogh paint your bedrooms simultaneously."

Albert gave us the rest of Raphael's biography, but I barely listened until he started talking about his death. The young genius never married but was rumored to have a voracious libido. Apparently, after a night of rigorous sex with his mistress, a baker's daughter, he came down with pneumonia, probably from too much sweating and exertion during a cold night of carnality. The story goes that Raphael didn't want to confess his debauchery to his doctors, so he lied about it. In turn, his doctors prescribed the wrong medical treatment for him, resulting in his premature death. In those days, having a high fever was often diagnosed as having an excess of blood, and the treatment in 1520 was to drain it using either incisions or leeches.

"He took fifteen days to die," said Albert solemnly, as if he'd known him.

"So, you could say the genius painter screwed himself to death," said Bo.

"Born 1483 and painted this portrait in 1513, so he was thirty at the time," I said, more to myself than anyone else. "He looks like a child—like a virgin adolescent."

Like the Russian.

"The portrait has been number one on the list of the most wanted paintings in the world since 1945 and is considered a national treasure to the Polish people. The Raphael's original frame hangs empty inside the modern Czartoryski Museum, waiting for its return to Krakow," said Albert.

"And you sold it," responded Bo reaching for the Dewar's and shaking his head.

"You insult me," said Albert impassively. By then, he'd had all his pride kicked out of him, and this slight defiance was now just show.

"Yes, Albert, I'm insulting you. Marty and I have a goddamn maniac assassin hunting us like it's a sport because you couldn't find the decency to do the right thing—give the damn painting back to the Polish authorities."

"I inherited the painting when my mother died."

"That would be your German mother, not your American mother," I interrupted sarcastically.

He stared at us, and for a moment, I thought we'd lost him again. His eyes looked past us into an unknown abyss. "When I first saw the painting," he said finally, his stare still vacant, "I recognized it immediately. I've become an expert on German history, the war, and Nazi confiscation. The portrait is world-famous. I even saw a show about it on the History Channel. I had no idea of its value, not right away. I had to do a lot of research. I knew, of course, that if I ever told anyone, I would be overrun immediately by lawyers and politicians. The painting would have been ripped from me like a kidnapped child. I would get nothing and probably be sued by the Czartoryski family or the Polish government for millions of dollars. I don't know which one has more money, but either could bury me in legal costs. I had to keep my secret, and did for many years, including the time you visited. I couldn't tell you about the Raphael because I couldn't trust you to keep my secret. I still don't."

"You never checked into a reward?" I asked.

"Of course I did. The literature will tell you there is a reward of $100 million, and it's the highest reward for any painting in the world. But it's nonsense. Rewards are for fools and children. The Czartoryski lawyers would have found a reason to cheat me. My mother held the painting for a generation and kept it willingly and covetously. The lawyers would smear me with her guilt. Paying a reward would be rubbing salt in their wound. They would blame me for its damage and sue me for defacing a national treasure."

He took a deep breath. "My greatest problem was that I didn't know what to do with it. I wanted to sell it, but to whom? I suspected there were buyers, but how would I find them? I am not an art expert and have never sold anything unlawfully. There are no signs that say, 'Black market, enter here.' I looked on the internet but found nothing that could help me. There were no chat rooms for Nazi loot; if there were, I couldn't find them. I also had no one I could trust. The reward is obscene and completely out of my reach, but for anyone else, it would be like winning the lottery."

"Why not have an attorney or someone else play the middleman," I reasoned. "Return the painting, collect the reward, and share it with you?"

Bo gave me a painful stare. I think he was uncomfortable with anything sounding like conciliation.

"Because my involvement would ultimately be discovered. The Czartoryski family would launch an investigation to confirm the provenance. I would be found out, and the legal proceedings would start." He smiled sadly. "The reward is a publicity stunt designed for the lucky idiot who might stumble upon it at a flea market or an estate sale—an accidental owner—not the person who held it illicitly for over six decades."

I nodded and poured cold tea into my scotch glass. I needed to stay sober.

"I met Nico several years ago at the Portland Charity Ball. He invited me to sit with him. I learned about his art business, and my instincts told me he could help me. I studied him for a while and decided he could be trusted, and after swearing him to secrecy, I showed him the painting. He sat in front of it for hours, just looked at it. Then he said he'd get back to me. That was it. I regretted it immediately. I was sure he would try to collect the reward and be a hero in the art world. I hid the painting and was prepared to call him a liar if the authorities came to my front door. There have been many false sightings and phony claims, so it would be his word against mine."

"I wonder why?" I asked.

"Why he never went for the reward," clarified Bo.

"I don't know," he shrugged. "He just told me he found a buyer." Albert gulped his scotch and poured some more. "He said an art dealer would purchase it. An art dealer named Natalya who facilitates transactions that are not always legal."

"She fences stolen art," said Bo.

Albert's head bobbed. "I asked Nico who her client was, but he wouldn't tell me. He said even Natalya didn't know that he knew."

"How's that possible? How would Nico know who Natalya represented if she didn't tell him? He must have lied," I said.

"How'd your German mother end up with it?" asked Bo, emphasizing "German."

"I know the life of this painting like it was my child, but I'll give you the short version."

"Can you give us the short version of the short version?" said Bo.

Albert bowed and recounted the painting's biography.

I'll summarize for you.

After bouncing around a couple of hundred years, Raphael's portrait was purchased by Prince Adam Jerzy Czartoryski in the early 1800s, along with two other significant works: Leonardo Da Vinci's *Lady with an Ermine* and Rembrandt's *Landscape with the Good Samaritan*.

These paintings—the Raphael, the Leonardo, and the Rembrandt—formed an exceptional triad of masterpieces called "the Great Three." The paintings languished for years at the Czartoryski estate. They were bricked up in a hidden room for a decade until finally, in 1882, they were brought to the new family museum in Krakow, where they were displayed for over 30 years. Then came World War II.

"To understand what happened to the Great Three during WWII, you need to understand the participation of another three—the German great three—Hitler, Goering, and Frank." Albert looked at Bo to be sure he was still paying attention.

"The German great three?" Bo *was* paying attention.

"Yes, you know Adolf Hitler."

"Yes, of course. Not a fan," said Bo.

"You know Hermann Goering?"

"Sounds familiar but don't remember."

I jumped in. "Number two Nazi. Big, fat, looked like beardless Santa with a swastika. Head of the military. Hitler's chosen successor. Started the Gestapo. Liked to wear white or powder blue uniforms—very GQ sassy—for a Nazi."

Bo studied me for a second. "You're starting to worry me."

"You know Hans Frank?" asked Albert.

"No, who was Hans Frank?" I asked.

"He was 'Reichleiter' or 'Reich Leader,' the second-highest position in the Nazi party, reporting directly to Hitler. He was also Hitler's personal attorney, and after the Germans overran Poland in '39, Hitler made him head of the Polish Provisional Government. He became known as 'The Butcher of Poland.'

"In August 1939, just before the war began, the Czartoryski family packed the three paintings into an evacuation trunk and sent them to their palace in Sieniawa, where they were locked into a secret attic room. The Germans attacked Poland two weeks later, and Nazi troops overran the Sieniawa estate and quickly found the Great Three. The paintings were immediately dispatched to the Kaiser-Friedrich-Museum in Berlin and then earmarked for exhibition at the planned Hitler Museum."

"Hitler had his own museum?" asked Bo.

"The museum was part of a huge cultural complex planned by

Hitler for his Austrian hometown of Linz. The idea was that after Germany won the war and converted the world to Nazidom, the Hitler Museum would become the largest museum in the world, filled with the greatest art plunder in human history. The Germans looted about one-fifth of all the art on the European continent, about 650,000 pieces, and this giant pile of booty was about to descend on Linz like a blitzkrieg. Hitler wanted the little city to become the Third Reich's cultural capital and one of Europe's greatest art centers, even overshadowing Paris and Vienna. Hitler hated Vienna because he once failed to gain admission to the Vienna Academy of Fine Arts."

"You know," I said, reverting to the Dewar's. "I applied to Stanford once and was rejected. Didn't start a war over it, though."

Bo smiled. "It's what makes you the better man."

Albert remained grave. Humor, like his pride, had been beaten out of him by our visit. "Hermann Goering was even more prolific than Hitler in his looting," he continued.

"OK, but what's all this got to do with the Raphael?" Bo's hands signaled him to speed forward.

"I'm trying to explain how the painting ended up in my hands instead of Hermann Goering's."

"In that case, please go on."

CHAPTER FIFTEEN

Wednesday Evening

The Baron's Wife

ALBERT CONTINUED THE STORY, TALKING QUICKLY, intent on cramming our heads with as much information as possible about a painting we'd known nothing about only an hour earlier.

"In 1940, Hermann Goering issued a special directive outlining how looted art would be distributed among the Nazi hierarchy. The first priority went to Hitler, and the second went to Goering. Third to the Nazi Institute of Art, and the fourth priority to German museums. This pecking order then kicked off a battle between Hitler and Goering. Goering wanted the Great Three for himself. Hitler, who was too busy destroying humanity to keep a watchful eye over them, was forced to deposit the masterpieces with Hans Frank, his attorney and the Governor-General of Poland.

"Frank was a repulsive man. After the Germans occupied Poland, he moved into the Wawel Royal Castle in Krakow as the country's top Nazi. While the war raged and everyone in Europe lived on rations, Frank luxuriated in splendor. He appointed his private suite with plush furnishings seized from wealthy Polish Jews on their way to concentration camps like Treblinka, Belzec, and Auschwitz. The 'Butcher of Poland' lived like a Renaissance Pope and considered the Great Three his prized trophies. He hung the Raphael and

Rembrandt in his offices and the Leonardo in his private bathroom because his son hated it.

"He enjoyed his lavish lifestyle for only a few years until the Russians counter-attacked in 1944 and began to press through Poland on their way to Berlin." Albert pointed a finger in the air. "Here's when certain events become critical for you to understand what happened to the painting."

He took a slight pause. "Much of the war's looted artworks were recovered by American soldiers called Monuments Men or by Russian soldiers called Trophy Brigades. Fortunately, the Leonardo and the Rembrandt, two of the Great Three, were found after the war in Hans Frank's Bavarian home by Americans, not Russians. Both paintings were eventually returned to the Czartoryski Museum in Krakow, where they are today. But the Raphael was never recovered. There's never been an explanation for its disappearance, only conjecture." He stopped briefly to refill his glass.

"Its vanishing is an irritating loose end in our social conscience, a mystery that grows over time, rooting itself in our culture, like the identity of Jack the Ripper or the whereabouts of Jimmy Hoffa."

"It's a lingering question for you and people like you," insisted Bo. "I've never lost a minute of sleep over it."

"Actually, Bo," I said, coming to Albert's defense, "he might have a point. Let's look at something." I pulled the baron's laptop closer, opened the browser, and typed "Raphael, *Portrait of a Young Man*." A second later, Google listed its findings.

"Look," I said, turning the display towards Bo. "There are over two hundred thousand search engine results. It's not trivial. The discovery of the Raphael would be huge news across the world. We're talking front-page *New York Times*, above-the-fold kind of news. Websites and art magazines would cover the story from London to Paris to Moscow to Tokyo. Every treasure hunter in the world would want to know how it survived. I think we're in this mess not just because someone wants the painting but because they also want it to stay lost. Albert is just putting it into perspective."

"Perspective! It's a goddamn bomb, Marty. We're in this shitstorm because Nico and Albert fucked up, and we're left to un-fuck it." Bo slumped and rolled his eyes. I looked at Albert, who seemed wearily grateful. Then he continued.

"There has been much speculation about what happened in those chaotic, lawless days when the painting disappeared. The German armies were in retreat, deserting soldiers, Polish refugees, and concentration camp survivors coursed through the country, scavenging everything that wasn't nailed down for food and shelter.

"Hans Frank and his small entourage of soldiers realized the war was lost, and they spent their last days rowdy, drunk, and feasting on a haul of food, schnapps, and cigars. They knew it was over for them."

"What happened to Hans Frank?" I asked.

"He was tried at Nuremberg and hung for war crimes."

"Hellooo." A high light voice drifted through the musty air.

Albert's eyes bulged, and he bolted upright and ran out of the room. Bo and I sat up and looked at each other. We heard some whispering, and then Albert came back holding a large bag of Chinese carry-out in one hand and a small blond woman in the other.

"Gentlemen, this is my wife, Baroness Chrystal Von Baltruschat."

Bo and I rose. I could tell Bo was as shaken as I was. We knew Albert was married, but we'd never given it a thought. She'd never been "on deck," so to speak. She was, for us, a vague fact, a marital cipher—the last thing we wanted or needed—just another vehicle in the growing pile-up.

She stood slightly behind the baron, timid and deferential, shielding herself from the strangers in her house. Slim and delicate, she gave us a shy smile. Her eyes were warm, obliging, and humble, and I knew the instant I saw her why Albert married her. She hadn't expected us, and I could tell from her somber face she knew we'd somehow terrified her husband.

"We have Chinese, I think, enough for all of us," said Albert.

I looked at my watch, 6:30—where had the hours gone?

We all ceded to our hunger, gathered around the tottering antique dining table, and feasted on Kung Pao chicken, fried rice, chow mein, dumplings, and spring rolls over the next half hour. The conversation was guarded but friendly. Like her husband, Albert's wife was highly social. She told us she was a German conversation teacher at the Portland German International School.

"What is a conversation teacher?" I asked her.

"I teach children during the day and adults in our after-school program how to converse in German. I get home late most evenings. I'm sure Albert has excused the terrible mess. All of our treasures packed into this tiny house like a suitcase."

I checked my messages during dinner—three calls from Nico's wife, Charley.

I excused myself and stepped out into the hallway to talk to her. I was afraid she might start calling Abbie or Katherine to find us. She answered on the first ring and immediately began berating me. I wasn't sure if she was hysterical or drunk, or both. I could barely understand her. She cursed the police for doing nothing and Nico for lying dead in a ditch somewhere.

She demanded to know what Bo and I were doing to find the man she now despised and intended to divorce right after she "cut his dick off and nailed it to his forehead." I told her we were visiting people who might have recently seen him. She wanted to know who, and I made the mistake of telling her that we were currently at the baron's house. She knew of the baron but little else. She insisted Bo and I search the dance clubs, and I told her that would be a job better assigned to Nico's brother, Dante. She complained that Dante was in Vegas and kept hanging up on her, and I followed his lead and hung up myself shortly after that.

///////////////////////////////////////

After dinner and more social banter, Albert told Chrystal that Bo and I knew about the Raphael. She became visibly alarmed, and the muscles in her soft face tightened. "That can put us in terrible danger," she said.

Again, the word "danger." Neither of them had a Beretta shoved in their faces. They'd never been threatened. Theirs was a different danger.

"What danger, Baroness?" I asked.

"Legal danger mostly. Albert and Nico violated serious laws governing art sales, especially national treasure art." She looked up at the ceiling to activate her memory. "US Military Government Law Number 59, Restitution of Identifiable Property," she proudly recited. "I read it online and memorized it, and there are other laws like that. International laws governing stolen art are very strict, and selling it is forbidden."

"The danger is civil as well as criminal," said Albert. "My German relatives would use it to destroy me, chop off the American branch of the Von Baltruschat family."

"That's very paranoid, Albert," said Bo. "I thought you were all one big happy family."

"Family, yes—happy, no," said Chrystal. "He's hated by his relatives who don't have his title, and they're unhappy that an American married into their family and became part of the gene pool."

It made sense to me. Baroness Chrystal Von Baltruschat had drunk the Kool-Aid. Albert had found a uniquely gullible and trusting young woman to marry. No one could enter that relationship without buying into its eccentricity and being willing to defend it. I privately sneered in my impatient and hostile mind because I dismissed her as a guileless simpleton.

For that, I am now profoundly sorry.

I could see that Albert wanted to change the subject. He became jittery whenever Nico's name came up, and I assumed he didn't want Chrystal to know Nico had been killed. "Just as you came in, sweetheart, I was about to tell them how my mother found the masterpiece," he said.

"She was a remarkable woman," she responded. "Albert, pour some wine."

As Albert did what he was told and Chrystal cleared the table of empty Chinese food containers, Bo coughed and showed me his watch. He didn't have to say anything. I understood him fully.

Time was inversely proportional to our danger.

We weren't killing time as much as it was killing us.

CHAPTER SIXTEEN

Wednesday Night

The Countess

"COUNTESS HELENE WAS GRAND," SAID CHRYSTAL. "She was a lady who wore hats and gloves and was elegant, never snobbish, just pleasant with everyone—so gracious. She moved to Oregon to be close to Albert. She was so alone in Germany. Everyone had died. Her husband's family shunned her. She told me once they were all typical German, arrogant and unkind."

Albert stood proudly behind his wife with his hands on her shoulders.

"Albert and I loved visiting her small apartment in Charbonneau, you know, the retirement-living complex up Interstate 5. Her home was like no other. The walls were covered in chartreuse and purple, with all these antique furnishings, much of it over 200 years old. It felt like stepping into the old world whenever I walked in. She hung a photo of the family castle outside her door. And then she died—87 years old—leaving everything to Albert. He was her sole heir."

"Did she hang the Raphael in her apartment?" I asked.

"Yes, but not so anyone could see it. It hung in her bedroom on the wall opposite the bed. It wasn't visible unless you walked directly into her bedroom, which you would never dare do. She'd just lay an embroidered veil over it when she wanted to hide it. She told us that she would fall asleep every night looking at it. She said it gave her contentment."

"She knew its value," said Bo.

"Oh yes," said Albert. "She told me it was her prize. Her compensation for a life she never wanted."

Albert brought us a yellowed photo in a silver frame. The picture showed a beautiful and poised woman with high, prominent cheekbones, intelligent eyes, and curly blond hair, and she wore a double strand of pearls.

"Helene was a model, you know." Chrystal ran her fingers over the frame glass. "This photo was taken in 1933 when she modeled at Bloomingdale's in New York. How wonderful that must have been. She went to all the elegant parties. She told me a chaperone always accompanied her in those days.

"At one of those parties, she met Baron Konstantin Albert Von Baltruschat. He was the German Ambassador for Foreign Culture Exchange, and he married Helene in 1936. How could he not? Look at how lovely she was. Helene became the Baroness Von Baltruschat…" Chrystal snapped her fingers, "…just like that."

I nodded. Bo stared into his lap.

"She expected a splendid life. She was the wife of a diplomat from a noble family back when nobility still meant something. But then, without warning, Hitler recalled the entire diplomatic corps because he was about to launch World War II. So, her new husband took her to Germany. Imagine the courage she must have had."

"So, how did she get the painting? This Hans Frank guy, the Butcher of Poland, gave it to her?" asked Bo, attempting to cut through another possible hour of irrelevant family history.

"She stole it," said Albert. "Not for herself, of course. She thought she was rescuing a bunch of paintings from the Russians. She knew nothing at the time about the Raphael. She was quite ignorant about art. She did a favor for a relative, who then betrayed her."

"Betrayed her," I repeated.

Chrystal sipped her wine and let her husband take over. She'd had her three minutes.

"As hard as the war was on her and the family, its aftermath was even worse. Germany was in anarchy. The cities were in ruins. Fresh water was in short supply. Food was nearly impossible. Everybody was starving. The country was overrun with refugees, deserters, and Allied soldiers. The cities had emptied. Farmers, estate owners—anyone with a large house—were required to offer rooms to shelter the people who arrived with tattered suitcases and empty stomachs. Czechoslovakian evacuees occupied all of my mother's Warendorf estate. Helene was able to save only her private room. She farmed the estate to keep it from being turned over to the Allies, laboring alongside refugees and POWs."

Chrystal lifted her hands off the table and studied them. "Helene would show me her old, knotty hands and tell me that the war had broken them." She demonstrated how Helene would model gloves at Bloomingdale's.

"By working the land, she saved the estate," said Albert. "She was lucky because she was American, young, and still attractive. She purposely befriended an American captain, who sent a soldier to the estate every day to protect her from the random deserters and Allied soldiers who came calling at night looking for women who might trade cigarettes or food for 'favors.'"

Chrystal interrupted, "She never said it, but I know she slept with the American captain. A woman understands these things. Helene told me that to be the girlfriend of an American officer meant protection."

"Where was her husband?" I asked.

"He was in a French POW camp for the first two years after the war, so she did what was necessary to stay alive." Chrystal said it like she had experience in post-war survival.

"One day, a distant relative, a maternal cousin, wandered onto the estate," Albert continued. "His name was Gunter Von Droster, and he was a scoundrel. He'd been a regiment leader on the Eastern front and had managed to retreat from the advancing Russians. He told Helene that he'd come from his family's hunting lodge in the Brandenburg Forest, from which he'd fled so rapidly he was forced to leave behind the family's valuables, especially a stash of paintings. He was desperate to find someone to return to the lodge and rescue them. He sobbed to Helene that he would go himself, but it was too dangerous. Russians were everywhere, arresting German men suspected of being former soldiers and throwing them into labor camps. Gunter convinced her she could travel safer than he could, and he would share whatever she could rescue and bring back. He made a point of describing a specific wood panel painting wrapped in presstoff."

"Presstoff?" I asked.

"It's a kind of artificial leather made from pressed paper. The Germans invented it to replace leather during the war. It was used for decorative purposes like the leather lining on clothes, binders, or cheap shoes—stuff like that," said Chrystal, wanting to stay relevant in the conversation.

"Yes, Gunter pushed her to find the wood painting wrapped in leather. Helene took one of the refugee women living on the estate with her, and they traveled across the war-torn country for three days. When they arrived at the lodge, they broke in late at night. The Russians had already ransacked it, but Helene found the paintings stashed in a cubby hole behind a giant wine rack, exactly where Gunter had told her to search. They cut the canvases out of their frames, rolled them up, and stuffed them into burlap potato sacks. She found the Raphael last. She didn't look at it because it was fully wrapped. Obviously, she couldn't roll it, so she pushed it into her large rucksack. My mother carried that damn thing on her back for three days through Russian occupation."

He paused, imagining her perilous journey. It was part of his raconteur schtick, artificial but effective. Then he continued, "God kept his eye on them, and they finally made it back to Warendorf, arriving late at night when Gunter was asleep. Before waking him, my mother hid the rucksack under her bed. I asked her once why she did that, and she said it was a feeling. She never liked Gunter—thought he was a coward and a complainer and didn't trust him to divide the paintings equally. She had no idea what was wrapped in the presstoff, but she knew Gunter wanted it the most, so she assumed it had value.

"After she woke him, they spent an hour looking at all the paintings and divvying them up. Some of the canvasses had been damaged when she cut them out of their frames. He asked about the wood panel painting, but she pretended not to have seen it, suggesting that the Russians might have found it. Gunter threw a tantrum. He demanded to wake the refugee woman who went with her to verify her story, but Helene slapped his face for his ingratitude and arrogance. True to her fears, Gunter separated the paintings unfairly, insisting on the better ones for himself and leaving her with the more damaged ones.

"Then Helene went to sleep, exhausted. She told me she'd never slept like that before or since. By the time she woke, Gunter had run off, taking all the paintings with him, including the ones he'd given her. The Raphael was the one painting he did not take because she was sleeping on top of it."

"Speaking of sleep, Albert, I am tired. I had a long day. I don't want to be impolite, but I will leave you, gentlemen, to your stories, take my bath and go to bed." Chrystal stood, shook our hands without eye contact, and began to exit. On her way out, she turned and said, "Helene never saw Gunter again. She was told he'd been killed the day after he snuck away from the estate by a roving gang of deserted German soldiers foraging for food. Served him right," she huffed and smiled. Then she left.

Bo and I looked at each other in agreement.

"So, this Gunter character got the painting from Hans Frank," I said.

"No," Albert turned the empty wine bottle upside down and watched a few drops drip into his glass. "Here is the answer to the mystery."

Finally!

"Two days before Hans Frank abandoned Poland and retreated to his Bavarian home, he drove to a small town nearby to visit Gerhart Hauptmann. He went without his usual entourage."

Albert showed us the palms of his hand. "Now, I know Gerhart Hauptmann is one more character, but he is the most critical person in the entire chain of events. Gerhart Hauptmann is why the painting was never found or traced to my mother. He is the missing puzzle piece, always overlooked by historians and treasure hunters.

"Gerhart Hauptmann was Germany's most prestigious novelist and playwright. He was admired by the Nazis and the Communists alike. He won the Nobel prize for literature in 1912, and Hans Frank was a huge fan. The Butcher of Poland considered himself a sophisticate, a man of letters, and a member of the aristocratic intelligentsia. He wanted desperately to be recognized as an equal amongst the few. He tried to win their favor, and Gerhart Hauptmann sat at the very top of the literary elite.

"Historians who've studied the last days of Hans Frank and the Great Three all know about his impromptu visit with Hauptmann. Just think about it—the Russian army was about to overrun his location, and he had maybe 48 hours to get away and flee to Bavaria with his men and their Nazi treasure.

"Gerhart Hauptmann lived only half an hour's drive away, and Hans Frank wanted to visit him so badly that he delayed his escape by a full day in the dead of winter to share wine and schnapps with the literary lion and ponder the big questions of the day. He wrote about it in his diaries, and the visit was also described in his son's biography."

Albert swallowed those last drops of wine and pointed both forefingers into the air. "What is not known, because Hans Frank never wrote about it, was that when he visited Gerhart Hauptmann, he brought along the Raphael hidden in the trunk of his Mercedes. Frank knew the war was over for him. At that point, he knew there would never be repercussions for anything he did regarding the Great Three. Hitler was already contemplating suicide in his bunker, and the paintings were Frank's to do with as he wanted.

"And that, gentlemen, is the big secret—the answer to the eternal question of what happened to the Raphael. The painting was never 'lost' or 'destroyed; it was merely gifted, like a belated Christmas present, to Gerhart Hauptmann to flatter and impress him.

"That coward Gunter Von Droster was friends with Gerhart Hauptmann. The Droster branch of the family was loaded with writers and famous poets, and they all knew each other. While retreating from the Eastern front, Gunter visited Hauptmann looking for a warm house and a clean bed. The thing to understand about that crazy time is that due to his rank—remember, Gunter was a regiment leader—he had a vehicle and cans of gasoline, things not available to ordinary soldiers.

"Gunter didn't tell my mother much about his short stay at Hauptmann's other than the great man had presented him with a historically significant painting which he took and transported to his lodge for safe keeping. My mother thought he stole it, but that's because she hated him for his betrayal. I don't believe Gunter stole it. I think he told the truth. My guess is Hauptmann accepted Frank's gift with equal reverence and repulsion. A Raphael masterpiece offered by a loathsome human being is still a Raphael masterpiece. I also think Hauptman feared that the advancing Russian army would invade and search his house soon. He was, after all, a Nobel prize-winning playwright, and he would never want the Raphael to fall into Russian hands. I'm sure he gave the painting to Gunter to protect it. Gunter then deserted and drove to his family lodge in Brandenburg to hide until the war was over."

"Where the countess picked it up, held onto it for the next sixty years, and then gave it to you," I added.

"Well, she never gave it to me," said Albert. "She died, and it was part of my inheritance."

"But how'd she bring the Raphael into the US? How'd she get it through Customs?" asked Bo.

"She never told me how she managed that." Albert raised his eyebrows and frowned. "I never asked. But look around you. When my mother decided to immigrate back to the US, she brought everything you see here in giant shipping containers. My guess is she shuffled the Raphael among all her other paintings. I remember the declaration list she gave to the Customs and Border Protection people was pages and pages long. CBP inspectors are no different from other government bureaucrats. They probably wanted to process her massive inventory as fast as possible. The woman was in her late seventies. She was a countess, not a drug mule."

Bo slapped his hands on the table, stood up, and stretched. "So, where is it?" he asked.

"I suppose in the hands of the buyer."

"No. That's the point, Albert. We're here because the Raphael is not where it's supposed to be," Bo persisted.

"Then it was stolen."

"How? By Natalya? By Nico?"

"I don't know. I turned the painting over to Nico last December and got the money in March."

"March—seven months ago?" I interrupted, frustrated. "Nico invested in Paladin in April, one month later. Why is this happening now in October? So long after."

Bo snapped his fingers. He had his epiphany. "I know what 'bad paintings' means now, and it doesn't mean stolen. It means forged. It took time for the buyer to figure out the Raphael was fake, and a good forgery would take time to discover."

"No, Bo, it's not possible," insisted Albert. "You've seen the photos. It's not a painting that can be forged. It's 500 years old! The wood is too old to fake, and the cracks and damage it received cannot be forged."

"Bullshit," said Bo. "You said yourself no one alive has ever seen the painting, and no one knows what it looks like today."

"Natalya saw it," I said.

"Did she inspect the real one or a fake? A good forger would know how to age it enough to pass a cursory inspection."

"Who could forge such a painting?" asked Albert.

"Benito Scava," I said.

"Do you think Nico showed Natalya a forgery?" Albert asked.

"If he did, the original might still be here in Portland," said Bo.

"Then let's go to Benito's," I said. "I've got my second wind."

Bo checked his watch. "It's almost ten—Benito's in bed, fully medicated. We'll get nothing but swearing and racist rants. Let's go tomorrow. I think we have to approach him carefully." Bo turned to Albert. "What did you do with the money?"

"It was all in cash, three suitcases. I don't know the details because I wasn't there. Nico told me he carried it off Natalya's private jet at Aurora airfield and then drove it here, and we divided it up."

"Albert," I interrupted. "You said the painting is worth at least $100 million, right?"

"Maybe more. Maybe much more."

"Then why sell it for only $10 million?"

"I wanted to get more. I tried very hard. But Nico said it was the best he could do. The going rate on the black market for looted art is around ten percent. The negotiation between Nico and Natalya wasn't for the price of the painting but rather for its market value. It's undetermined because it's never been priced. How do you value something that's not supposed to exist? Natalya valued it after her inspection. Nico said she picked $100 million because of the reward and would pay ten percent. I wanted him to bargain harder and try for more. But he wouldn't. I think he was worried about screwing up the deal. I gave him $1 million commission, and I have the rest."

"You have $9 million in cash? In this house?"

"No."

Bo and I knew he was lying.

"It's late, Albert. Too late to dig through all your shit to find where you hid it. We're going home now. You'll have the money for us tomorrow morning, all of it. God help you if you spent any of it. We'll need to take it to the Russians."

"You cannot do that, Bo. You will leave me with nothing."

"Albert, you have so much junk in this house that it smells like a furniture bazaar. You spent the afternoon telling us about your family and its wealth. You want to scream poverty now?"

Albert stared at his empty wine glass, twirling its stem. "I have nothing. I have a lot of broken things. I have interesting stories. The painting was all I had."

"Bullshit. You'll make a fortune on eBay," I said optimistically.

Bo took a step closer and looked down at him pityingly. "The painting will kill you. It will kill all of us. I think it's cursed. Nothing good happens to its owners."

"If we find the original, can I keep the money?" he asked.

"You can negotiate any deal you want with the Russian. Think about Chrystal."

"I am thinking about her and protecting what is mine." A sliver of his arrogance had returned.

"It was never yours, Albert. Just like you're not a true Von Baltruschat. You're just a guy from the Windy City with a great aunt who lived the life you wished you did." Bo stuck the knife in as deep as possible.

Albert looked like he was about to burst into tears. To his credit, he held himself together.

We left, agreeing to pick him up the following morning to go with us to Benito's.

As we drove out of the unlit cul-de-sac, I saw the silhouettes of two men sitting in a Cadillac. I said nothing to Bo. I was determined to keep my paranoia in check.

CHAPTER SEVENTEEN

Thursday Morning

A Change of Plans

THE NEXT TIME I SAW THE BARON, he was tied to a wooden armchair. A black plastic garbage bag draped his head and shoulders. The bag was secured by a tight ribbon of duct tape wrapped around his neck, creating an airtight sheath. The rest of the bag was pulled over his shoulders and chest. His wrists were taped to the arms of the chair, which sat in the center of the same blue tarp from the cabin. The stacked boxes and furniture surrounding the tarp gave it a theatrical effect.

Left of the chair sat three grey Samsonite roller suitcases, zippered shut. Right of the chair lay a long-handled pruning lopper, and in a large puddle of blood that had pooled around the right front leg lay two fingers, an inch apart, where they'd fallen. My eyes traveled up the leg of the chair and fixed on Albert's blood-soaked hand where his pinky and ring finger had clotted over into bulbous purple stumps.

"He said he didn't know where the painting was," said the Russian, following my eyes. "I wasn't sure with the first finger. I was sure with the second."

Bile surged into my mouth, which I immediately swallowed. My body felt like it was trapped in a swaying cage. My equilibrium kept shifting.

Bo stood silent. His fisted hands hung at his sides. "Is he dead?" he asked.

"You see him breathing?" responded the Russian.

"I can't tell."

"He's not breathing," I said.

Holding the same Beretta he had in the cabin, the Irishman stood outside blood spatter range as before. We didn't have to see the baron like that, but I'd insisted. The Russian had told the Irishman to take us to see him, and he had snapped sharply, "It's not necessary."

"I think it is," countered the Russian firmly. "You understand?"

Then, for a moment, they stared at each other in outward conflict, and although the Irishman held the Beretta, he did as he was told. We single-filed our way through the furniture to the steps and descended into the baron's windowless basement. The Irishman brought up the rear and then stood against the wall by the basement door cradling the 9mm across his chest, his left arm holding up his right. For the first time, I saw he had a wedding ring.

His face looked different to me. Three nights ago, in the cabin, he had appeared calm, almost uninterested, until the shooting. Now, in the dim yellow light of the baron's basement, he looked hostile and incensed. His lips were pressed so tight they could have been surgically stapled, and his eyes were focused entirely on the Russian, not us. I remember thinking if he shot anyone, it would be his comrade.

//

Bo and I'd left the baron's house the night before, drunk on certainty and counterfeit courage. We figured we had the money, at least most of the money, and a sense of where the Raphael was hiding. Why Nico would try to forge an unforgeable masterpiece was still a mystery, and why it took over six months for the Russian to find us was also unknown. But we were close; we felt it in our bones.

After Bo dropped me off at the office to pick up my car, I drove around until midnight, so I wouldn't get home until everyone was asleep. I wanted to avoid all contact with Abbie and any questions she might have had about Harry Callahan. I was sure Christine had mentioned Harry to Abbie when she picked up Boomer.

Who's Harry Callahan? Isn't he the Clint Eastwood character in Dirty Harry?

No, Hon. He's a psycho killer who kidnapped Boomer and has threatened to kill all of us—you first—if we don't bring him the most valuable Nazi-stolen painting in the world.

I could see how that conversation could quickly get away from me.

Boomer met me when I quietly opened the back door, and we both crept to the TV room, where we spent the rest of the night. I wrote an email to myself detailing everything that had happened to us since Monday. I wanted a record to be found if, like Nico, I went missing. I assumed someone would check my emails sooner or later. I fell asleep on the couch like I'd been sedated, Boomer at my feet.

I woke to my face being licked and slowly realized the house had emptied, and Abbie had not disturbed me. Again, I raced through my morning routine and called Bo to pick me up, which he did. I dug the rifle out from behind the dryer and threw it back into Bo's trunk, and as I got in the car, I smiled and said, "Today we find the stuff dreams are made of," quoting a famous line from an old movie. I had adrenalin to spare.

The fresh, clean air from the day before was replaced with a damp, depressing chill. After years of living in Oregon, I'd learned never to let my mood be determined by the weather, especially in October. I'd have become bipolar in a week.

Before pulling into the baron's driveway, we passed the black Cadillac I'd seen the night before without its two silhouettes. I could now see the car had rental plates.

"I saw two guys in that car last night when we left."

"Yeah, so?"

"Well, it's just odd cause it's parked on the side of the street, not in a driveway, or even near a driveway, and it's facing forward, right at the Von Baltruschat's."

"You think we were followed last night?"

"I don't know."

"I think we're OK," he said, pulling into the driveway. Bo was focused on the mission, and randomly parked cars would not distract him.

We walked to the door. I knocked while Bo rang the bell. The door flew open, and a Beretta 9mm barrel pressed into my forehead. I cringed and crouched, but the barrel followed me. Bo hunkered with me. It all happened in a second.

"Don't," said the Irishman, his brogue seared into my memory. Behind him stood the Russian. Bo and I straightened, and the Beretta moved from my forehead to my right eye.

"You still have a gun in your pocket, boss?" asked the Russian calmly.

"No," said Bo.

"Where is it?"

"In the car."

"Glovebox?"

"No, in the trunk."

"Come in."

"No," Bo's voice was sharp and defiant.

"You think I will hurt you, yes?"

"Yes," I answered for Bo.

"You think I will only shoot you inside, not outside? You see anyone on the street? It is dead-end street. I promise I will not shoot you. The gun is just in case you had yours, and we had to negotiate."

The Irishman stayed silent but lowered the gun from my eye and held it behind his back.

"I'm not coming in," repeated Bo.

"Maybe I would do the same thing," said the Russian. "But I

talked to your friend Albert, and he told me everything. I know you had nothing to do with what happened. You are not thieves. But I still need to find the painting. Albert didn't know where it is. You can help me." He waved us in like a doorman. The Irishman took a step back to make room.

"If I wanted to shoot you, I would have done it when I opened door," said the Russian, as if he'd held the Beretta himself.

I stepped around the Irishman and into the house without saying a word. Bo curled his hands into fists, narrowed his eyes to let me know I'd pissed him off, and followed me.

The Russian's clothes, still the same, looked rumpled and disheveled. He and the Irishman had been up all night, and it showed.

The house smelled different. Gone was the stale storage smell, replaced by a strong odor of gasoline. I looked down the hallway and saw a red two-gallon gas can next to the tall clock. The Russian weaved through the furniture and ducked into the kitchen. The Irishman motioned with his head for us to follow. He kept the gun behind his back. When we turned into the kitchen, the Russian poured coffee into the teacups we had drunk from the day before.

"Coffee?"

"No," we said in unison.

The Russian handed a cup to the Irishman, and then he opened the refrigerator, reached for a quart of milk, smelled its open spout, and poured some into his coffee. "So, where do you think the painting is?" he asked.

"Where's Albert?' I countered.

"Not here."

"Bullshit. You said he *didn't* know where the painting is, which is past tense."

The Russian looked at me and cocked his head.

"I've had to pay attention to my words lately," I said. "You forced that on me. Words like is, was, didn't, doesn't. They have more meaning for me these days."

"English is not my mother tongue, you understand. But I said it correctly." As he spoke, the Irishman moved the gun slowly from his back to his side but did not raise it.

"Jesus Christ," Bo whispered. "Chrystal?"

"Talking about Albert and Chrystal is not helpful. It's distracting. We need to focus on the painting."

"We don't know where the painting is. We only know where the money is," I said. I started feeling light-headed and put my hand on the island counter to steady myself.

"Yes, I know where the money is too. I have most of it. There is some missing, but you know that."

"We don't have it," said Bo.

"I know," said the Russian. "The baron was very…" he paused and made a *tsk* sound, "…open. He told me everything. It was distressing. Getting information from a man like him is always easy, but…" he made another *tsk* sound, "…unpleasant."

He looked at me directly. "You understand?"

I met his stare but said nothing.

"I will confess something now, yes?" He sipped his coffee. "I didn't know very much about the painting. I was told to get $10 million and a Renaissance masterpiece. I don't know shit about the Renaissance. I never learn about it in school. You understand? I saw a picture of the painting in a book. But it didn't mean much, just a painting of a *mal'chik* in a fur blanket. But now, I know more."

"Did Natalya hire you?" asked Bo. The Russian registered no surprise. He knew now what we knew—or didn't. We'd become the loose end I'd agonized about.

"I think maybe we both made mistakes. I thought you were thieves. You sell bad art to finance your little company. And you thought I was hired to put you out of business. But we were both wrong. You don't sell fake art, and I don't get hired. I do a favor for a family friend, a friend who didn't tell me enough."

"A favor?" Bo scoffed. "You killed someone. Where's Albert? Where's Chrystal? How is all this crazy shit just a favor?"

"Because crazy shit happens, Bo. But a favor is still favor."

"For Natalya?" I repeated Bo's question.

"I don't like using names. In the old days, names were OK, but names are too easy to find today. The internet makes us all neighbors, you understand. The less you know, the better for you."

The old days? When did this adolescent psychopath get started? When he was four?

"Do we still call you Harry?" I asked.

Harry nodded with a pensive frown.

The Irishman's feet were shifting. He was getting uncomfortable. He rarely spoke, and when he did, I always paid attention. "We're actin' the maggot and need to move," he said to Harry, not us.

"Move where? We only have a hunch." I said.

"Then we follow your hunch together. I go with you," said Harry.

"No," said Bo.

Harry sighed and looked directly at me while answering Bo. "I will not bring a gun. The gun stays with my friend. My friend stays behind, so he can finish the job if I suddenly become ill. You will leave your gun in the car trunk. I will be unarmed, and you will be unarmed. We make a treaty—a cease-fire. You understand?"

"Where are Albert and Chrystal?" I asked again.

"Chrystal is upstairs, and Albert is downstairs."

"Can we see them?" I asked, not sure I wanted to.

"You don't want to see them. Maybe you piss your pants again." The Russian knew what buttons to push.

"I'm not going anywhere until we do."

It was then that he told the unwilling Irishman to lead the way. As we snaked our way to the basement, I counted three more gasoline cans.

///

After we climbed the basement stairs and returned to the kitchen, the Russian asked, "You want to go upstairs now? Visit with Chrystal."

Both Bo and I shook our heads. Then the Russian said to the Irishman, "You know what to do here, yes? Break things. You know what needs to burn first."

The Irishman nodded.

"What are you doing?" I asked as my bowels began to hurt, and nausea rippled through me again.

"We have a robbery," said Harry. "Albert liked to brag about his treasure. I know because he framed and collected newspaper clippings about it and hung them here on his walls—'The Portland Baron'—ha! It's like he was begging to be robbed. So, he will be robbed. Fire makes a good *uborshchik*, you understand, cleaner."

"Harry, we can't do this." I felt dizzy.

"We? You will do nothing. You were never here."

CHAPTER EIGHTEEN

Later Thursday Morning

Fake Masterpieces

THE EVIL THAT HAD INVADED MY WORLD was metastasizing, and I was staggered by its escalating savagery. Before that week began, I'd succeeded in avoiding life-threatening jeopardy. Even in war, I braved only a tenuous peril, like a tourist wandering through a seedy part of town.

Let me digress a moment into an anecdote—one of those fitting short stories I'm so good at telling.

One day in Vietnam, I was working traffic control, and a UH-1 helicopter crashed in the jungles after I'd cleared it for takeoff. It carried two crew members and a new pilot freshly graduated from Fort Rucker's flight school. They were on a standard Dustoff medevac training exercise. About an hour into their mission, they'd crossed into Laos and radioed the tower to let me know they'd had engine failure and were forced down in enemy territory. Hostile locals from a nearby village immediately set upon them with machetes, axes, and farm tools. The crew carried only sidearms, which they fired until they were out of ammunition. I scrambled an F-4 and three Hueys to the crash site for their evacuation. The pilot stayed on the radio, transmitting landmarks and coordinates to aid their rescue. He shouted into the radio as his crew was hacked to pieces. I could hear their death screams. Near the end, he implored God to help him as the machetes reached him, and he was cut down. I listened, cried, and threw everything that wasn't nailed down, but I was never in danger. I was merely an audience—death's earwig.

I'd lived my entire life like that, always a safe distance from the carnage. But now, since Monday, carnage's clammy hands were around my neck and tightening.

///////////////////////////////////////

We took Bo's car. The Russian told us to put our phones in the glove box. He put his in first, and we grudgingly followed. He sat in the back seat like one of my kids. Bo was twice his size, probably twice his age, and there was no doubt he could put the bastard down in a few seconds. Even I could put him down. It might take a little longer, but I could do it. I imagined punching his adolescent face, crunching my fist into his bones, and wiping away that puerile expression. Then I turned and saw his steady eyes regarding me without fear. If anything, his sneer grew more confident.

I thought about the arsenal in Bo's trunk, but I knew that if anything happened to the son-of-a-bitch, the Irishman would report back to "his family," and they would take revenge. Maybe burn down my house with my family in it. So, Bo and I reluctantly formed a temporary partnership with a murderous psychopath built on fear, distrust, and hate—the three pillars of every healthy relationship.

"Harry, did Natalya tell you to kill Nico?" I asked. "Was that part of the favor?"

"No. Maybe scare him a little."

"Why Bo and me? Why'd you set up a meeting for us in the cabin? Why not Nico?"

"Natalya only knew Nico, but she said he had business partners. I checked you out. You have nice website, and it gave me the wrong idea. I make mistake. I added two plus two and got five." He nodded his head in resignation. "I thought you were *moshenniki*, swindlers.

I looked at your rank on website, and I thought Bo was boss man, you understand?"

"In the cabin, you said we stole from 'a rich man.'" I used air quotes. "You know who the buyer is?"

The Russian snorted a laugh. "I was playing role, and I say what was in my head, you understand?"

"Then, why not say a rich woman? Natalya's a woman." I was annoying him.

"OK, we stop this now."

The streets were dry, but I could see the coming rain. As I hung onto the handgrip, I wondered if Bo was driving to scare the Russian or impress him. He steered sharply into every curve, drafting vehicles whenever possible. Harry and I said nothing for the next few miles, listening to each other breathe, captivated by Bo's road rage. How we didn't get stopped by a traffic cop, I don't know.

When we pulled into Benito's dirt driveway, a light rain began to fall.

"I hate the rain here. It's cold. At home, it's warm. After we find painting, I will leave here fast, like a man who owes money." He smiled an ugly smile.

I exited the car and told him, "Benito is not balanced. He's old and not always rational. You should wait for us in the car."

"You think I am your dog? You say sit, and I stay? I think I go everywhere you go. I hear everything you hear. You understand?"

Bo looked like he was thinking about his gun in the trunk. As we started for the portico, Melina bolted out of the front door, grabbed Bo by the arm, and dragged him back into the house as we followed.

"Have you seen Nico?" she asked. Her hair was pulled back into a tight bun and looked unwashed. Her eyes were tired and anguished, and she'd removed her lip ring.

The Russian watched her and straightened his spine like readying himself for a fistfight.

"No, we haven't seen him," said Bo clasping both her shoulders like he wanted to prevent her from lifting off.

"Where is my bastard son?" bellowed Benito from his living room.

"He's freaking out," said Melina, slapping her open hand to her forehead. "I got here an hour ago, and the house was trashed. He's throwing stuff. I gave him his meds, but he's off the chart nuts now. Nico hasn't visited for almost a week." She looked at the Russian. "Are you a doctor?"

"No," said the Russian dismissively as he studied the display of sculptures flanking the foyer.

"What do you want to steal from me today?" barked Benito, lumbering towards us. He wore a badly stained bed sheet with a hole cut in the middle for his head and underneath an equally stained T-shirt and underwear. It was probably his sleeping outfit. The stench of body odor advancing with him was so pungent I cupped my hand over my mouth and nose.

"You never come to see me," he said, forgetting our earlier visit. "You hate me, like my son. He hates me. He steals my work—you help him—I have proof. Melina, call the police. Tell them there are thieves in my house. Tell them to find my bastard son."

He ranted, raved, and marched back and forth in the foyer for another ten minutes until we coaxed him back to his living area and pushed him onto his sizable and chunky Chesterfield couch. His living room didn't look much different from his studio. Half-completed sculptures were everywhere. Painted and unpainted canvases leaned against much of the campaign furniture. Deer and cougar mounts hung on the walls between tapestries and paintings. The fireplace hearth was black with a year's worth of burned wood and ash.

Benito started to calm down. His hysteria had exhausted him. He'd been manically transporting his large frame around for several hours before we arrived, bringing him close to cardiac arrest. Now he sat in a gasping stupor, panting like a colossal mastiff and staring at us with agitated eyes.

"Melina wants to leave me. Everyone wants to leave me. They all want me to die."

"I need to call someone. I need to get out of here," Melina said, looking back and forth between Bo and me.

"Try calling Dante," I suggested.

"He's in Vegas," she answered.

"I heard. Why? When's he coming back?"

"He's gorging on drugs," growled Benito. "He's an addict, don't you know that? Nico is with him. They are both drug whores. They hate me, so they leave me to die. They should both die before me. They only steal from me." He stopped and studied the Russian sitting opposite him on a chesterfield wing chair. "Who are you?"

The psychopath who killed your son.

"No one," said Harry.

"My son has left me. He owes me money," whined Benito.

"Me too," Harry said with a slight nod and a grin.

"Melina, I'm sure we can talk to someone. Isn't there a doctor?" I asked.

She stood in the doorframe, looking like she would break away at any moment. Now that we were there, she could flee with a clear conscience. "I have his doctor's number, but what can he do? He's not going to drive over here."

"No, but he could dispatch an ambulance, or maybe he knows home care professionals."

"We need a wheelbarrow of Xanax. I gave Benito his regular dose this morning, but it's not enough."

"When was the last time you ate, Benito?"

"I'm not hungry. I eat, and I shit. It's all I do anymore. I need to work, and I need to get paid." His eyelids grew heavy.

"Melina, get some food for him. I'll bet his sugar level is low."

"I got old pizza and cold KFC."

"That'll do," I said.

We needed to keep the old man awake and semi-coherent,

especially with the Russian attached to us like a tumor. Melina disappeared, and I prayed she wouldn't escape out the back door.

"Benito, we're looking for a painting," said Bo.

"Everyone looks for a painting. Talk to Nico. He decides my projects."

Bo stood in front of him, blocking the Russian. "No, we don't need you to paint. We are looking for an existing painting. An old masterpiece."

"Everything I paint is a masterpiece. Have you seen my bastard son? He left me to die."

"Did you forge a masterpiece?" asked the Russian, peering around Bo.

"I don't forge anything. I wouldn't waste my time. People forge me."

It went on like that for a while. Even the Russian understood Benito was impossible to interrogate. If he had information hidden in his decaying brain, it would have to be coaxed out of him, not pulled out with coercion or torture. Benito would not lose his fingers.

Melina brought food, which Benito consumed like a ravenous animal, and his breathing stabilized. Bo went to sit in a distant chair. Benito's eating was always disgusting to watch up close. While stuffing pizza into his mouth Benito bent the Russian's ear about his skin sores and how he no longer showered because the warm water would soften the scabs, and they would hurt and refuse to heal. Harry listened to him in awkward silence—we all did. I remember thinking Benito could make even an assassin cry with enough time.

We carefully asked more and more questions about Renaissance masterpieces, and he finally said something interesting. "I don't need another masterpiece. I have too many already. I tell my sons all the time, stop—no more."

Bo came out of his chair. "How many masterpieces do you have? I've never seen them."

"I don't let people see them, you idiot," rumbled Benito. "It's a secret."

"What secret?" I asked.

"My secret—a Scava secret—we have many masterpieces. I've told the boys they must never talk about it. It has to stay in the family. But they never do what I tell them. They steal from me instead. They steal my masterpieces."

"Benito, I don't understand," said Bo.

"You want to steal a masterpiece? Go ahead! You steal everything else. Go to my room, my bedroom. Steal my masterpieces."

The Russian was on his feet and into the hallway before Bo or I could stop him. We followed him as he instinctively navigated his way to the bedroom. I think he followed his nose. The reek from the bedroom was as pungent as Benito.

Hanging on the wall above the headboard of Benito's rumpled and filthy bed were three Van Goghs. I recognized two of them immediately as *Painter on His Way to Work* and *Vase with Five Sunflowers* from an article I'd read the previous night about Nazi-looted art. The paintings were believed to have burned in air raids during the war. On another wall hung a Degas, a Picasso, and a Courbet. I remembered the Degas, from the same article, was called *Five Dancing Women* and was lost in 1940, and Gustave Courbet's *The Stone Breakers* had been destroyed in '45 near Dresden when allied forces bombed its transport vehicle.

Each wall in his bedroom was covered with a cluster of unframed paintings that I recognized from my research as lost, stolen, or destroyed masterpieces.

"Holy shit," was all I could say.

"These can't be real—can they?" Bo was transfixed.

"I don't see the Raphael," said the Russian, displaying his single-minded purpose.

"Calm down, fellas," mocked Melina as she strolled into the room behind us. "I stayed quiet 'cause it's fun to watch your reactions. They're not real. Benito's just crazy. They're copies. It's not such a big secret. Anyone who works here knows about it."

"Then why call them secret?" asked Bo.

"It's how Benito talks about Dante's work. Nico convinced him that Dante's hobby could get them all in trouble. It's not true. But Nico wants to keep Dante's skill a secret because he doesn't want people to know what he's actually doing with him." She paused and rubbed her eyes. It was mid-morning, and she was already exhausted.

"As I told you before, Dante has a gift. I don't understand it, and I've never known anyone else to have it. I wish it was a disease, a family virus, something I could catch 'cause I would have sex with Benito himself if I thought he could give it to me."

Bo and I studied the canvases and touched them to ensure they were real.

"Dante can look at a painting and duplicate it perfectly," she said. "He told me once he doesn't know how it happens. It's like his brain is photographic, but only with art. He failed math and just about every other subject in school. Sometimes he can't remember the day of the week. But if he looks at a painting long enough, his brain captures every brushstroke, accent, color, flow, and rhythm. He sees the image in his head like it's in front of him. He told me it's even more vivid when he's high. He'll binge on ganja for a week and create a perfect copy of any painting. It's freaky and wondrous."

"So, all those paintings in Nico's house—the Matisse, the Chagall, the Warhol—are all Dante's? All fake masterpieces?" My mind spun.

"Yes, of course. But the paintings are not forgeries," she explained. "Forgeries are more malicious."

"Malicious?" asked Bo.

"Yes. Paintings have history, just like you have history. Art is not created in a vacuum. It's the product of the artist's knowledge, experience, and talent—the essence of his spirit. Great art can be identified by the artist's style, not just by their signature." She was in her element now, the art major tutoring her students. "Forgeries falsify that history. They rip away the biography of the art. A copy of a painting is just a perfect image without pretense or perception, but a forgery is a copy with a manufactured biography. Forgeries have the intention to betray people, dealers, and buyers mostly. On the other hand, copies are homages, tributes to the artist; they don't betray anyone. Dante is a human Xerox machine, not a forger."

"But he would be capable of forging a masterpiece if he wanted to," said Bo.

"Of course. He does it all the time, but not this stuff." She strode out of the room, leaving us to stare at Benito's gallery of counterfeits. The Russian followed her.

"What do you mean not this stuff?" he asked.

"There's a difference between painting a perfect replica of a known masterpiece and creating a brand-new original in the artist's style. In one, you recreate the work; in the other, you recreate the artist—their talent—like occupying their soul."

"Who's soul is Dante occupying these days?" asked Bo as we caught up to her.

She stopped short of the living room and looked at Benito lying on the couch, his eyes closed, mumbling to himself. Then she detoured us to the foyer and whispered, "Most of Benito's work is done by Dante now. Nico said I must never tell anyone, but I don't owe him anything if he stops paying me. I watch Benito struggle every day. He's losing his talent slowly, like it's sweating out of him. He starts and then forgets what he's done and starts over. Sometimes he gets frustrated with his hands, and he punches the clay and destroys his work. I've been here longer than any others, and I haven't seen him finish anything in my time. Even the portrait of that baron douche is mostly Dante."

"He's not a douche," I interrupted in Albert's defense. It seemed the least I could do.

"Nico tells Dante what new images will sell in the galleries, and after a few days in the barn, Dante delivers a new Benito Scava sculpture. It's how Nico fills his inventory. I think deep down, Benito knows it. Things haven't gone completely dark for him. I think all that crying he does about Nico stealing from him is his bitching that it's God who is stealing from him, but he's too close to dying to insult God, so he substitutes Nico." She frowned. "But, I'm no shrink."

"And Dante is in Vegas," said the Russian.

"Dante needs his binges, so he disappears for weeks. That's when Nico and Dante fight like rabid dogs." She chuckled to herself. "Dante's addicted to weed, and Nico's addicted to strippers."

"So, Nico's using Dante to build inventory before his factory shuts down and dies," I said.

"He's been doing it for a long time. I'd bet every gallery that carries Benito has fakes. Nico and Dante can keep the scam going for a long time, claiming Benito left a trove of unreleased works in his studio." She shook her head. "Nico promised to pay my tuition for graduate school if I kept my mouth shut."

"What about the piece Benito bragged to us about just the other day?" asked Bo.

"All Dante; that's why I think Benito knows what's going on, even though he throws his tantrums. He's a good actor when he wants to be. He touches the mold, talks about his God-given talent, and the world sees what it wants to see."

"Why is the brother in Vegas? Why not party here at home?" asked the Russian.

"He has biker friends there. Dante is weird. He's shy and with-drawn, but he hangs with a couple of biker freaks, getting high together. I think they hang out with him because he makes stuff for them. Last year he spent three months working on a life-sized bronze chopper sitting in front of their clubhouse in Vancouver."

"Vancouver?"

"Yeah, I met them once; they're Canadian. The Devil's Sons of British Columbia," she said with a smirk. "They're associated somehow with the Hells Angels, like a minor league club where the members hope to get sent to the majors someday. They meet in Vegas, where they own a motel."

"You know a lot for an assistant," said the Russian.

"Yeah. Dante and I were a thing for a while when I arrived. I was totally drawn to him when I saw what he could do with his hands. Talent's an aphrodisiac for me. I slept with him, and he told me things when we shared a cigarette. I will never understand why that idiot has such a gift and does nothing with it. It's why I stopped sleeping with him. I wanted him to do something more with his genius, and we fought about it."

"Did he tell you when he'll be back?" I asked.

Melina laughed. "I'm not his girlfriend. He doesn't check in with me."

"Do you know where he is in Vegas?" asked Harry.

"Nope."

She gave me Dante's number, and I called him. No answer. I left a message. Then Melina called, and he picked up. I threw my hands in the air—why don't people answer when I call? Melina walked into another room while we stayed in the foyer, avoiding the napping Benito.

"He said to piss off," she announced, returning a few minutes later. "He's on vacation, and if we want to talk to him, we can call Nico. I told him Nico had disappeared, and all he did was laugh. He said Nico disappears all the time. A few years ago, he decided that the women in Iceland were hot, so he flew to Reykjavik for a week. He said maybe now Nico's hunting hookers in New Zealand. However, I managed to find out Dante's staying at the Lucky Break Motel. I told him Benito was going nuts, and he said Benito's been going nuts for years and I should call his doctor. He doesn't care. I think he and Nico stopped caring about their father years ago."

"If they ever did care," I said dryly.

I looked at Bo, who looked at the Russian, who looked at me.

Long story short: we were going to Vegas.

CHAPTER NINETEEN

Thursday Afternoon

The Flight

WE HUDDLED UNDER THE PORTICO, out of earshot of Benito and Melina. Light rain continued.

"I'm not getting on a plane with you," declared Bo resolutely.

"Why not? What can I do? I can't even take a nail clipper on the plane. I go with you or without you."

I continued to be impressed by the Russian's stoic calm, a kind of belligerent civility. It's odd and disturbing to envy the qualities of someone so pestilent, like admiring the serenity in a corpse.

"Why go to Vegas anyway?" Bo persisted. "Call Dante and ask him if he forged the Raphael and what happened to the original."

"Why would he tell you? Why would he confess to you?" Harry's questions were valid.

"He won't," I answered. "Dante doesn't know what happened to his brother. If Dante forged the Raphael, then Nico was in on it. Dante won't tell us shit without Nico's permission—certainly not over the phone. If we want to get information out of him, we've got to do it face to face." I looked at my watch. "There's a flight to Vegas every hour."

I'll spare you the verbal brawl that ensued. In the end, the Russian walked to the car and pulled his phone out of the glove box. He asked us for our birth dates, which we gave him, and he walked out of hearing range.

"Nico's got galleries worldwide selling fraudulent art," I whispered. "That's probably why he never turned in Von Baltruschat for the reward. He couldn't afford the publicity or scrutiny of being a hero in the art world."

"Yup," said Bo. "You can't spend $100 million in prison."

The Russian meandered back through the drizzle.

"I hope to hell you know what you're doing, Marty," Bo muttered. His instinct was to walk away and find a different solution, but I knew he wouldn't abandon me.

"I don't have a goddamn clue what I'm doing," I answered, wishing I did.

"But I do," said Harry rejoining our huddle. "We will find a valuable treasure."

"It's not an adventure, you idiot," I flung back.

The Russian stepped forward and leaned into my face, exuding malevolence. "Be careful. You understand."

I didn't flinch. Without his gun-wielding Irish shadow, his power to go from charm to harm in an eyeblink was much less intimidating.

We left Benito asleep on his couch and drove to the airport. Melina agreed to stay with him until she contacted his doctor.

Once we'd parked in the airport lot, the three of us walked in opposite directions to talk privately on our phones.

I called Abbie. There was a weariness in her voice. "What's in Vegas?"

"Chasing money, another investor pitch." Lying to Abbie was becoming perfunctory, like knocking on wood for luck. "How'd your meetings go?"

"With the bank or with Tom?"

"Both, I guess."

"They went fine. The bank feels better. Tom feels worse. We can talk about it when you get home tomorrow." Her words felt like small punches to my chest. "Do you have a change of clothes?" she asked after a strained pause.

"Yes," I said. Abbie knew I kept a fully packed overnight bag in the office. It wasn't just for travel; I'd spilled more coffee on myself than any man alive and learned to keep spare clothing nearby.

"Why'd you sleep in the TV room?" Another uncomplicated question.

"I didn't mean to."

"Hmmm. You've slept in your clothes three nights in a row." She hesitated, and I let the awkward silence linger. "Who's Harry Callahan?" Finally, the question I was expecting. "Why'd he bring Boomer to the office?"

I smiled, realizing suddenly from her voice that my earlier concern had been unnecessary. As I feared, Christine had told her about Harry Callahan, but while anyone familiar with Clint Eastwood movies would know the name immediately, it meant nothing to Abbie because she'd never watched them. She's a Jane Austen rom-com girl. To her, "Harry Callahan" was just a name, allowing me to heap on another lie. "Just a guy from the dog park who found Boomer wandering his street. He knew where I worked but not where I lived."

"Well, that's very coincidental."

Too far. She's sensing something, time to hang up.

I told her my plane was boarding and that I loved her. She hung up before I got to the "love you."

Once inside the airport, Harry told us to wait in the central terminal area while he wandered up to the Southwest Airlines counter to get his boarding pass. After he returned, he had us wait a few more minutes while other passengers got their passes, and then Bo and I went to collect ours.

"Evil bastard is good," said Bo watching him. "We can't get his real name the way he did this."

We shuffled through security. Harry held back, allowing several strangers to get between us in line. Southwest Airlines boards its passengers in groups. There are no assigned seats. Harry had made sure he boarded with the A group; he probably paid extra, while Bo and I boarded with the B group. As soon as we were on the plane, Bo grabbed the first aisle seat he could. I looked down the rows and saw the Russian was seated in the exit row, which had only two seats instead of the usual three, to leave space for the emergency door. I thought briefly about it and then took the seat next to him.

///////////////////////////////////

"Why'd you take my dog?" We were airborne, with no one sitting in front of us and two young women in the row behind us with earbuds firmly planted in their ears.

The Russian looked sullen. "I don't like you," he said quietly. "I think you make trouble for me. You are…" He paused a moment. "*Khui*…you understand?"

It sounded like he said, hooey. "No."

"It means, dick, a prick   you are a prick." He paused. "And *'suka*, a bitch. You piss yourself." He reached up and adjusted his airflow nozzle and then continued. "I took your dog because sometimes, talk is not enough. Sometimes you must do deeds. I went to your house to end your dog. Cut his throat. Make you piss your pants again, maybe in front of your wife and kids—raise your fear—keep you controllable."

"But you didn't."

"Your wife… she will leave you, so I changed my mind."

I stared at him like he was an oncoming train and I was tied to the track. "How the fuck do you know that?"

He shot me a knowing smile. "I heard her talk to her lawyer."

"You bugged her phone?" It took all my energy to keep my voice to a loud whisper.

"You think I'm CIA? I can bug people's phones?" He chuckled.

I snarled. "How did you hear her?"

"We visit your house. The door on your deck is unlocked. Not safe. It's very dark part of house, you understand? The door slides open very easy, no sound." He looked between the seats to check on the women behind us. "So, I open it a little."

"What is wrong with you?" I rasped. "My whole family was home!" My breathing became labored, and I clenched and unclenched my hands to avoid hyperventilating. The psychopath stayed composed. It was like we were in two different conversations.

"We saw you leave your house with the dog. Without a dog, doors are easier to open, and I listened for a little while."

I felt cold, especially my fingers. "How long?"

"I don't know. I don't look at clock. Your house is quiet at night, like it is empty, like no one lives there." His words were disorienting. "But then, I heard phone ring, and your wife said, 'Hello, Tom,' so I think maybe Tom called. I didn't hear much, but then she walked into the room, and I stood against the wall next to open door." He arched his back against his chair. "At first, I think it's a lover, and she came into room to hide conversation from children. I got a little thrill, you understand. The room was dark, and she never looked at door." He separated his thumb and forefinger by an inch. "It was open very little. She sat at dinner table and talked about getting advice. Then I knew she was talking to lawyer. I think he ask her why because she said," he lingered, "...let me remember exactly... something about big ambitions and lost causes." His black eyes stared into mine. "She was talking about you, yes?"

I said nothing.

"I learn you will lose wife soon, so I let you keep your dog. You will need a friend. And then you came home. You made more noise than a drunk woman at a party. You cried about falling and bleeding." He pointed casually at my forehead. "You and Abbie go upstairs to fix your big wound."

"Don't say her name," I hissed.

He took in a long breath. "We have a saying in my country." He said it in Russian, then translated. "The husband is the head, but the wife is the neck, and the head always looks in the direction the neck turns, you understand?"

"Fuck off," I said to him, and then under my breath, "scumbag."

We didn't talk for a while. I could see the back of Bo's head tilt casually to one side. I think the drone of the plane had lulled him to sleep.

"We…you said *we* saw you leave," I said quietly. "Your Irish buddy listened as well?"

"No. He went into forest after you. You talked loud to your dog, so he followed your voice." He grinned, "Maybe you buried the money."

I shook my head a little. "If you decided not to kill my dog, why'd you take him?"

"He came to visit me after you go upstairs. He put his nose out the door and sniffed. He is friendly dog, not a good watchdog. I decide to take him with me. It was a feeling, an impulse. I want to send you a message, you understand? Fear has big eyes."

"Why'd you come to the office then?"

"It felt like good idea. I think you were plotting something, and I wanted to get rid of stupid dog. It was another impulse."

"Yea, self-control's not your strong suit," I said dryly.

He didn't like my comment. His manner changed in a beat, like a cat sprayed with water. He narrowed his eyes and said, "You are lucky I didn't end your fucking dog. I went to all-night Walmart and bought a leash. I walked him. I watched him take a shit. He never sat still in the back seat. He whined like you. I thought about throwing him out of moving car."

"I'd have killed you."

He snorted. "Barking dogs don't bite."

"Why'd you shoot Nico?" Adrenalin surged through me.

"It was not intentional."

"Albert and Chrystal were intentional."

"No. They were necessary—not intentional."

"If they were necessary, then Bo and I are next. We're only alive because you don't have the painting."

"Look, *mudak,* I never wanted to end anyone. This trip supposed to be quick in and out. But I was too optimistic. I was put in compromising positions." He rotated and looked out the window for a minute.

Turning back, he said, "Big thieves hang little ones, you understand? Albert was a little thief. I know many like him." He took a breath and leaned closer. "I knew this guy once who decided he will steal a big shipment of Swiss chocolate. He planned it all out; the perfect *krazha,* heist. He found a buyer. He knew the truck and the route. There was no security because it was just chocolate. And so, he highjacked truck. After driving around for a while, happy, he stopped to check his cargo and maybe take a few bars home for his wife and kids before driving to the buyer. But when he opened back of truck, he saw something went wrong. He stole the wrong truck."

He stopped and looked down the aisle to ensure no one was near us. "The truck was not filled with Swiss chocolate, not a chocolate bar in sight. Instead, it was filled top to bottom with Swiss watches, hundreds of Rolexes, Patek Philippe, Omega, Tissot, Tag Heuer—you name it. The guy almost shit himself. You think it was good news for him? No, it was not. He couldn't sell a truckload of watches. He was a little thief who could handle a thousand dollars in chocolate, not a million dollars in watches. He had no buyer.

"In business language, you say he had supply but no distribution. He was a little bit fucked; you understand. So, in desperation, he went to one of my comrades in family and asked him for help. My friend took one look inside the truck and agreed to help him. But the little thief never realized he made big mistake. He escaped the wolf, but he ran to the bear instead."

I knew what was coming.

"My friend was the bigger thief, and he cut the little thief's throat, fed him to alligators, and then sold the watches. But first, he let his other comrades feed a little." He rolled his left sleeve back and showed me his gold Rolex Daytona.

"Money doesn't stay long with a fool. Maybe Albert thought he was a big thief. But he was not. Like you, he didn't have the *yaytsa*, you understand—the eggs." He flipped his hand like he was batting away a fly.

I looked straight into his dull, dark eyes. "You cut the fingers off a helpless man. You tortured him when he was tied to a chair. Where are the eggs in that?"

The Russian stayed silent for half a minute, annoyed at my candor. Then the corners of his mouth turned up slightly. "That fat goat told me he didn't have the painting, and I didn't believe him, so I made sure." He paused and purred, "Sometimes, the devil taps me on the shoulder and says...I wish I thought of that." He pulled his lips back and showed me his teeth.

I winced. "You know how sick you are?"

"You have a brave mouth when you're not pissing your pants."

We said nothing for a long time.

"You're Russian mafia, aren't you?" I finally asked.

"I am Russian, not mafia. Russia does not have mafia. I am in brotherhood with other Russians."

"And they're in business with you?"

"Don't be stupid. I am independent businessman. We all work for ourselves, and sometimes we help each other. We never work for outsiders, never for others; it's against the rules."

"You have rules?" I was oddly curious.

"We are a family. All families have rules."

"Tell me one."

"Don't talk about the family."

"That's an easy one; tell me another."

"Give up old family for new family—no wife or children. Loyalty travels alone down a narrow road."

"That sounds like a religious cult. Can't you marry? Are you celibate?"

"I take any woman I want," he answered quickly and defensively. "But in brotherhood, women are not relevant. They are second to comrades, and the brotherhood stands above all."

"That other guy with you, the Irishman, he has a wedding ring."

"He is not part of family. He is Irish, IRA, but his soul is Russian. He works for other comrades and me. He's a *shestyorka*, a sixth."

"A what?"

"A sixth. You know, the lowest card in a *Durak* deck. He is an associate. A helper. A lookout."

"You told Finley you were in the drug business."

"No, I said my family is in drug business. In America, drugs are excellent business, but I have other business—construction and entertainment."

"Entertainment? Is that what you call it in Russia? Here it's called sex trafficking."

"Marty, you are not smart. I will tell you only one more thing to show you how stupid you are, and then we stop, you understand?" He waited for a passenger on his way to the lavatory to pass. "I don't traffic women. Sex slaves are for movies to sell tickets. I don't own women. It is better to own where they work. I own motels, you understand?"

The captain came on the radio and told us we were beginning our descent to McCarran International and would be on the ground in twenty minutes. I could see Bo stirring awake.

"Now I ask you a question," said the Russian, checking his seat belt. "You know how much paper is $10 million?"

I shrugged.

"Very much paper! Very heavy. Hard to carry. Hard to count. And one of the suitcases at Albert's was half empty. Albert told me

Nico got a $1 million commission, and I think he shared it with you. Maybe you thought it was his money. But it was not his money, you understand?"

"We don't have any money," I said firmly. It was not a lie. All the money we'd received from Nico was long gone, spent on lawyers, programmers, salaries, and keeping the lights on.

"I think Nico made investment using my money."

"What difference does it make? It's gone."

"Marty, if you steal my money and buy a new car, I own your new car."

"I don't know what you're trying to say. Maybe Nico invested his commission money, maybe not. It doesn't mean you own my company. We have many investors. You can't just own a company. It doesn't work that way. But if you want to talk about new cars, Nico has plenty of nice ones. I suggest you rummage around his man cave—let me know what you think of the train."

He looked puzzled. My sarcasm was lost on him. "Do you know Nico's brother well?" he asked, abruptly changing the subject.

"No," I replied. "I just know Dante's a genius with a paintbrush, and he loves weed."

"He is an addict," he asserted.

"I don't know if it's an addiction or just a bad habit," I said.

"In my country, we say, a bad habit is a shirt you wear till death."

I looked at him, and muttered under my breath, "In my country, wearing the wrong shirt doesn't get you killed."

CHAPTER TWENTY

Thursday Night

Las Vegas

ETA FOR VEGAS WAS 7 P.M., and we turned onto final approach precisely on time. Having had enough of me, the Russian sat silent and stared out the window, watching our slow descent into a shimmering sequin robe floating on a black sea.

While disembarking, I turned my phone on. I was staggered by the number of messages I'd received: two voice messages from Abbie, one from Charley, one from Benito, which I assumed was Melina, and even one from Katherine. My three text messages were all from Abbie.

The first one read, "Call me immediately." The second read, "Call me as soon as you land." The third one read, "The police are looking for you."

By the time I caught up to Bo, he, too, was anxiously scanning his text messages. The Russian walked alongside me as we spilled onto the concourse, so Bo and I spoke again to each other without speaking.

Me: "Something bad has happened."

Bo: "I know."

Me: "We've got to ditch the asshole."

Bo: "I know."

Me: "I'm going to the bathroom."

Bo: "I know."

In the men's room, next to each other at the urinals, I whispered, "The cops are looking for me. I don't know why."

Bo whispered back, "Katherine sent me three panic texts, all 911. I need to call her now."

"I'll call Abbie."

"No! Don't talk to a freaking soul until I talk to Katherine!" he snapped. "We can't have different stories. Let me find out what's going on first."

I listened to Abbie's first message as I walked back into the airport.

"Martin, let's figure out a time this weekend to talk. You slept on the couch, and I don't want that. I don't want to be angry all the time. Call me later tonight. OK?"

Then I listened to her second message.

"Martin, the police were just here. They're looking for you. I called Katherine. They were at her house as well, looking for Bo. They wouldn't say why. What's going on? Are you in trouble? I'm scared. Call me as soon as you get this message."

I looked for Harry. He had wandered to the other side of the concourse, reading magazine covers in a self-serve kiosk. He looked utterly composed. Evidently, his phone had not exploded with messages during the flight. I was a little rattled by his casual affability as I paced in a tight circle until Bo rejoined me and started whispering fiercely.

"Cops came to our house and scared the shit out of Katherine," he said. "She thought they were there to report I was dead."

The Russian started sauntering back toward us.

"They didn't tell her why or what, just that they wanted to talk to me. She said Abbie called her right after and cops had also come to your house, which means it's a coordinated search." His speech accelerated, and he turned his back to the approaching Russian. "I also checked a voicemail from Melina, who said all the news channels are broadcasting the baron's house burning to the ground, and the police believe it was a home invasion. They found two bodies."

We marched through the airport to the car rental while my sense of foreboding increased.

///

We rented a Mustang convertible from Alamo and were soon navigating the broad river of bumper-to-bumper traffic down the main strip, top-down, immersed in the pulsating lights and vibrant entropy of an early October evening in Vegas.

We drifted with the heavy traffic. The late dinner hour had pulled much of the population out into the open, an army of gamblers, ramblers, and vacationers swarming the sidewalks and walkways like foraging ants. Vegas has a deliberate casualness unlike anywhere else, and the three of us fit in well, just a trio of low-rollers on a bad-luck streak.

My phone buzzed. It was Abbie. The Russian was in the back seat, attentive, so I answered, holding it tightly to my ear. "Martin, what the hell is wrong with you? Katherine just called me to tell me Bo just spoke to her. Why haven't you called me?"

"I'm sorry. I was about to call. There's more going on than I can talk about right now."

"Talk about to who? Did you bother to listen to my messages? The police were here looking for you. Katherine said something about Nico vanishing. What is going on?"

"I'm sorry I didn't tell you, but I couldn't. Nico's disappeared, and we're trying to find him, and I can't just talk about it because of investors—"

"Goddamn, you and your investors!" Her words drummed through the phone like pelting rain. "Who do you think I am? Have you lost all perspective? I'm your wife! Your business partner disappears, and you don't tell me? Are you in Vegas looking for Nico or meeting an investor?"

"To find Nico." I could feel the Russian's eyes on my neck.

A tormented sigh followed the short, predictable silence. "So, you lied to me…again."

"Nico's wife reported him missing early Tuesday. I thought the cops might wait a few days before taking the report seriously. I'm sure they came to the house to talk about Nico's disappearance. I don't know anything more than they do. Bo and I are trying to find him. We're in Vegas to talk to Dante, his brother."

"You're not making sense. You can call Dante on the phone—you don't need to fly to Vegas. What are you not telling me?"

"I'm home tomorrow. I'll tell you everything then."

The distress in her voice continued. "The kids were home when the police knocked on our door. Martin…damn it! They know something's wrong. I told them not to call you, but they might anyway."

"Abbie! I'm fighting more demons than I can count. Nico, his brother, his father, the company, and now the cops. For the love of God, stop piling on."

I could hear her breathing, even over the welter of street noise. "I wanted you to quit the company, Martin. I never wanted you to quit us." Her voice wobbled a bit. "I'm sorry." She hung up.

That ledge I was on was getting smaller and smaller.

"The cops came to your house?" asked the Russian coolly.

"They came to my house as well," responded Bo.

I stared intensely at my phone. I wanted to call Abbie back and tell her something heroic. Explain to her that I was in Vegas not to find Nico but to save her life. But her potential killer was sitting behind me, and I wasn't sure how much she would believe or appreciate. More likely, she would scold me for the decisions I'd made.

The Russian sat back and dialed his phone.

"It's me." Pause. "*Da.*" Pause. "*Derr'mo'.*" Long pause. "*Blayd!*"

Pause. "*Nyet.*" Pause. "It is unnecessary." Pause. "I don't like that." Pause. "Do what you want…*ero piz'dets.*"

He hung up and said, "The cops are investigating robbery and arson at Baron Albert's house. It's on the news. Big three-alarm fire. Lots of TV coverage." He stopped for a minute and thought about what to say next. "I don't think the cops come to your house looking for Nico. The cops don't care about Nico. They come because you were at the baron's house last night."

Bo slammed his foot on the brake, and the car behind almost rear-ended us. "What?!"

A horn blared, and he reaccelerated. My stomach clenched, and I stopped thinking about Abbie.

"A friend told me someone told the cops you were at Baron's house last night."

"The Irish guy who carries your gun?"

"No. A different friend."

"Who the hell knew we were there?" asked Bo. "We didn't tell anyone."

"Shit! I did. I told Nico's wife." I recounted the call Charley and I had the prior evening. "She wanted us to search the clubs and not waste our time at the baron's house. She barely knew who he was. Why would she tell the cops we were there?"

"Because she's scared, Marty! Scared people do crazy things!" Bo went into racing mode again, his standard road-rage protocol. He started weaving through the heavy traffic without success, helplessly changing lanes amid unending columns of cars. From the traffic helicopter, I'm sure we looked like a drunken firefly in a slowly advancing battalion of lightning bugs.

"Maybe someone saw us…a neighbor," I said, seeking a different reason to alleviate my guilt.

"Neighbors wouldn't know us from aliens," replied Bo. "It was Charley."

The Russian stayed silent, but I sensed more; something else was bothering him.

Remembering I'd also received a voice message from Charley, I checked it. Her shrill intensity surged into my ear. "Where are you? Why don't you answer my calls? You're ignoring me. I'm not important enough for you to pick up. You're just like everybody else. No one will call me back. No one gives a damn about Nico. No one gives a damn about me. You know that guy you said you were visiting last night? That baron guy? Well, he's all over the news right now. His goddamn house burned to the ground! They're saying two bodies were found. They're not reporting the identities yet. What is going on? Call me…damn it!"

"Yeah, her fear is growing into panic," I conceded, putting the phone back in my pocket. "She's nearly hysterical, and it sounded like she was about to do something stupid."

We remained snarled in traffic for an hour, finally arriving at the Lucky Break Motel and parked in its empty lot. The place was a dingy, single-story U-shaped disaster at the end of an unlit street lined with windowless commercial buildings. A neon sign of a four-leaf clover and a dimly lit entrance area offered the only light. It didn't look inviting or even in business.

"No one stays in this dump, not even cockroaches," said Bo.

Two Harley-Davidson choppers were parked in front of rooms 12 and 14. There was no 13, and I smirked at the cheekiness of it. We sat quietly for about ten minutes and finally decided to come back later after searching for food. We found an Arby's and ordered beef sandwiches and curly fries. Then we returned to the Lucky Break's empty lot, backed the car into its darkest corner, and waited. Like an onyx statue, the Russian sat silent and motionless in the rear seat. The open-air Mustang kept me from feeling claustrophobic.

My phone vibrated, and it was Charley. I stepped out of the car and receded into the inky shadow of the lot's perimeter fence.

"Where are you?" she hissed.

"Back off, Charley!' I growled back. "I don't work for you. I don't work for your husband, and I don't have to report to you about anything. Nothing! Do you understand?"

No response.

"I know you're scared. I am looking for Nico, so back up and breathe." I pictured her tired and wan face. She'd been lurching between anger and fear for the past thirty-six hours.

"I think Nico is hurt," she said. "The cops wouldn't give me the time of day. Nobody pays attention to me. I can't even get his goddamn father or brother to call me back. Everybody thinks he's whoring around. But it's been too long. Nico would never go this long without calling me. Something is wrong, and I know it."

"I'm doing the best I can."

"What happened at that baron guy's house last night? You told me you were there. Who is that guy?"

"Just a customer. Benito's doing his portrait. He owes Benito money, which Nico was supposed to collect, so we went to ask him if he'd heard from him." There was truth in my lie, and I told it spontaneously. While I spoke, I listened to myself. Did I sound rational? Would the cops accept the same explanation?

"I called the cops and told them you and Bo were there last night."

"What is wrong with you, Charley? Do you know how stupid that was? The police came to our homes and scared the hell out of everybody. How does that help you find Nico?"

"The cops wouldn't return my calls. I told them about you, and for the first time, I got their attention. They came to my house and sat down with me. They took notes. Now they're listening to me."

"Who'd you tell that to, Charley? Who knows you called the cops about Bo and me being there?"

She hesitated for a second, "Alex Danilenko, the owner of Shangri-La. He's the only one who returns my calls. I talk to him all the time."

"Listen to me carefully, Charley." I took on Bo's anger cadence.

"The cops don't give a damn about Nico. But they give a giant damn about arson and murder. Stop using me to get the cops to pay attention to you. If I find out anything, I'll call you. Report me to the cops again, scare my wife and children again, and I will burn down your house. Don't call me. I'll call you." I hung up.

I repeated the conversation to Bo back in the car. Harry's black silhouette did not stir. "Alex Danilenko is your spy…your so-called friend," I said bluntly. "You get all your information from him. From Charley to Alex to you. That's how you knew we took a photo from Nico's house. It's how you found out about Von Baltruschat. You never heard of him before Alex told you we were there."

I was reminded briefly of Alex's joke about the Charley Express and its efficacy.

"I told you before it is not good to know my sources," said Harry.

"Listen, dirtbag," snarled Bo. "You took us by surprise the first time. It won't be that easy next time. You're not so scary when you don't have your Irish buddy protecting you; you're just creepy."

We sat in hostile silence, and I worried we were at the wrong motel. I stepped out of the car again to pace. Reviewing my messages, I realized I'd not returned the call from Melina and called her. She answered on the first ring and spoke softly and immediately.

"Marty, be careful with Dante."

Her opening comment caught me off guard. "Why?"

"I called Dante. Something's off." She stopped to take a drag from a cigarette. I could hear her exhale. "Nico's fallen off the planet. He's gone completely dark. You guys claim to be looking for him. His wife, Charley, calls me twice a day, freaking out. I've kept Benito away from her by hiding his phone. I put it in my pocket and then pretend to help him look for it. You asked questions about that baron clown, and I told you about his deal with Nico. Then a day later, his freaking house burns down. It's seriously crazy. I called Dante and told him about the baron's house and that you and some Russian kid were looking for Nico and coming to Vegas."

"So, he knows we're here?"

"Holy crap, Marty, he acted like I'd kicked him in the balls. He got really agitated and wanted to know where Nico was. Like I know? Like I haven't been looking for him? First, he tells me Nico's probably hunting whores in New Zealand—his words, not mine—and now, just a few hours later, he goes berserk."

"Are you still with Benito?"

"Yes, the doctor has a nurse coming tomorrow at 8 a.m., and I'm Florence Nightingale until then. He's heavily sedated. I double-dosed him. He'll sleep till noon."

We talked a little more, and I thanked her for the heads up. I felt bad for her and made a fumbling effort to separate Bo and me from the baron's burning house, but I probably made it worse. Then I hung up and returned to the car.

"I'm not sure Dante's here anymore," I announced, returning to my seat. "Melina told him we're in Vegas, and he was not happy."

"Well, we've been here for over two hours. Might as well wait a while longer." Bo leaned back to nap while Harry sat stone-still, a brooding, malicious silhouette. By contrast, I felt charged and energized. I hadn't slept more than a handful of hours since Monday, and I knew I was due for a collapse, but right then and there, the inevitable crash felt like a long time off.

About an hour later, a cab pulled into the empty lot, stopped in front of the choppers, expelled three passengers, and peeled out as if its driver had doubts about his welfare. Two large shapes staggered to room 14, while the third shape stood next to the choppers for a few seconds, bent over, looked like it would vomit, but then straightened up and kicked its head back to stare at the starless sky. It was Dante. Bo was as attentive as I was. His head jutted forward, and he studied the moving figures like they were numbers on a balance sheet. No one spoke.

Room 14's light came on, and a small portion of the lot lit up like a lantern in a cave. I could see Dante's friends through the curtainless window. Muscled, tattooed, and leather vested, one had a massive beard covering his face, neck, and upper chest, while the other was beardless but had a ponytail that reached the middle of his back.

They left the door open and shuffled around in the room. We made sure not to slam the car doors and strolled towards the light. I wandered into the room first, with Bo immediately behind me. Dante looked up, burst out, "Son-of-a-bitch!" and lunged at me. The guy with the ponytail turned to see what Dante was hollering at and charged directly at Bo.

As Dante slammed me into the adjacent wall, I watched over his shoulder. With a speed and grace I had not seen before, Bo ducked under the outstretched arm of the charging biker and slipped effortlessly behind him. He quickly wrapped his arms around the guy's midsection and picked him off the ground as he purposely fell backward, taking the entire flailing bulk with him. The biker's head and upper body slammed first and hard onto a round table by the window, shattering it into kindling. Without hesitation, Bo rolled the stunned bruiser onto his belly, straddled him like he was riding a horse, intertwined his legs with the biker's, and jammed his elbow deep into the base of the man's neck. The entire maneuver took less than five seconds, and its brutal agility temporarily stunned me. Dante had me pinned to the wall, but I managed to wrap my hands around his neck, felt his Adam's apple, and squeezed while shouting into his face, "We're not here to hurt you! Get the fuck off me!" Dante took a step back as his eyes registered recognition, just as the second biker, the one with the beard, blasted out of the bathroom, straight at the Russian who had just stepped into the door frame.

Harry lowered his head and hurtled himself at the stampeding bull without fear or hesitation. They collided in the center of the room, with the Russian surprisingly landing on top and clawing for the knife holstered in the biker's belt. I freed my grip on Dante's neck, shoved past him, and grabbed Harry's arm before he pulled the knife. Bo pressed his elbow deeper into the neck of the writhing biker, who grunted and swore. He struggled to get up, but Bo had him pinned like a schoolyard bully. Dante started clamoring for everyone to stop, and slowly we began to untangle.

"I know them," Dante said several times breathlessly, rhythmically, until everyone was upright and glaring at each other. Then he asked, "Where's my brother?" His voice was slurred. They'd been drinking, which explained how the three of us got the three of them under control so quickly.

"He's not here," I panted. "We're here for the painting."

"Piss off, Marty. What painting?"

I rolled my eyes. There was no reason to be coy. We were either right or wrong, and I wanted to find out quickly. "Jesus Christ! Stop being an asshole," I yelled. "The Raphael, the one you forged, the one Nico sold to Natalya."

Dante was as good with secrets as his brother. Only his eyes hinted that I'd surprised him. "Who wants it?" He demanded.

We were right.

"The buyer, you moron! The guy who paid $10 million for it," heaved Bo, standing coiled in front of the equally coiled and gasping biker. "Von Baltruschat got paid $10 million, and now the buyer's a bit irate at not getting what he paid for. We think he got a forgery. You know anything about that, Dante? Or are we just wasting our time here?"

Over the next minute, we assembled ourselves, straightened our rumpled clothes, arranged the furniture—except for the table that had become a permanent casualty—and sat well apart, spread out over the two beds and three chairs. Dante introduced his biker friends as Biker Mike, the ponytail guy, and Beard. Neither was particularly sociable. Mike grunted and arched his back, which had taken the brunt of Bo's wrestling souffle, and Beard checked his knife sheath to ensure it was secure. Neither spoke.

Biker Mike was clearly a gym rat. He wore an old Gold's Gym T-shirt with the sleeves ripped off at the shoulders to showcase his massive triceps and tattoos. His hands were huge and fat, and he sported an impressive pewter ring of a skull with tiny ruby eyes on the middle digit of his right hand. Beard doesn't need a description. Just imagine a big burly biker with more hair than face.

Dante handed out Budweiser cans to everyone before sitting on the bed nearest the door, leaning hard against the faux leather tufted headboard.

"Nice place," I said.

"It's ours," said Beard. "The club owns it…bikers only. A place to unwind."

I nodded and thought about the stress of being a biker—all that grooming and hygiene discipline.

"I need to find my brother," said Dante, and his voice cracked.

"You have the painting?" asked the Russian.

"Who the hell are you? I don't know you."

"I'm Harry. I represent the buyer."

"Natalya?"

"Yes."

"Piss off," said Dante. He gulped his beer and belched. "Natalya was never the buyer. She was the go-between."

"What difference does that make? You cheated her buyer, and he wants his painting," I interjected.

"Did the buyer burn down the baron's house?" Dante asked.

He's connecting the dots.

"Yes. Listen, the buyer is not happy. He's going scorched earth. Tell us where the painting is so we can stop this insanity."

"I need to know where my brother is," said Dante, flashing us the palms of his hands. "He's disappeared, according to everyone. The painting is my only leverage, so I need to talk to Nico first. Do you know if he's safe? Is he being held for ransom?"

The conversation was going sideways, and I had to get it back on course. "Dante, look at me," I said and waited for his red-mottled eyes to settle on mine. "It's not important where Nico is right now, and finding him won't fix anything. Only finding the Raphael will fix things. Where is it?"

"In the hangar. Nico's hangar at the Aurora airport. Where he keeps all his art inventory, and his boat, and the Briccones."

A tense silence followed, disturbed only by six men breathing. I checked my watch. Friday, 2:35 am, and we'd located the painting—mark it. The disembodied bits of the puzzle had been assembled. We'd accomplished what had seemed impossible just three days earlier.

"So, we were right. Nico sent a forgery to Natalya and kept the original. What the fuck was he thinking?" I demanded, feeling like a relieved parent scolding his recovered lost child.

Without warning, Dante's upper body crumpled into a heap on the bed, and his fists beat the worn and shabby bedspread. His beer tipped and emptied, and he slapped it, sending the can rolling to the floor.

"He didn't!" he cried. "Nico never meant to send a forgery." He straightened up and wiped snot away with his forearm. "He never knew."

"What happened?" asked Bo.

All eyes stayed on Dante. No one moved, not even Biker Mike and Beard.

"Fucking Nico!" Dante wailed, mucus bubbling from his nostrils. "My stupid son-of-a-bitch brother! He promised me $100,000 to make him a copy of the Raphael. You know how big a deal that is for me? He pays me crumbs for all the work I do for him. He promises big money but never pays me. He tells me he has no money. I do all of Benito's work now. Everything that goes out the door is mine. All the art you sell for your company is my work. I'm supposed to get thirty percent. You know what I get paid? Pennies!" He shook his hand, and Mike got up to get him another beer.

"So, I laughed when he came to me and said he had Raphael's original *Portrait of a Young Man*."

"You know the painting?" asked the Russian.

"Of course! It's one of the most famous paintings in the world. Fortune hunters have been looking for it for years. I once considered painting it as part of my masterwork collection for Benito. They're hanging in his house. Nico steals the ones he likes best for his own house."

"We've seen them," I said.

"So, when Nico showed me the real thing, I nearly wet my pants from the joy of touching it. He told me about Von Baltruschat and said he had a lead on a buyer but wanted a perfect copy for himself before selling it. Maybe he planned to sell it someday, but I didn't care. The challenge was enough. So, I made Nico a perfect copy, not like the others I copied from photos. I had the authentic. I could study it. Run my hands across the paint. Study its brilliance. See how it'd been punished by time and stupidity. I could make a true copy front and back. It took two months. I locked myself in Benito's barn and never left. I let no one in, not even Nico. The barn had everything I needed, a bed, paints, chemicals, and a commercial oven. I used it not just to bake my masterpiece but also the pizza. Can you believe it? I lived on pizza for two months." He paused and wiped his nose with the bed pillow. "I also smoked a bucket of hash. It was crazy. I can't describe it. Living every day with a masterpiece, melding with it, was like one long orgasm."

"So, if Nico didn't intend to ship a forgery, how did it get to the buyer?" asked Bo.

Dante began to weep again. His face collapsed, and once more, he punched the much-maligned bedspread. "While I worked on the masterpiece, Nico confirmed his buyer. Nico's a genius at finding buyers. I heard about the baron and Natalya, but I didn't much care. I wanted to paint and get paid. When I finished, I showed the copy to Nico, who loved it. Then I wanted to party. I'd created my greatest work and lived in a barn for two winter months. I wanted to celebrate because I hadn't seen or talked to anyone other than the pizza delivery guy. Get Mike and Beard together and party here in warmer weather."

Mike and Beard nodded bovinely.

"I wanted my money!" he cried. "But Nico kept putting me off. He said he hadn't been paid, so he didn't have money for me. But it was bullshit. My brother has short-changed me since I was born. He had the money, just not for me. He always has money for himself. Christ! You've seen his barn! His house! You know how many thousands he spent building his little choo-choo train?" He took a long drink from his beer. "He'll spare no expense when the liquor runs low in his fancy bar. Shit, he pays a kid to come over and polish his Ferraris once a month. Nico doesn't even drive them. The kid wipes off dust! But pay me for my greatest achievement? Suddenly he has no money. Son-of-a-bitch."

I could tell Dante's anger was born of frustration, not hate. "What happened, Dante? What did you do?" I already knew by then, but I needed to hear him say it.

"Natalya came to inspect the Raphael, and she crated it and sealed it herself. Then she left to report to the buyer and get the money."

"Natalya left? She took her eyes off the Raphael?" The Russian was surprised.

"It wasn't a big deal. Nico dealt in good faith. He charmed her, and she was satisfied with the painting's provenance. Nico told her about the countess and how she found it but said he'd never reveal her name, or the seller's name, just like Natalya would never identify her buyer. It's all a game—each of them could dig deeper, but they jointly agreed to lay down their shovels."

"How is it possible that Natalya would agree never to meet Von Baltruschat," I said, dumbfounded. "Didn't she have to verify the painting's history?"

"It wasn't necessary. Nico told me that Natalya was less guarded than usual 'cause the painting is so renowned it falls into a separate category. She told Nico no one in their right mind would offer up a fraudulent Raphael, and it helped that Nico was an unknown from Portland 'cause that appeared more authentic. It's always been assumed if *Portrait of a Young Man* was ever discovered, it would be found in the basement of an obscure nobody, maybe a soldier or the son of a soldier. It wasn't stolen in a heist. It was lost in the chaos of war. If it were ever recovered, it would be under banal circumstances."

I could see Biker Mike and Beard squint at the word "banal." They were either impressed that Dante knew the word or trying to figure out its meaning.

"But Nico's an art dealer. He and Benito are not obscure," I said.

"Hah!" he hacked. "Trust me, in the art world, the high-end art world, Nico's a nobody. And so's Benito. The snobs that control that world are all arrogant elitist shitbags. They wouldn't sully themselves with sculptures of wild animals or cowboys. It's too pedestrian." Dante paused, allowing his insight to linger. Then he continued, "Nico told me Natalya knew the Raphael was real the second she saw it. And it was. She inspected the real thing. Then after she left, all hell broke loose. I wanted my money. Nico and I went at it. I don't remember how it started, but it was biblical—Hiroshima and Nagasaki combined—screaming and throwing shit like we've done our whole lives. It was a true Scava brawl. In the end, I didn't get my money, and my brother told me to piss off." He stopped talking, and his eyes began to moisten again. "So, fuck it…I switched the paintings in the crate. Screw that bastard! I'll keep the damn Raphael until he pays me." He hiccupped and cleared his throat. "Then he can have it back."

What was by then obvious was still shocking when he said it.

Bo's hand cupped his mouth. Biker Mike and Beard lowered their eyes and stared at the shag rug.

"You allowed Nico to hand over a forgery to Natalya." I shook my head.

"I am so sorry. I screwed up. I was mad. I was crazy stupid."

"Bullshit!" said Bo. "This happened...what...seven, eight months ago? Why haven't you ever said anything? You're so pissed at your brother that you want him to get blamed. You want Nico to get killed."

"Killed? Jesus, what are you saying? Killed!"

I think Bo dropped the word purposely to see what would happen.

"Why the hell didn't you tell Nico?" I jumped in to divert him. "You had months!"

"I don't know," he whacked the bed again. "I stayed pissed at him for weeks, maybe a month. I got high a lot. It's all a haze now. Then, later I was too scared to tell him. After four months, I convinced myself that the buyer was happy with it. I know my copy is near perfect, and no human alive would know the difference without serious analysis like microscopy or x-ray. I figured the buyer could never risk putting the painting under detailed inspection. I convinced myself to shut up about it. I guess I went from being scared to the opposite of scared." He straightened his spine and took a deep breath. "If I could get away with it, I wanted to own it myself. Maybe figure out how to collect the reward."

"But Nico wanted the fake, right?" said the Russian. "He never asked about the fake?"

"I told you." Dante looked at Harry, his eyes puffed and nearly shut. "I didn't speak to my brother for a month after the fight. When I started talking to him again, he said he'd pay me, but I told him I destroyed the fake in a rage and burned the damn thing. I can lie as well as he can. In the Scava family, everybody's nuts. Growing up with Benito, we never question a good tantrum. So, he said he'd pay me if I did it again. But I knew he'd screw me, so I never got around to it."

A few silent seconds passed, and Dante looked at Bo, "Why did you say killed?"

Bo turned away from him. "I don't know, let's get to the airport.

Dante, you need to come back with us. We need to get the painting out of the hangar. Why did you store it there?"

"I knew it would be safe there. It's where Nico hides all his toys, all the sculptures, the APs, and the molds—everything he smuggles away from Benito before he dies, and it all gets trapped in an estate battle, not to mention an IRS audit. My brother robs Benito a little more every week and stores it in the hangar. He keeps it a secret. He's like Gollum with his ring. The hangar is where he keeps all his 'precious.' After Benito dies, he'll probably even keep the urn there."

Suddenly, it occurred to me that Dante and Nico referred to their father only by his name. I guessed Benito never considered himself a dad, nor did they.

"If it's in his hangar, why'd he never see it?" asked Harry.

"I was smart about how I hid it."

Mike and Beard got up and left the room to smoke outside. Dante pushed himself off the bed to join them. "We got to find Nico," he said on his way out the door.

I checked my watch, anxious to catch the first flight home.

"We go to the hangar, and we're done," Bo told Harry after we were alone. "You get the damn painting, and we get our lives back."

"Natalya is on her way to Portland," he said quietly. "My friend told me when I called."

Bo and I stared at him in disbelief.

"Stop the friend bullshit," I said, irritated. "You mean Alex, the owner of Shangri-La. You're saying Alex Danilenko knows Natalya?" I shook my head like I wanted loose pieces to fall back into place.

"Why is she coming?" asked Bo. "Why today?"

"She has a private plane. She's probably on her way already." He looked at his Rolex Daytona. "It's 3 a.m., so it's 6 a.m. in Florida. Maybe she is leaving soon."

"You didn't say why," said Bo.

"She is coming to pick up the painting."

"You're lying, Harry. You made that call to Alex over six hours ago. Remember, we were stuck in traffic, and you didn't know we had the painting then."

"It doesn't matter why…she is coming."

I looked out the window but couldn't see Dante. Biker Mike and Beard were puffing and mumbling between themselves, but Dante was gone. I jumped from my chair to the door in a single step. I could see Dante marching down the motel's inside perimeter, his phone cupped to his ear, his head down, listening intently. It didn't feel right.

Who was he talking to?

CHAPTER TWENTY-ONE

Thursday Middle of the Night

Vasili Bobrov

AFTER HIS CURIOUS PHONE CALL ENDED ABRUPTLY, Dante rejoined Mike and Beard in their cigarette huddle, and a few minutes later, they single-filed back into room 14, with Dante bringing up the rear. I started talking about flying back to Portland as Mike discreetly positioned himself next to and slightly behind the Russian. While I was reciting departure times, Dante bobbed his head slightly, and Mike sucker-punched Harry before he could sense anything coming.

Biker Mike's fist struck Harry an inch below his right ear with the devastating force that could only come from decades of bench pressing his body weight four times a week at his favorite gym. I watched Mike's right fist, the one with the skull ring and ruby eyes, disappear deep into Harry's flesh, and he dropped like a pair of trousers.

The blow caught Bo and me by complete surprise.

Bo instinctively lowered his shoulder for battle, but Dante walked past him, stood over the semi-conscious Russian, and spat on his face. "You killed my brother!" he screamed. "You piece of shit. Die motherfucker! Die!"

Close enough to grab Dante by the back of his shirt collar, I pulled down hard, causing him to fall against me and then butt slam onto

205

the carpet. Bo shoved his open hand into Beard's face, and Beard stood rock still with his fists clenched.

Dante tried to twist away. "Let go of me! That shitbag killed Nico!"

The Russian twitched, and Mike kicked his steel-toed Harley Davidson boot into the back of his head. He lay still like a fallen soldier.

"He killed my brother," repeated Dante, slumped between my legs. Either he was trying to convince us, or he was so deep into an adrenalin rage that he couldn't think to say anything else.

"Stop! He's not alone," Bo shouted at Biker Mike. "He's got friends. They're watching my house, Marty's house, and our families. Anything happens to him, and our families get hurt."

I pulled Dante to his feet. "He's Russian mob," I said. "You kill him, and we all die."

"You never said nothin' 'bout Russian mob," said Mike. "What's Bratva got to do with it?"

"We're not sure. We think the buyer was a Russian." I pointed to Harry. "And he's here to collect."

Harry twitched again and let out a low moan, but instead of another head kick, Mike walked over to the bedside table, pulled the phone cord out of the wall, and used it to hog-tie him. Mike and Beard then dragged the limp Russian into the bathroom, lifted him into the bathtub, drew the shower curtain, and rejoined us, shutting the door behind them. "He's gonna be punch-drunk for about an hour, maybe two," said Mike.

"Dante..." I spoke slowly, fearing his rage blinded him to rational conversation. "We have to get back to Portland, and Harry told us Natalya was flying in to pick up the painting."

"His name's not Harry; it's Vasili." Dante spat out the words. "Vasili Bobrov or something...Russian prick!"

"How do you know that?" asked Bo.

"Alex told me. I just talked to him outside. I was trying to find

Nico. He practically lives at Shangri-La, so Alex is always a good bet. I've been to the club plenty of times. I told him you guys were here with some Russian kid named Harry, and he said his name's not Harry; it's Vasili Bobrov, and he's not a kid; he's major trouble." Dante straightened his collar. "I asked him what kind of trouble, and he said bigger than he ever expected. He said that dick destroyed his entire life. Cried that he could lose everything, his club, his house, even his life. He was pretty intense on the phone—like I had something to do with it—like he was blaming me for something." He took a deep breath. "I'm just hanging out with my friends in Vegas, for cryin' out loud. So, I told him I didn't care about this Vasili guy. I'm just trying to find my damn brother, and Alex freaks out like he's crazy and starts yelling into the phone that I'll never find Nico cause Vasili killed him. Shot him in the head. He screamed about how he's in deep shit cause it was his gun and his cabin. I couldn't follow him. He wasn't making sense. He yelled so loud I had to pull the phone from my ear. I started to feel sick, and he kept screaming, so I hung up. Then I told Mike to take that son-of-a-bitch down."

He turned to Mike. "Thanks, buddy."

Mike nodded.

Dante was trembling and bouncing from one foot to another. He was in a full adrenalin spasm and panting like he'd run a mile. "Alex said you guys know everything, and if you talked to the cops, he'd go to prison. He's seriously scared. Talked so fast it hurt my head."

"Call him back," ordered Bo. "Call that duplicitous bastard back and tell him to meet us at 10 o'clock at the IHOP by the Portland airport. I want to know what he knows. Remind him we will talk to the cops."

"This time, the Charley Express has consequences," I injected.

"And we need him to go with us to Aurora airport. We've never met Natalya, and we need him to identify her," Bo concluded.

Dante stopped bouncing. He pulled the tattered bedspread off the bed and used it to wipe the sweat that drenched him.

"What about that murderous piece of shit?" he asked, evil-eyeing the bathroom door.

"Leave him in the tub," I said, looking at my watch. "We're two hours from take-off. By the time Harry gets out of there, we'll be home. If we get the painting to Natalya, maybe she'll call off her dog."

"Vasili," said Dante. "His name's Vasili."

I watched Bo go into the bathroom, look behind the curtain, come back out, and shut the door. Tension shrouded his face. "We've got time," he said.

I picked the Russian's phone off the filthy carpet and stuffed it into my pocket.

"If you take his wallet, he won't be able to fly," suggested Mike.

"Getting back to Portland isn't my worry," I said, appreciating his advice. "He's got buddies in Portland waiting. What we need is a few hours head start. If we can't make a deal with this Natalya woman, then we need enough time to get to the FBI before he or his crew retaliate."

Dante threw his arms around Mike and Beard and said goodbye. Bo and I shook hands with them, and we smiled at each other.

We were all comrades-in-arms now.

CHAPTER TWENTY-TWO

Friday Dawn

Natalya

ON THE WAY TO THE VEGAS AIRPORT, Dante called Alex and instructed him to meet us at the IHOP at Cascade Station, near PDX. Then he curled in a fetal position across the back seat, cried quietly, and mumbled to himself. It was 5 a.m., and the streets were empty. The blazing lights on the strip made me feel like the night was beginning, not ending. I leaned toward Bo and whispered, "Back at the motel…very impressive."

"College wrestling team." He grinned. "I was All-Conference champion in my freshman year. It's muscle memory. I'm fatter and older, but you never forget the basics. Between wrestling and football, I've still got skills."

///////////////////////////////////

While waiting to board our flight, Harry's—Vasili's—phone vibrated, and I pulled it out of my pocket. The caller ID said Natalya, and I quickly answered so it wouldn't go to voicemail. Bo and Dante walked toward me, but I waved them off.

"Hello?" I started.

A long silence. "You are not Malysh."

"No, I'm not."

"But you answer his phone."

"Are you looking for Vasili?"

"Yes. Malysh…Vasili."

"Vasili isn't here right now…he's tied up. Are you Natalya?

"Yes."

"Natalya, my name is Martin Schott. Do you know who I am?"

"Yes, I think so. You are with Nico Scava."

"Do you know that Nico Scava is dead?"

"Yes," she said, followed by silence. Then after an uncomfortably long time, she continued, "But I just found this out. I was not told everything. I am flying to Portland. I am flying to the same airport as last time, Aurora airfield, and will arrive about 1 p.m. your time. Will I be meeting with you?"

"Yes, and with Bo Bishop. I also think with Alex Danilenko. I understand he knows you."

She chuckled. "Yes, I know Alex quite well. Do you have my painting?"

"Yes. I don't have it this minute, but I know where it is, and I will have it when you arrive."

"Thank you. I will appreciate that."

"Natalya, did you send Vasili to kill us?"

"No. I asked Malysh…Vasili, to talk to Nico because I bought a painting from him, and he cheated me. Vasili is doing me that favor, but I did not instruct him to do more. I spoke with Vasili every day, but I just learned he didn't tell me everything. He left…holes." Her English was very clear despite a distinct Russian accent. "Alex called me last night and filled in those holes."

"I am not sure Alex filled in all the holes, Natalya, because I'm not sure he knows all of them. Did he tell you that the lives of our families have been threatened? Did he tell you that the police are searching for us? Did he tell you about the baron?"

"I don't want to discuss this over the phone, especially not Vasili's phone. I called him to instruct him to stop his actions immediately and come home. But instead, I am talking to you."

"We are holding him here in Vegas until we can get back to Portland and get the painting."

"You are holding him…how?"

"We locked him in a motel bathroom. Two men are watching him."

"Martin, may I call you Martin? I want you to listen to me. You do not understand Vasili. Those two men are in danger. Let Vasili go and bring him with you to the airfield today, and I will take him home. Will you do that for me?"

"I can't. He's in a shitty little motel off the strip, and I'm at McCarran, ready to board the flight back. I want as much distance between me and that maniac as possible. My friends will let him go after we land in Portland. They can take care of themselves."

"I don't think that is very smart. Vasili is not like other people. I've known him all my life. He can turn on you without warning. He is a grenade in your pocket—sometimes a useful weapon—sometimes it blows off your legs. Either way, it leaves a mess. You understand?" The way she said "you understand" sent a jolt down my spine.

"If Bo and I give you the painting, can you make him stop? Can you put the pin back in the grenade?"

"Yes, but he is unpredictable. If he decides to seek revenge, I will not be able to stop him."

Thinking back on it all now, that was the moment I made my decision.

"I don't have the money, the $10 million. Vasili does," I said as the boarding announcement came over the loudspeakers.

"If you give me the painting, and it's the real one—the one I saw—I don't care about the money."

"Natalya, my plane is boarding. I will see you at Aurora at 1 p.m. today. We can discuss everything then."

"I will pick up my painting. I am not sure we need to discuss many more things."

"Now you sound just like Vasili."

"Do not presume you know me, Martin. I look forward to meeting you." She hung up, and I caught up with Bo and Dante and repeated the call to them from memory.

CHAPTER TWENTY-THREE

Friday Morning

A Forger's Work

WE SAT ON THE PLANE THREE ACROSS with Dante in the middle. The plane was half empty. No one was sitting in front or behind us. The flight attendant encouraged us to separate and take advantage of the open seating, but we declined.

"You know we can't give art to investors anymore," said Bo. "We can't have anything to do with forged art."

"I warned Nico," said Dante. "I always thought his 'art for equity' plan was bad. It's too much volume in too short a time. It'll hurt Benito's brand and valuation. The other day I saw one of his sculptures go up on eBay. Thank Christ, Benito's too far gone to ever know about that. If he ever saw his work on an internet auction site, the few brain cells he still has would explode. But Nico doesn't care. He is not an artist. No artist can keep up with Nico's need for money. It's why he glommed onto you. Paladin was going to save him. He planned to sell his stock and live large. He promised to give me 30 percent of all his equity in the company for doing the work. I've never seen a single share."

"You can keep the shares he paid for," said Bo.

Dante's head dropped as if it was too heavy.

"Must have been easy for you to paint the Raphael," I said

casually to get his mind off his brother. "You didn't have to work from memory."

"Have you guys ever heard of Ely Sakhai?"

Both Bo and I shook our heads no. "Well, he's an art dealer who owned a big Manhattan gallery. The guy made a fortune on forged art. He used to buy minor, lesser-known works from big-time artists and bring them back to his gallery, where he had an entire forgery operation working on the upper floor. A bunch of Chinese immigrants working for peanuts copied the works he bought. These Asians were good, and Sakhai instructed them to reproduce the pieces exactly, including any markings on the back of the canvas and frames. Then he'd attach the certificates of authenticity from the originals to the fakes and sold them overseas. This guy had some balls on him. After a few months, Sakhai would order new authenticity certificates, which were easy to get cause he still had the originals. Then he'd sell the originals with their new credentials into the American market.

"But Sakhai's greed got the better of him, and he sold the real ones too soon after selling the fakes. One day, Sakhai decided to sell an original Paul Gauguin called *Vase de Fleurs* through Sotheby's."

"Hey, now that you mention it," I interrupted, "I vaguely remember reading about that. Wasn't there a big brawl with Christie's or something?"

"Yeah. It turns out that Sakhai's customer in Tokyo, who bought the fake *Vase de Fleurs*, decided to sell it, coincidentally at the same time, but through Christie's. The two auction houses don't talk to each other, so neither knew what the other would offer in their spring season. Both Sotheby's and Christie's put out their spring catalog, and the Gauguin was on the cover of both. Oh my god, the chaos!" He laughed, and it sounded just like Nico's laugh.

"To make things even worse, when the two paintings were compared side by side and studied for their authenticity, the fake—the—freaking—fake—was considered so good that it was nearly impossible to tell the difference!" He laughed again. "The damn

Chinese forgers were so good they matched the original brush stroke for brush stroke. That's my point. There's a difference between copying an original before you and copying something from a photo or memory. It's why I was able to duplicate the Raphael perfectly."

"So what happened to the Sakhai guy?" asked Bo.

"He's still in jail. The experts finally figured out which painting was fake, but not by studying the paintwork; the individual strokes were copied flawlessly. They did it by studying the entire product, and the original just looked older. You can't fake age. You can try, and there are tricks, but no one can truly fake time."

"How'd you fake it with the Raphael?" I asked.

"Talent," he said with pride. "I also got a lot of help from World War II," he chuckled. Bo cocked his head like Boomer does when he's puzzled.

"There are fake paintings, fake provenances, and sometimes both," Dante continued. "That's what provenance is; the chronological ownership of the artwork traceable back to the artist."

I was impressed with Dante and regretted never getting to know him better. Nico had described him as a drug-addled ne'er do well when, in fact, he was articulate and intelligent. I realized we could have been friends, and it dawned on me that Nico had disparaged his brother to keep Bo and me away from him. Dante was too important to roam free. He was Nico's true precious.

"With the Raphael," he continued, "World War II was a friend. The fact that the painting was boosted seventy years ago cut a truck-size hole in the provenance that any rational story can fill. No one alive has ever seen the original."

"You're saying any good story would be acceptable because the chain of custody had been irreparably broken," said Bo.

"Right. Nico told me the whole Von Baltruschat story, and by the way, that is one weird dude."

Bo and I nodded in accord.

"But I didn't paint a forgery. I painted a perfect copy. I just wanted it to pass the superficial inspections, like UV light analysis and craquelure examination. That's where the war helped me out the most. There are very few pre-war photos of the Raphael; I think only one is in color, and a few are black and white. There's no recorded pattern of the craquelure. The photos aren't detailed enough to capture it, so whatever evolved from my make and bake process would be acceptable. There's nothing to compare it with except the original, which I assumed the new owner would keep lost forever."

Dante spoke in a low voice, slightly bent over. The flight attendant came by with refreshments. Bo and I asked for coffee, and Dante asked for a Coke. After the cart proceeded down the aisle, Dante continued.

"I never expected the painting to pass detailed lab analysis. I only wanted it to pass the eye test. First, I needed old wood. Finding old wood that's still smooth, not warped or splintered, is not easy. I caught a break when I scoped out the antique stores in Portland and found this old file storage cabinet. Damn thing was all hard maple and stood up to my chin with thirty drawers. Probably used to hold architectural drawings or shipping manifests. It was expensive, a typical 'statement' piece, yuppie furniture, over a hundred years old. But the bottoms of the drawers were perfect; old, flat, clean, and close to the ideal size. The store was empty. You know how those old warehouses are, crammed with furniture and no one around to answer questions. So, I pulled two drawers out and walked out a rear fire exit with them under my arms."

He took a long drink from the Coke and belched. "You know that lattice on the back of the panel? I used old wood splints, rusted some nails, and spent extra time constructing something sloppy because the original cradle was poorly built.

"I prepped the panel with rabbit glue gesso and mixed up an oil-based primer of raw umber for the first layer. I mixed in turpentine as a quick-drying agent and even a little powdered dirt. I ordered everything I needed from a website in France, even lead-white, which you can't get here anymore, FDA regulations, and all that garbage. I had it delivered express; very expensive.

"I researched Raphael's technique, so I knew he used walnut oil to bind his pigments, but I used linseed oil instead because it dries faster. See—the trick in copying an old masterpiece is not in the drawing; any good artist can do that; it's in the aging. More specifically, the drying. It takes years for the oil to dry completely. I didn't have days or weeks, or years. I had hours. The best way to fix that problem was to bake the painting."

"Like you bake a cake?" asked Bo.

"Cake, pizza, cookies, Hot Pockets—yes-siree. Bake an oil layer at 240 degrees for 90 minutes and it's dry. But there's one other secret ingredient." He tapped the side of his head with his forefinger and leaned forward, causing us to follow, and he whispered, "phenol-formaldehyde." Then he fell back into his chair with a satisfied grin. "Pick it up at your local Ace Hardware store. Mix equal parts of linseed oil and phenol with half a part of Liquin, bake, and you have a dry oil painting with craquelure. It's magic."

"How the hell do you know all that?" I asked.

"I've read every book ever published about art forgery. Forgers have massive egos. They all want to brag. So, when they get caught, they write a book, like crooked politicians. Each has a formula, and they're eager to pass it along. I've experimented with all of them."

We got refills of coffee and Coke, and Dante kept going. "First, I outlined the portrait's composition in charcoal like Raphael did most of the time. He liked to sketch things out. His work is very geometric and harmonious. But as I got further into it, I started to doubt if the damn portrait is even a genuine Raphael."

"What? The Raphael isn't genuine?" Bo almost spilled his coffee.

"I checked, and there've been questions about its authenticity forever, even before the war. Some scholars think a Raphael student painted it after his tutor died as an homage to him. Others are convinced it's a true portrait done by the master. But even the owner, the Polish dude—help me out…" He snapped his fingers lightly.

"Prince Czartoryski," I said.

"Yeah, that guy…Jesus, what a mouth full, and I'm Italian. So, what's-his-name—that guy— tried to sell the portrait back in 1850 for less than a hundred K, and no one took him up on it for over three years. Did you guys know that another Italian forger in the 1600s created Raphael forgeries? Maybe the portrait is a four-hundred-year-old forgery. Wouldn't that be insane!"

"And?" I pressed.

"I don't know if it's real, but I can tell you that if Raphael did paint it, he got lazy or bored with the damn thing."

"Why?"

"Because there are places in the painting where things fall apart. It's like some days he was really into it; other days, it was just a bloody chore. You can tell by the brush strokes. Like the fur robe, for example. Beautiful and rich. I had to put my whole body into those strokes; gorgeous, powerful, dense. Then as you recede to the far-right corner of the painting where the robe trails off, it's just a formless flow of indifferent dabs and dashes casually applied. When I get bored with a painting, that's what I do. I fill in gaps with some hurried strokes to get it done.

"Another example is the neck. Raphael was on par with DaVinci and Michelangelo. He was a master of the human form. But look at the guy's neck; it's too long. Not symmetrical with his head or body. And that hat…oh my god! That insane beret. Are you kidding me? I had a hard time painting it 'cause it's just so wrong. The damn thing is so big and awkward. It should be sliding off the back of his head. Instead, it sits like a faceless animal nesting in his hair."

"Why does he look so young?" I asked. "Raphael was in his thirties when he painted it. He looks like a girl."

"No, that's OK. It's normal for that period. Raphael was a

naturalist, just like Michelangelo. The androgynous look was very in fashion."

"So, how'd you make it look old, including that damage line? That bubbled vein down the whole center of the painting."

"Flaking paint around a crack isn't hard to fake. It's just another layer baked on top, and then I used a heated needle to peel the paint. It took me several days. But remember, the damage happened after all the pre-war photos were taken, so whatever I created would be new to the viewer. I only paid attention to two thin cracks, starting at his left eye socket and running to his cheek. They were in the pre-war photos. I recreated those cracks perfectly. Nico told me Natalya used a jeweler's loupe to look at them. She probably studied the pre-war photos before she came to inspect it. I figured Natalya kept all her research limited to the internet and a few books. She couldn't just call up experts on Raphael and ask questions about one of the most hunted treasures in the world without catching attention.

"Anyway, the whole thing is layer after layer of paint, glaze, and varnish, and I baked every layer. You can only bake for about 90 minutes, or you'll burn the oil, so I set two alarm clocks in case I fell asleep. I put one alarm across the room so I'd be forced out of bed to turn it off. Sometimes, I'd let the painting sit under ultra-violet lamps when I smoked a bowl to bake it even more and oxidize the varnish."

Dante looked hard at me, then turned and did the same to Bo.

"Last but not least, my secret formula. I took a standard varnish, mixed it with some brown stain, and applied it very thinly, like a dental veneer. After it dried, I poured cold coffee on the whole damn thing and added some vacuum cleaner dust and cigarette ash. I let it dry and then washed the entire portrait carefully with light soapy water." He took a deep breath. "Finally, I spread a fine layer of powdered rottenstone on it. That's a polishing abrasive. I let it sit for a few hours and then blew it off with a hairdryer set on low. The powder makes the whole thing look a little dusty. My masterpiece was done. Took me two months. I never got laid or ate a decent meal. That was my sacrifice. No need to thank me." He smiled.

The pilot came on the speaker to advise everyone sitting on the plane's right side to look out the window and enjoy Mt. Hood, which we all did in silence. Yesterday's clouds had again disappeared, letting us look down on a rolling carpet of verdant forest. We began our slow descent into Portland.

"How did Nico ever find Natalya?" I asked.

Dante turned to me, his eyes trembly with grief. "Funny story," he lamented. "Nico told me it was a sequence of fortunate mistakes." He stopped, and his body buckled as he silently wept again. A woman sitting across the aisle wearing a sweatshirt that read "I lost it all in Vegas" stared at us, and I pointed to Dante and mouthed the words "lost everything." She smiled understandingly and went back to her morning nap.

Sitting back up, he said, "You know the Vatican sculpture, *Joan of Arc on Horseback*?" Bo and I nodded. "Well, it's supposed to be an exclusive edition for the Pope. No one gets another *Joan of Arc*. It would insult the church, and Benito would never allow it. But you know my brother 'Mr. Volume'; he cast another one. He never sold it, of course; he's greedy, not stupid,"

"Isn't the original mold of a sculpture supposed to be broken after the edition is filled?" asked Bo.

"Ha! Do you think Nico works with a foundry where he can't bribe the owner? They break *a* mold, but Nico always gets the original."

I noted that Dante had as much difficulty talking about Nico in the past tense as we did.

"One day, Nico showed up at Shangri-La, dating Charley at the time, and saw the *Joan of Arc* in Alex's office," Dante smirked, remembering. "Nico told me he almost had a coronary. There was a miscommunication with Manuel, the guy who manages Nico's sculpture inventory. Manuel accidentally delivered the *Joan of Arc* to Alex to cover a debt. It was bubble-wrapped or something, and he mistook it for something else. Nico didn't want to draw attention to its value, so never said anything. He figured the unauthorized *Joan of Arc* would dwell forever in an obscure nook in Alex's home. My dear brother had already stolen the mold from Benito, so he could always make another one.

"A year later, Nico reads an article in *ARTNews* magazine about some rich Russian guy, and in a photo, this guy's sitting in front of the *Joan of Arc*. So, unless the Pope gave sculptures to Russian billionaires, he immediately calculated the provenance, the chain of custody, from Benito to Nico to Alex, to the oligarch. But how did Alex Danilenko know a Russian billionaire? Alex had already told him he'd given the sculpture to his stepmother, and that's when Nico connected the dots and figured out the missing link was Natalya."

I almost swallowed my tongue. "Natalya is Alex's stepmother?"

"Yes. Nico figured Natalya received the sculpture from Alex and then sold it to the Russian. He never told Alex about the magazine, and I doubt Alex reads *ARTNews*. Nico told no one about the photo except me. He just asked Alex to put him in touch with his stepmother, which he did."

I understood now how Nico knew Natalya's buyer without her knowing.

Dante began to weep again.

CHAPTER TWENTY-FOUR

Later Friday Morning

Biker Mike

BIKER MIKE TEXTED DANTE TO CALL HIM as we hustled through PDX to keep up with Bo's purposeful pace. He arrived at his Mercedes well ahead of us, pulled the snub-nosed .38 out of the trunk first thing, and stuffed it into his pants pocket. There was something a little desperate in his motion and mood, and I took it to be the same fatigue pushing on me.

Dante climbed into the back, placed the phone on the center console, dialed Biker Mike, and pressed the speaker button. It rang long, and I was worried it might jump to voicemail.

"Yeah," Mike grunted.

"It's me," answered Dante. "We're in Portland."

"Good. I need to get outta Vegas. The Russian is gone, and Beard's dead." His cold composed words felt like fist blows. I stopped breathing for a minute. "You still there?" Mike coughed and wheezed. "You hear me?"

"What happened!" Dante burst out.

"I made a breakfast run; was gone maybe a half hour. I don't know what happened. Maybe Beard went to check on the Russian, maybe the Russian ambushed him, either way, the bastard pig-stuck him. He got untied somehow and must've pulled the towel rack off the wall 'cause he rammed it through Beard's neck. He's layin' in the tub with a chrome bar stickin' out of his beard. I didn't even find him until after the Russian left.

"I came back carryin' breakfast, walked into the room, and he stuck me in the chest with Beard's knife. Never saw it comin'—upper right pectoral. Fucker knew what he was doin'—held the knife and twisted it. Told me to sit down on my hands, palms up. Said it was my fault and that he's always bein' put in compromisin' positions."

I recognized Vasili's words.

"Said he's bein' forced to clip people against his will. I told him as far as I was concerned, he could leave. I wasn't gonna do nothin' anymore. Son-of-a-bitch is crazy; he had his shirt off…probably to keep it clean of blood and stuff. He's marked up, Dante. He's inked front and back. Typical Bratva tags." He hawked mucus from his throat and spat; it sounded painful. Then we only heard breathing.

"Mike?" Dante's voice faltered a bit.

"I superglued the cut to stop the bleedin'. Hurts like hell. I know a vet who'll sew me up and stop any infection. You got to be careful, bro; that dude's seriously bad news. I sat on the floor, bleedin', Beard's knife in my chest, and watched him put his shirt on in front of the mirror like he was dressin' to go out for dinner. All tucked in and nice. He put his jacket on, checked his face for blood, straightened his hair, and talked to himself about how a simple job turned into a shitshow. He took Beard's phone, and then he got in my face and told me he stuck me high instead of low cause he wanted me to live and tell you he's excited to meet you all at the hangar. As he was leavin', he said he liked my skull ring, an' if he ever saw me again, he'll take it, finger first. Don't know where he went, but I'm guessin' he walked to the main street and caught a ride for McCarran."

"What about Beard?" I asked, a creeping sensation rippling over my skin.

"Who's talkin'? Marty?"

"Yes."

"Well, I can't leave'm here. I can't call nobody. This never happened. The Sons are associated with the Angels. We're a puppet club. If I bring cops down on the Sons or the Angels, I'll be countin' worms."

"What're you gonna do?"

"The Lucky Break's fine. Nobody scheduled this time of year. I'm gonna get my chest stitched up, then come back here, clean things myself, wrap up Beard, ride him into the desert, and bury him. Then I'm gonna take a long ride down to Mexico and hang out there for a few months."

"What about other club members? Won't they ask about Beard?" I asked.

"I can cover for him. I'll hide the bike. I'll tell the club he went to Mexico with me and disappeared one night. I'll say he got into a beef with a cartel guy in a bar or somethin'. People disappear down there all the time."

"That's it? No more questions?" I was confused.

"Fuck, Marty. Nobody talks 'bout missin' members. You don't ask to join, an' when you're gone, you're gone. Listen, I gotta go. I'm startin' to bleed again. Dante, I'll be in touch but not for a long time." And the line went dead.

A horrible silence hung over us.

"How'd you get involved with bikers?" I asked Dante. It was all I could think of to break the bitter dread saturating the car.

"I bought weed from them. Mike and Beard run the distribution for The Devil's Sons in Seattle and Portland. So, I'm a big customer. Mostly I paid in cash, but sometimes I paid in art." He shrank into the backseat. "Will Natalya kill me for switching the portrait?" he said, partly to himself.

I didn't answer because, truthfully, I didn't know.

"You think he used Beard's phone to call the Irishman?" asked Bo. "You think our families are safe?"

"Irishman?" Dante cried out, his voice bordering on hysteria.

"When Vasili killed your brother, two other guys were with him. One of them had an Irish accent," said Bo.

Dante's eyes expanded, and his lips trembled again. Fright was eating him in small relentless bites.

"I think they're OK," I said to Bo, looking at my watch. "It's 10 o'clock. Wives are probably doing their thing, out and about, and the kids are in school."

"Ten o'clock?" Bo's aggravation was palpable. "You think that animal operates on a clock? Nobody gets killed before noon?"

"You want to be an asshole right now, Bo? Really?" My face reddened, ready for a fight. He wasn't the only one tired and angry.

"You talked me into this nightmare, Marty! I wanted to go to the cops, remember? We have four people dead, and I'm trying to figure out our limit. What's the magic number? At what point will the 'protecting our family' defense no longer hold up?"

"We haven't killed anyone!" I shouted.

Dante pushed deeper into the back seat as he reached for the door handle

Bo leaned into my face. "We're not innocent victims anymore, Marty! That stopped with Albert and Chrystal. We're players now! Accomplices! Nico died in spite of us—Beard died because of us!"

CHAPTER TWENTY-FIVE

Friday Midday
Alex Danilenko

THE IHOP WAS HALF EMPTY, and we found Alex Danilenko sitting in a corner booth near the kitchen, a mug of coffee steaming in front of him. Bo and I slid in next to him on both sides, locking him between us, and Dante pulled up a chair and sat opposite. Alex's fleshy head and hands poked out of a loose black cashmere sweater. His jeans and shoes were the usual black. He had no jewelry other than the diamond ear studs, no watch, bracelets, or rings. He was aggrieved and dressed the part. We didn't exchange pleasantries.

Dante recounted what happened to Biker Mike in one long fierce whisper. Alex listened carefully, and I could feel a simmering fury radiating from him. I took over from Dante when he started to hiccup, and his eyes teared up again.

"Natalya is your mother," I said bluntly and irritably.

"Stepmother," Alex answered. "But I am very fond of her. We are excellent friends."

"Where'd she find the Russian animal?" demanded Bo.

"He is her nephew, my cousin, but not by blood." Alex's usual rowdy bluster had been replaced by grim sobriety. He spoke in a low, controlled voice and spent the next few minutes trash-talking his "not-by-blood" cousin.

I'll spare you the details and summarize.

His name was Vasili Bobrov. He was a soldier, a *boyevik*, inside the Miami Russian Brotherhood, also called the Miami Bratva. His criminal nickname, or *klichka*, given to all who join the fraternity of thieves as a symbol of their new life, was *Malysh*, which means boy or man-child. It had been assigned to him because he had the unsettling and creepy peculiarity of having a face trapped in adolescence.

"It's a glandular condition," Alex said. "It's his marker."

Vasili started with the organization when he was only twelve, shortly after setting foot on American soil with his aunt Natalya. She had taken custody of him after his mother, Natalya's twin sister, had committed suicide on his tenth birthday.

I wondered if Vasili had been the cause.

His first job was as a *shestyorka* or errand boy for the bulls, who liked to show off by having a kid fetch cigarettes. He officially became one of them on his 20th birthday. He was popular. Leaders in the organization had tagged him early as a potential torpedo—an assassin. It was evident to anyone who knew him that his malignity could be harvested.

The Irish guy, according to Alex, was Brody Lynch, not a lunatic like Vasili but ruthless enough to legitimize the word goon.

"Are our families in danger from that guy?" asked Bo, breaking the narrative; his face was only a hand's width away from Alex's.

"You mean from Brody? No, he is going to Aurora airfield to meet with Natalya like we are. He's got the money they found in the baron's house and will meet us there. Vasili, however, called me half hour ago. He was still in Vegas but boarding a flight back. He is pissed that I interfered by calling Natalya to tell her what was happening."

Bo slumped back against the booth padding, looking like a boxer after a hard round. The waitress appeared, and I ordered coffee all around. No one was hungry. My mouth tasted like mulch, and everything above my waist felt heavy and hard to lift.

After the waitress delivered three more mugs and a full pot,

Dante leaned across the table and said to Alex, "On the phone, you said something about your gun and your cabin; were you involved in killing my brother?"

Alex fiddled with his coffee mug, rotating it back and forth. I smelled shaving cream and impulsively checked for stubble on his naked skull.

"A week ago," he said slowly, "Vasili showed up at my house. I knew why because Natalya called me a few days earlier and screamed that Nico had cheated her. I told her I would fix it, take care of it, and talk to Nico. She said if I talked to Nico, she would cut off my balls and hang them around my ears. She said that bastard needed to be given a lesson. He needed to feel shame."

Alex looked at us, linked his fingers as if in prayer, and explained, "In my world, shame is a big deal…worse than death. So, I never talked to Nico. It is not acceptable to meddle in family business. Then Vasili came here, to my home. We are not friends. I never liked him, even when we are same family, but he is in Miami, and I am in Portland, so there is a positive distance between us."

He thought for a moment, ran a flat hand over his naked skull like he had hair, and continued. "Vasili planned to get back the $10 million and maybe the painting, but he is crazy and came into town too eager and heated. Like a guy with an erection looking for a place to put it—fucking bedbug. I see men like that every night—too eager. Smart dancers at the club know how to work them to get big tips. They are called 'bedbugs' because they're always bugging the girls to go to bed. Dancers say, 'I'm working the bedbug at table nine.' It means…" he snapped his fingers quickly, looking for the right word, "… very persuadable…easy mark.

"That was Vasili, *peregretyy,* overheated. Then, he got me worked up too, and I told him everything I knew about Nico and you, his new business partners." His head rotated between us. "We drank too much, and I think the wheels in our skulls turned too fast."

No one responded. We were all studying the reflections in our coffee.

"Vasili was convinced you were all part of scam to cheat my mother and I didn't oppose him. He said your little gang would unravel like a badly folded footwrap if he applied force." He snapped his fingers again. "He just needed a private place to put the scare into you. That's when I made big mistake and told him he could use my cabin near Rhododendron. He also wanted my gun. I gave my Beretta to Brody and told him to be careful because I changed the trigger weight."

Bo nodded in understanding while I looked puzzled.

"I go to shooting range all the time," he responded to me. "I compete in marksmanship competition. It's a hobby. A new Beretta has about 10 pounds of squeeze, and in a contest, the stiff trigger can throw off my aim just enough to hurt my score, so I reduced the weight of the trigger squeeze to about two pounds, which is like nothing. It's a hair-trigger. If you're not careful, you shoot off your toes. But Brody never told Vasili. Brody never thought Vasili would go cold crazy like he did. *Mudak!*"

He started to breathe faster. "No one was supposed to die in cabin. You think I offer up my cabin to be a coffin? But Vasili never expected Nico. He only wanted you two; to scare you. He thought you're the brains. Erasing Nico is big problem for him. He is not here on Bratva business. Outside of brotherhood, he doesn't have approval to remove people…" he waved his hands about, "…on impulse."

He shook his head. "Remember Monday night? We talk about Nico at club." Bo and I nodded. "Well, Vasili called and told me I lost my best customer. I laughed because I thought he was pulling my balls. Then I realized that fool was not making a joke. That *khui* brings shit into my life and tells me about it like he forecasts rain for weekend. No *izvini,* no sorry—nothing. *My* gun! *My* house! *My* friend! *Blyad*!" Alex practically spit his words. He'd been marinating in a rage since Monday.

Bo grabbed his forearm, held it down, and said, "Why didn't you call Natalya right then and tell her what the hell was happening?"

"Because Vasili told me he spoke to Natalya every day. He followed her instructions, and I believed him like you believed him when he said he'd kill your family and like he believed you when you said you'd get the money and find the painting. We are all here now because we believed each other."

Alex was right. Our deceptions had turned us all into colliding marbles.

"What happened to Nico's body?" Dante asked, keeping his voice muted.

"I don't know. Maybe his parts are spread over the mountain. I don't want to know. Vasili and Brody are not virgins; they know how to make a body disappear."

"Nico's wife told you we were at the baron's house Wednesday night after I talked to her, and you told Harry, I mean Vasili."

Alex hung his head. I could see the beginning of a back tattoo peeking out from under the neckline of his sweater. "*Da*, Charley called me. I talk to her many times. No one else talks to her, so I am again her best friend. What she tells me, I tell Vasili. That baron guy meant nothing to me. I don't know him. But yes, I told Vasili. It was mistake." He spoke directly to his coffee, saying something in Russian, then translated. "My cousin is like a dancer who blames his testicles for tripping. When I heard about house fire the next day, I called Vasili, but he never answered. I think he was on plane with you to Vegas, so I called Brody."

"The Irishman," I confirmed.

"He is more pissed than even me. He is friends with Vasili, but no more." He took a deep breath, "Brody told me he and Vasili drove to Von Baltruschat's house after I told them you were there. I don't know how they got the address, maybe internet. They saw your car in the driveway, so waited for you to leave. He said Vasili had a theory. Vasili figured you guys had the money—or most of it—and you were running around to replace what you spent. He also thought you sold the painting to another buyer, and the baron was maybe that buyer. After you guys left, Brody and Vasili broke into house."

He straightened his back and checked if anyone had moved close enough to hear. "I will tell you everything because I want to show you we are allies." He spun his glossy head from Bo to Dante to me. "You are in trouble with cops, and I am in trouble with cops. We are just bystanders, but it was my cabin and my gun, so I have more shit splash on me than you, yes? I tell you everything I know, but we must trust each other and help each other, we agree?"

Dante nodded, but Bo and I sat silent. We both knew it was too early to negotiate.

Alex continued in a slow, solemn voice barely above a whisper. "Brody said they took the baron guy to basement. His wife was upstairs in bedroom, and Vasili tied her down. He told Brody she was hard to control, scared and struggled while he wrapped her head with tape over her eyes and mouth." He circled his arm around his head.

"Vasili swore she was fine when he left her, breathing OK, spread out, and tied to bedposts. Then a while later, Brody went to check on her, and it was bad news. She'd vomited, and because of the tape, it came out her nose, blocked her breathing, and she choked. Brody said it was a real mess."

We all sat mute with horror.

"With a dead wife, you must kill the husband; without question, there are no other options. Brody told me he and Vasili had a big fight, and Brody was fed up and wanted to get out. Go home. The baron guy had already told them where he hid the money. He didn't put up any fight. He was so scared he vomited many times. The money was in the basement in an old cupboard meant for dresses and shoes."

Alex snorted and sipped his coffee.

"But Vasili said they couldn't leave," he continued. "There were too many prints and DNA. So, they decided to make it look like a robbery and burn everything to the ground. Brody went out to find gasoline to torch the place, but it was around four o'clock in the morning, and there were no open stations for miles. He drove to the airport, found a truck stop, bought containers, and filled them with gas. It took him over an hour, and when he finally got back, Vasili had killed the baron."

I clenched and unclenched my hands under the table.

"Brody was furious Vasili cut off the fingers." He refilled his cup and blew on it hard enough to cause a ripple. "Brody said he only came to Oregon because Vasili wanted help to do a quick job, a favor for Natalya. Brody had never been to Oregon, so he said OK, but now he is neck-deep in shit and dead bodies. He wants to get out of Portland."

"So, no one is hunting our families," said Bo.

"Not Brody, for sure. But I cannot say for my cousin. Vasili is an important man in the brotherhood. He has much influence. Brody told me Vasili is the *obshchak* for the *Pakhan*. That means he is the bookkeeper. He collects the skim from the bosses. He is also the security man for the *Pakhan*, like an enforcer. He can take life without permission."

"*Pakhan*?" I asked.

"Yes, the boss of bosses. The leader of the organization. The *avtorityet*…the *kapitans,* report to the *Pakhan*. But Vasili is here on personal business, not official business; the organization probably doesn't even know Vasili is in Portland—shrinking our population."

"Will Brody follow Vasili's orders?" Bo asked.

"I told you, Brody won't hurt your families. He wants to fly back with Natalya and go back to Ireland. When the *Pakhan* finds out about Portland, he thinks someone will pay a price, and he wants to get out of line of fire."

"Vasili told me Brody is former IRA," I said.

"*Da*. Vasili said Brody came to work for the brotherhood about five years ago after a drive-by bombing in Derry, Ireland. The street whisper was that Brody drove the car. He came to Miami to lay low until things cooled but never left. His wife liked the warm weather."

"There was another guy in the cabin who never said a word. He taped us to the chairs," said Bo.

"I know. I don't tell you his name because he worked for me, and I promised never to talk about him. He was a bouncer at the club. Vasili thought he needed another guy, so there would be three against two. It would look scarier for his little game. I asked my guy to go, and I'd pay him triple for the night. He was just a prop for the show. Vasili told him to look scary and follow along. Vasili never thought Nico would be with you, and when he showed up, my guy got nervous he might be recognized. He was more scared than you and left town that night. I think he's hiding in San Francisco now." Alex paused and drank more coffee.

Dante asked, "Will Vasili come after you for talking to us?"

"He wouldn't dare touch me. I'm Natalya's stepson. She works with the organization and is friends with the *krysha*."

"*Krysha*?" I said it with a fake accent, as if Alex was tutoring me in Russian.

He gave a short chuckle, and I recognized the old Alex. "Marty, I will tell you more than I should because we are friends, yes?" He motioned to the waitress for a refresh. The young girl looked annoyed. Four men were taking up her booth, drowning in a six-dollar pot of coffee. I reminded myself to leave a generous tip.

"*Krysha*...means roof in Russian, like protection. Every organization pays for protection, you know this, yes?" We all nodded like kids in class.

"In Russia, there is no difference between the *vorovskoi mir*—the world of thieves—and the world of business. They're intertwined like mating snakes. *Krysha* is not just payment for protection; it is a whole enterprise, like an industry run by *Vory*, with much violence.

The *Vory* today is not like yesterday, not like in the movies. Today they wear suits and hide their tattoos behind white shirts."

"*Vory?*"

"Yes, Bo…*Vory v Zakone*. It means Thieves in Law. In Russia, *Vory* is like the Mafia in Sicily. The gangs started in the gulags under Stalin but are now part of Russian culture. In old days the *Vory* were hard men who tattooed their resume and rank on their bodies. But over time, traditional ways were replaced with new methods. Still very dangerous but more hidden, more skilled, more…" he looked to the ceiling to find the right word, "…polished."

"Vasili," I said.

"You said Natalya is friends with the *krysha*," said Bo. "You mean the mob provides her protection?"

"First, Bo, mob is not a word you should use for them. It is not respectful. 'Brotherhood' or Bratva is better. In Russian, it means boys or guys or chaps."

"Words I would name my dog," Bo said.

For a moment, Alex stared at Bo in silence. Like Bo, he wasn't used to being ridiculed, but I think his guilt for our mess caused him to retreat from confrontation. "No, I mean that Natalya is close friends with Dmitry Chernyshevsky, an oligarch and good friend of Vladimir Putin. In Russia, he is very powerful and dangerous man. The street whisper is that Chernyshevsky is the protector for Moscow Bratva, which controls the Miami Bratva, that's Vasili's syndicate."

"And he's the buyer of the Raphael," said Bo.

"Yes, I think that is true, but no one alive will ever confirm it." Alex fidgeted in his seat. Perhaps he was uncomfortable saying Chernyshevsky's name. Beads of sweat started forming on his shaved skull, and he pulled up the sleeves of his black sweater, exposing the sword and the cross tattoos. "They have a long history together, back in Russia."

"Your stepmother and this oligarch," I clarified.

"Yes, Dmitry was business partner with Natalya's first husband, the one before she married my father. They were young KGB offi-cers when the Soviet Union collapsed in '91. When KGB dissolved, Dmitry went into private enterprise and hooked up with his friend who had become a gangster, a *Vor*."

"Natalya's first husband was a mobster who protected the oli-garch," clarified Bo, punctuating mobster to make a point with Alex.

"We read about this when we looked up Chernyshevsky," I broke in, sounding proud of myself. "It said Dmitry's business was built with *Vory* friends."

"All Russian business is built with *Vory* friends—some more than others. The *Vory* is Russia's version of American venture capitalist," said Alex with a slight smirk.

"I'm not sure there's a clear difference," said Bo with a bigger smirk.

"So, Dmitry isn't just Natalya's client…he's an old friend," said Dante.

"And she knows Dmitry's hobby is collecting Nazi loot," said Bo, connecting the same dots Nico had.

"Why'd Natalya get divorced?" I asked.

"Natalya is not divorced; she is a widow. Natalya told me that after Dmitry received Putin's oil contracts, he became super rich and powerful inside the *Nomenklatura*, the elites in communist party. Dmitry is so powerful the *Vory* doesn't protect him—he protects them. This created a power vacuum in organization and a mutiny among the *kapitans*. Natalya was almost killed with her husband, but she escaped."

"How'd the wife of a dead crime boss get to be a renowned art dealer?" asked Bo.

"After her husband was killed, she feared for herself, so she took Vasili and came to the States. Dmitry helped her. He, how to say, *dernul za nitochki*—pulled the strings. When they got to Miami, she went to Miami boss, who had worked for her dead husband,

and he took Vasili in as a *shestyorka* and sent Natalya to my father, who owned an art gallery.

"My father, Mikhail, was good man, wise and educated. He taught art history at the University of Moscow. After my mother died, we came to America. We had nothing. My father borrowed money from the Miami Bratva, just a small gang back then. He convinced them to fund an art gallery because it was the perfect business to launder money. My father had many interactions with the brotherhood but also made the gallery very successful.

"When Natalya came to work for him, he was already in his fifties, and I was a young man." He smiled. "A real pistol; I gave my father a hard time. Natalya was still a young woman and a beauty." He projected both his thumbs in the air. "My father fell in love the second she walked in his door. He taught her everything. He became her English tutor and her art teacher. My father proposed to her three times. She said no because of their age difference. Finally, on the third time, she gave in, and she became my stepmother."

"Why are you in Portland?" I asked, wondering if Natalya had banished him.

"My father sent me here after he married Natalya. He didn't want me to be involved with the brotherhood like Vasili. The *Vory* life was a big temptation for me, but their sacred rule is to, how do I say this, forsake the parent. My father wanted none of that, so he sent me to other side of the country. He bought me a rundown dance club in Portland. It was a dump. I renamed it and built the best club in the Northwest." He looked at us for validation.

He breathed through his nose, and it gurgled a little. "Then my father got the cancer like my mother. He took a year to die. When Natalya married him, I wasn't sure she loved him, but how she cared for him and grieved convinced me she did. Natalya managed the business, and she built an even bigger international reputation. One day Dmitry Chernyshevsky called her and flew her to Geneva, where he hired her to broker a deal for some paintings. They rebuilt their friendship. She doesn't talk to me about Dmitry out of respect for my father, but I am sure they are more than friends now. She is flying here in his Hawker 800."

"Did Natalya adopt that animal, Vasili?" asked Bo.

"No, she never like Vasili. Natalya had twin sister who was not a kind woman—drug addict. Vasili's mother never cared for him; she let him run wild. By time her sister died, Vasili was already dangerous. But the bond with a sister is very strong, especially twin sister. Natalya believed Vasili was her responsibility. Also, the sister never knew who the father was. She bartered sex for favors, so there were too many men to keep track. She had sex with American diplomat once and put his name on the birth certificate. Natalya said it was helpful to get immigration papers quickly. So, Natalya became Vasili's guardian. She looked after him, but *ostorozhno*—carefully—like he was a baby wolf. She told me she always worried when the baby wolf grew up...it might turn on her."

I looked at my watch. We needed to get to Aurora. I pushed myself out of the booth to go to the bathroom, and Dante followed me. Standing beside me at the urinals, Dante swung his head around to see if we were alone.

"Funny how Alex told you he was sent to Oregon because his father didn't want him to join the brotherhood. Nico told me that's his standard story."

"What do you mean?" I asked.

He coughed, and it echoed through the bathroom. "Alex came to Portland because his father was scared he'd get beaten or killed by the Bratva boot-boys because he's queer."

I was dumbstruck. "Alex is gay?"

"Charley told Nico, and Nico told me. It's why Charley liked working for him. It's why his club gets all the hot women. He doesn't try to bang them or pimp them. He just runs the club. Women are safe around him—at least as safe as they can be in a dance club."

"He hides it well."

"Maybe he has to," said Dante knowingly. "He has a murderous maniac for a cousin who's a member of the most powerful Russian mob in the country."

"Yeah," I remarked, "what could possibly go wrong?"

CHAPTER TWENTY-SIX

Friday Afternoon

The Hangar

"I'M NOT GOING WITH YOU!" declared Dante in the IHOP parking lot as a panic seizure puffed his grief-stricken face into an obstinate mask. "That Russian maniac will kill me. I know it. I told Mike to take him down, and I switched the painting. He'll want payback. I can't be anywhere near that lunatic."

"Then stay here," said Do. I could tell from his voice he wanted Dante to stay behind. One less person to worry about. "Tell us where the Raphael is."

Dante described the hangar and gave us its number and location. "Go in through the side entrance. A blue Briccone hanging directly over the door has the Raphael taped to its back." His lips quivered as he spoke.

Alex stared coldly at him. "Hiding from my cousin will not save you from him," he said.

"What is a Briccone?" I asked, getting in between them.

Dante straightened his spine and breathed deeply. "The hangar is filled with them, stacked everywhere and hanging from the walls, maybe a hundred or more."

"They're paintings," I said.

"Yes, they're modern abstracts, very Rothko-esque…kind of a poor-man impasto style. Nico had this idea a few years back to become a great artist like Benito. He had no talent except a good eye for color, so he decided to throw paint at a canvas and lather it on with rollers and spatulas, rich, vibrant colors blended...."

"Yeah, I don't care." Bo cut him off. "I've had enough art lessons to last a lifetime. Anything else we need to know about locating the Raphael?"

"Briccone is a pseudonym," Dante continued as if Bo had not spoken. It was his small way of hanging onto some dignity. "It was Nico's joke. It means rascal in Italian. He was going to sell them as high-end carpet art—when the painting has to match the carpet and drapes." He paused, and we all looked at him. Then he spoke to his shoes. "I'll get a cab to Benito's and hang out in the studio barn."

"You do that," said Bo. "We'll call you. If you don't hear from us by nightfall, plan to join Biker Mike in Mexico."

///

We were several minutes down the road when Alex, sitting in the back, strapped on his seatbelt. He'd figured out Bo was as lethal with a car as his psycho "not by blood" cousin was with a gun.

Comfortable with Bo's racing antics, I turned and asked, "Alex, when did you introduce Nico to Natalya?"

"Mothers are not common conversation in a bar filled with naked women, yes?" He smiled, his eyes fixed on the road over Bo's shoulder. "Nico just asked me one day to make an introduction to her. He knew she was an art dealer. I told him to call her, but he said he needed a good referral. I said no because my stepmother doesn't recommend dancers to me, and I don't recommend artists to her. But then Nico made me..." he paused as Bo steered into oncoming traffic to pass a truck, "...a very persuasive offer."

He gripped Bo's headrest and watched the road like he could steer the car that way. "I set up a conference call between them. They talked, and Natalya called me an hour later and asked many questions about him. I said good things, even if they weren't true. I vouched for him, and that's why Natalya is pissed at me."

"You got a Ferrari for your trouble," I reminded him.

"I earned that Ferrari. After everything, I deserve it."

It infuriated me that he'd made a craven alliance with his psycho cousin, and his reckless mouth resulted in Albert and Chrystal's torturous death.

"Did you know about the deal?"

"Natalya told me nothing at first. She is very secretive. Her business requires it. I thought Nico made a deal for his father's art. She came to visit me twice in March. I figured it was to see Nico and maybe visit his father. But I found out later it was to inspect the painting and then, second time, to pay for it. She took me for dinner at El Gaucho's—great place—best cigar lounge in Portland. Natalya doesn't smoke but likes the smell of a good cigar. Someday I will own a place like that."

"It's October. Don't you think it's odd that Natalya took half a year to figure out the Raphael was fake?"

"No." He waited as Bo shifted the car through a series of corners, following an imaginary racing line. "It probably spent a few months in freeport."

"Freeport? What's that?" asked Bo. I could see that Bo speaking instead of concentrating on the road bothered Alex.

"A freeport is a warehouse at an international airport, like Geneva or Singapore. It's located on airport property and is very secure, crazy secure, like nuclear bunker secure. It's how rich people escape taxes and customs fees."

"I don't understand," I said.

"If an item is held in a freeport warehouse, it's considered in transit, like in international waters. Governments don't tax it until it arrives in the destination country. Natalya told me the Geneva Freeport has over a billion dollars of art, gold, antiques, cars, and valuable things. Stuff gets stored there for months, sometimes forever.

Natalya has freeport storage in many countries. She says you cannot be an international art dealer if you don't have freeport storage."

"So, the fake could have sat in a warehouse for the last six months," I said.

"I don't know, but yes, it's possible."

///////////////////////////////////

The airport's low-rise buildings and metal mono-pitch hangars came into sight, and I checked my watch: 1:10 p.m. I scanned the few taxiways and hangar aprons visible from the speeding car and announced I didn't see a Hawker 800, as if I could identify a Hawker 800.

"It's gunmetal grey with pink lettering," said Alex. "Very stylish."

I smiled agreeably.

Bo fishtailed onto the entrance road. "You might want to be careful," I warned him. "The last thing we need is airport security coming down on us."

"There's no airport security here," he snapped back. "I've flown out of here several times. Single runway, small tower, many single-prop Cessnas, student pilots, countless touch and go's."

Nico's space was near the perimeter fence along the northeast row of hangars, furthest from the tower. We drove across multiple aprons passing puddle jumpers parked alongside turboprops and a few charter jets. We veered onto a narrow side road that took us to the last row of hangars, and I spotted a silver Nissan parked in the gravel, facing the hangar with its driver door propped open.

Alex whispered loudly. "That's Vasili. It's a rental car."

Bo hit the brakes so hard Alex's head almost collided with the driver's headrest. We sat silently for a minute, staring at the car and the hangar. "You want the rifle?" asked Bo.

"Yes," I answered before he'd gotten the word "rifle" out of his mouth. My insides pressed on me again. I was suddenly frightened, but it was a prudent fear, wary and alert.

I knew what needed to be done.

Bo turned off the ignition, and we quietly climbed out of the Mercedes. Bo opened the trunk and gently lifted the Browning out. Before handing it to me, he bolted it and unlocked the safety. "I left the scope at home," he said. "It's got a suppressor, which cuts the noise in half, but it's still loud."

Bo looked at Alex standing next to me. "I don't need anything," he said. "Vasili's not going to hurt us. Brody told me he still has my Beretta, so Vasili is probably unarmed. He wants the painting; we're not in combat."

"The last time I saw that crazy piece of shit, he was hog-tied in a bathtub." Bo pulled the .38 out of his pocket. "It feels like combat to me."

I heard rumbling from the hangar, and something banged against the wall from the inside. "That you, Bo? Marty?" Vasili called out. "Come inside, guys. I could use some help."

Bo and I crept to the hangar's side door, which had been kicked open. Alex hung back about thirty paces. We peered in.

The place looked like an abandoned art seminar with a dozen H-frame easels standing haphazardly about. Overturned canvases lay on the ground. Bins of paint tubes had been thrown onto the smooth grey concrete floor, its surface so dotted with dried paint splatter that it was an abstract painting itself. Under a ripped and dirty tarp in the far north corner was the outline of a giant cigarette boat resting on its trailer. Next to it were rows of sculptures, maybe a hundred or more. Behind the sculptures, against the far wall, stood metal racks loaded with plaster and clay molds. Long lines of metal cable had been strung along the steel walls, and hanging like laundry on the wires were colorful abstract images, canvases coated in thickly applied acrylic, like cake frosting, flamboyantly signed "Briccone."

"There you are. I've been waiting." Vasili's words reverberated throughout the hangar. "I started looking without you. I hope you don't mind."

He looked surprisingly neat. His white shirt was wrinkled but stainless, and his cashmere jacket retained its shape. His adolescent face looked haggard, but his eyes were alert. He reminded me of a teenager arriving home prom morning.

"We'll give the painting to Natalya as soon as she arrives," said Bo. Once again, I envied his sonorous voice.

"Well, Bo, I want to give her the painting myself. It makes me look bad if you give her the painting while I'm standing around holding my dick, you understand?"

"I think holding your dick in front of your aunt would be impolite, Vasili," said Bo.

From Vasili's cold expression, I could see he was surprised that Bo knew his name and that Natalya was his aunt.

"You've been talking to my brain-dead cousin."

Everyone stood silent for a while, including Alex, still far behind me in the tall grass. Bo asked quietly. "You have a gun?"

"What do you think," he scoffed, then walked casually to an empty easel.

"He doesn't need a gun," I said. "He killed Beard with a towel rack."

"That was unfortunate but necessary," he responded defensively. "I let Biker Mike live so he could update you. Let you know I will help you search for the painting."

"Keep the rifle on him," said Bo in full voice as he stepped further into the hangar, the .38 in his right hand hanging to his side.

I centered myself between the door jambs and aimed the Browning at Vasili's head.

"Look at the tough guy," Vasili jeered. "Big man with rifle. Have you ever fired a rifle? Have you checked your pants, Marty? Are they wet?" He sniffed the air. "Maybe this time you will shit yourself."

Bo took careful, restrained steps forward. The Russian's baby face began to flush red. The easel next to him had a screwdriver resting on its ledge.

"I think we all need to calm down and wait for Natalya to get here," said Bo. "We can tell her the whole story and have a good laugh." He stopped about twenty feet in front of Vasili. "What do you think?"

"You and your pissing monkey want to embarrass me to Natalya. If you shame me, I swear you will regret it."

"You have most of the money, and you're here when we give Natalya the painting," said Bo steadily.

"Then tell me where the painting is. I want to hand it to her," said Vasili.

My head felt light. No sleep, no food, a gallon of coffee. I stopped breathing. Then the voices started.

He is unpredictable. If he decides to seek revenge, I will not be able to stop him.

Vasili picked the screwdriver up from the easel and pointed it at me. "You think I worry about that loser? He was born without testicles. He just pretends."

Vasili didn't bother to look at me. He wanted to lessen his humiliation by swelling mine.

In my world, shame is worse than death.

Vasili winked at Bo. "Maybe I won't end his wife. Maybe I fuck her instead. Let her see what a man can do for her."

I think I will kill your wife first. I can find her easy. Maybe she walks to her car in a parking lot, maybe with groceries in her arms. I drive by slowly, wave to her.

Sweat trickled down my back, and my shirt stuck to my skin. Vasili looked down at a paint splatter near his feet as if pondering something important. "If you give me the painting now, I might not kill Marty's dog after I fuck his wife," he sneered.

Sometimes, the devil taps me on the shoulder and says...I wish I thought of that.

Vasili stared at Bo with contempt. "Natalya is close. I can hear her jet taxiing. Give me the fucking painting. I want her to receive it from me."

You don't commit suicide by stepping onto the ledge. You commit suicide by stepping off.

The voices in my head shouted to be heard over the roar of the taxiing jet.

Vasili stabbed the air with the screwdriver.

Barking dogs don't bite.

I pulled the trigger. The Russian fell where he stood.

Bo crouched and raised his gun towards Vasili but realized the shot had come from behind him. Alex, standing in the grass, ran towards me. I could feel him coming, and without looking at him, I thumped the rifle butt into his chest, and he staggered backward with a grunt.

Bo stared at me as if my face was bathed in blood. Alex pushed me aside roughly, ran up to Vasili, bent over him, and felt his neck for a pulse while exhaling the word "fuck" steadily like a clucking hen.

I knew there would be no pulse. The bullet hit Vasili where I had aimed it, between his eyebrows just above the nose. It tunneled through his head, exiting just above the brainstem with a spray of blood and bone that formed a pink mist coating the black and yellow Briccone that hung yards behind him, shaking it gently as if a breeze had touched it. The bullet then pierced the thin-steel hangar wall behind the painting, breaking free to destinations unknown. The suppressor dispersed the rifle's deafening crack, and it melded into the roar of the taxiing jet.

Bo's face composed itself quickly. Panic was never allowed to live there long. "You OK?" he asked.

I didn't answer.

"This is bad," gushed Alex.

Without a word, I handed the rifle to Bo, found a ladder, and used it to climb up and pull down a four-foot by four-foot dark and light blue Briccone hanging above the door frame. It was heavy, and as I finessed it down the ladder, I felt something pulling and stretching the canvas. A bubble-wrapped package was tied to its back with black Gorilla tape.

"Let's get something to cover him up," said Bo. He found a white cloth tarp folded neatly on top of a waist-high stack of Briccones, shook it like he was making a bed, and let it descend over the body.

I don't remember much about the next few minutes.

///////////////////////////////////

A woman knocked firmly with a gloved hand on the open door. "Allo?"

She wore a belted black trench coat with a Tiffany-blue pashmina wrapped around her neck like a large ascot. She looked urbane and assembled but in a completely natural and unaffected manner. Perhaps it was her hair, thick and blonde, parted on the right and pulled into a casual bun, or her face, sans makeup, dignified and strong, with gentle creases and sculpted eyebrows arching over and protecting deeply set brown eyes.

She looked at Alex, whose naked head and face had drained of all color. "Alex, *moye syn*—introduce me, please." Her voice was better than on the phone, deeper, huskier, like Cher's contralto. Alex pointed at Bo. "Bo Bishop." Then he pointed at me. "Marty Schott." Then he stood like a soldier ordered to stand at ease.

Natalya's brow immediately furrowed. She knew something was amiss, and her eyes surveyed the hangar and came to rest on the blanketed mound. I felt like I'd been dragged in front of my mother after breaking her favorite vase.

"What is this?" she asked. As she came closer, she saw the red stain across the top of the tarp, and her expression twisted to dread.

No one said anything for an excruciatingly long time. "Is it

Brody or Vasili?" she finally asked, but her voice betrayed that she already knew.

"Vasili," said Bo.

"Let me see him."

Bo flipped the tarp over, exposing what I assumed was Vasili's blood-soaked head and torso. I didn't look at him. Instead, I watched her. She never flinched, and her breathing never changed. Her eyes had no sadness, just a prescient certainty as if she'd reached a foretold destination.

The door creaked, and we all turned to see a muscular, bearded man in a blue windbreaker with epaulets step into the hangar. "Can you give us a minute, Frank," she said to him, and he responded by stepping back out and closing the door behind him. "My copilot."

"I think he saw Vasili," said Bo.

"That's all right," she answered, motioning for Bo to flip the tarp back over him. She looked at me and the Briccone, still in my grip. "That does not look like my Raphael."

I rotated the painting to show her the package taped to its back. She looked hard into my eyes. "Was it you?"

I nodded my head yes.

"Did he attack you?"

I shook my head no.

She stared at a circle of dried paint in front of my shoes and said, "But he put you in a compromising position."

I nodded yes.

"It is a problem, you understand?"

I nodded again. I couldn't speak. I felt drained. My brain had pulled its alarm, and energy poured out of me like souls swarming out of a building, leaving behind a silent, empty structure.

"Where is the money?" she asked.

"With Brody," said Alex. "He's bringing it here."

I could see her mind working. "This will need to be explained."

"Who knows Vasili's in Portland?" Bo asked.

"That is not relevant. What isn't known now will become known. This will not be our little secret. I will have to describe things as they are. To hide anything would only make matters worse."

"Explain to who?" asked Bo.

"The man he works for."

"Will that man want revenge?" Bo emphasized the word *revenge*.

"Maybe," she answered blandly, distracted suddenly by the .38 still in Bo's hand.

The door opened, and the Irishman walked in. He saw Natalya standing by the blanket mound, and his scowl told me everything. "*Privet sudarynya.*" His Irish brogue attempting Russian sounded clumsy.

"*Zdravstvuyte, moy drug.*" Her eyes followed his to the shrouded Vasili. Everyone stood silent for a moment.

"If I tell a story about what happened, Brody," her voice reverberated in the large hangar, "can I count on you to back me up to *brat'ya*?"

"They're not me brothers, Ma'am" He pronounced Ma'am like Mum. "I work for 'em, but no more. I'll be goin' home to Derry,"

"That will be convenient," she said. "I think Vasili was going to shoot Martin, but Martin fired first. It was self-defense. He was protecting himself and the painting. Vasili threatened to put bullets through the Raphael—my Raphael."

"How'd he get a gun, Mum?" Brody asked.

Natalya sighed, not hiding her annoyance. "Why do you care?"

"I don't, but he just got off a plane and came 'ere directly, so people will ask me."

"Oh," she said, bringing a gloved finger to her lips. "Yes, very good. *Spasibo.*"

She thought a moment and looked at the .38 in Bo's hand. "He took the gun from him," she nodded at Bo. "Then a struggle. Vasili will shoot Martin and my painting, but Martin shot first."

"That would never happen," Bo interjected quickly. "That psychopath would never get my gun."

"You are not part of this conversation, Mr. Bishop. And do not refer to my nephew as a psychopath. He is dead now. That is punishment enough." She turned to Brody, "Is the money with you?"

"Two full bags and another 'alf-empty, didn't count it, but it feels between eight and nine."

"Can you ask Tony and Frank to help load it onto the plane? Take Vasili as well. Ask them to help you clean up this mess." Then she looked at Alex. "*Moy mal'chik,* I saw two cars outside, and one looked like a rental. Is that Vasili's car?"

Alex nodded.

"Please return it to the airport now. Then go home. I don't want you here. You were never here, you understand, yes?"

"But I can back your story, like Brody," he said.

"*Nyet!* No!" she said firmly. "I don't want you involved. You were not here and only know things before last night. The final thing you know is Vasili went to Vegas—nothing about that other man—that baron person. You did not call me, or warn me—*vy nikogda ne govorili o Vasili.*"

Alex continued to nod. She may have become his stepmother after adulthood, but he deferred to her as if he were twelve.

Natalya slipped off her gloves, tucked them into her pockets, and walked towards me, stopping just inches away. With a gentle but confident touch, she gripped the Briccone, and I spontaneously let go. We studied each other's faces in silence, and I caught a trace of Chanel from her. She carefully ripped the tape from the back of the canvas, tucked the bubble-wrapped package under her arm, and scanned the hangar, not for better lighting, but for a spot away from Vasili. She walked towards the boat, picked an easel off the floor, and stood it upright. Then she carefully peeled the wrapping off the painting, like a nurse removing gauze from a healing wound.

Bo, Alex, and Brody joined her as she stepped back to look at the portrait of Raphael Sanzio. Watching her unwrap the masterpiece, my brain sputtered like a pull-start mower. My inner voice instructed me to go and look at the painting. I walked over to Natalya, stood as close to her as I dared, and gazed at it with sudden and unexpected reverence.

The portrait had meant nothing to me for the past week. It was just an object in a deadly treasure hunt. But now, a flood of feelings washed over me, and my eyes began to tear up. After five centuries, the painting kept its power, spirit, and energy. I wasn't sure if my emotional rush was for the painting or in consequence of it. I could visualize Raphael painting it in my rebounding mind, his brush charting his tired, doleful eyes.

I turned and walked away so I could blink and regain my composure. I did not want Natalya to see me weep.

"That is the painting I saw the first time," said Natalya in a reverent whisper.

"One hundred million dollars." Bo exhaled a loud sigh. Then he shook his head. Bo was rarely impressed by art, but he was always impressed by money.

"I think we walk now a little," Natalya said to Bo and me. She rewrapped the painting and gave it to Brody. "Please put this on the plane. Be delicate. Treat it more carefully than the money or my nephew, you understand?" She gave the instructions while pulling her gloves back on. The weather wasn't cold enough for gloves, and I thought perhaps they were illusory armor for her, like wearing clothes at night was for me.

The hangar apron was nearly empty, and we walked towards the airport tower and a small administrative building with a sign advertising coffee and donuts. She wore stylish but comfortable shoes, the heels making a soft tap as we walked across the tarmac. Bo and I flanked her, and she began our conversation by saying, "Tell me everything...leave out nothing."

Bo talked, rarely letting her interrupt, briefing her on every detail as if she were our commanding officer. I was self-conscious at how easily he and I fell into obedient compliance. I credited her imposing style and bearing. She was as formidable to me as my wife, and I instinctively knew we could have been friends if I hadn't killed her nephew.

We sat on opposite sides of a picnic table on a small patio outside the coffee shop and drank bottled water from a vending machine. Her patience was as short as Bo's, and she would spool a gloved index finger when she wanted to accelerate the narrative. She was most interested in understanding the countess's story and how the Raphael transferred from Hans Frank, the "Butcher of Poland," to Gerhart Hauptmann, the Nobel Prize winner.

"I am interested in the provenance," she said. "Nico told me some of it, but you have filled important holes. I studied the history of the painting and Hans Frank. I read his son's book. He truly hated his father, but I think his loathing was exaggerated to make himself look a little better in the eyes of history, yes? When your father ships thousands of Jews to Auschwitz and Belzec, I think you work very hard to thin the blood, you understand?"

I smiled not at her comment but at her verbal tick. In a small way, Vasili was still with us.

"There's a section of the son's book," she continued, "where he pours great scorn on his father for leaving his troops in the cold of winter, just days before Russian soldiers arrived, so he could visit with Gerhart Hauptmann. Hans Frank himself wrote about it in his diaries. It never occurred to anyone that he might have given the painting to Hauptmann." She shook her head and removed her gloves again. "Hauptmann would have made it public someday, but he died soon after the war. If Hauptmann had held onto the painting, it would have become the property of Stalin. Poland was part of the Soviet Union for so many years. The Russians would have returned it to the Czartoryski Museum after Stalin died. It is on the market only because that crazy old woman found it. Anyone else, and the masterpiece would have been returned to its owners."

Her insight impressed me.

Bo explained how Dante had switched the original with his copy. She'd already connected those dots, but the specifics still disturbed her. "You're saying this mess is the result of a prank."

Bo and I nodded in unison. Then she asked, "Did you get any of the money I paid to Nico?"

"We think so. It's hard to tell. Nico invested a million with us, but we received only half."

"He gave you cash?"

"We would never take cash. It would raise too many red flags. He wired us money from a bank in Panama."

"Banco Alaido?"

"You know it?"

"It's a popular bank in Panama. I have an account there myself." She interlaced her manicured fingers and placed them under her chin. "Tell me about your company."

Bo and I went into our standard pitch as if she'd abruptly transformed into a potential investor. She asked a few questions, all of them astute and discerning.

Later we told her what happened in Vegas. "I told you not to hold him," she reminded me.

"Natalya, why'd you send Vasili to deal with Nico?" I asked. "Why not yourself? You knew Nico wasn't dangerous."

"No, I didn't know that. I made a reasonable decision." She looked at me sternly. "Three masterpieces were stolen in 1990 from the Isabella Stewart Gardner Museum, and they've never been recovered. Do you know what the reward is offered today for them?"

I shrugged.

"It is $10 million; a Vermeer, a Rembrandt, and a Flinck. That's $10 million for each painting. That is a lot of money, yes?" She took a deep breath and arched her eyebrows. "But the Raphael reward is

$100 million. It is the highest reward offered for a single painting in the world. It is so high because no one believes it will ever be paid, but that doesn't change anyone's motivation. I bought a painting Nico could turn over to the authorities for ten times what I paid him. You understand? That much money can buy much treachery."

I nodded.

"How did you find out it was a fake?" asked Bo.

"I cannot tell you that, and I cannot tell you who my client is. Yes, it is an open secret, but I have never violated my contract by speaking his name."

"Did he tell you the Raphael was fake?"

"He didn't. He doesn't know, even now. If he did, I think you'd have much bigger problems." She tapped a finger lightly on the table like a metronome. "If you cheat me, you steal my commission and hurt my reputation. If you cheat my client, you steal $10 million and shame him. The consequences are much greater."

Those words stayed with me for a long time.

CHAPTER TWENTY-SEVEN

Two Months Later

The Closing

IF IT IS TRUE THAT WE AGE NOT BY YEARS BUT BY STORIES, then I should already be a ghost. I've told this story reluctantly, not because it's hard to tell but because it's hard to believe. It is a confession of sorts, and while there is no statute of limitations for murder, the truth is not always convincing and, absent any proof, invariably refutable.

I survived, which brings its own regret because survival is an end, not a beginning, and certainly, for me, carries no redemption.

I killed an evil man.

I have parsed those words more often than I can count and always reach the same conclusion. The words *I killed a man* consistently drown out the word *evil*, which leaves me, at times, feeling...empty.

Although we never talk about it, I believe Bo resents me for burdening him with unwanted complicity. He didn't pull the trigger, but he is forced to hold the secret; to be a lifetime accomplice.

To my uneasy surprise, our lives dropped back into place somewhat quickly. Although scraped and bruised, we'd briefly traveled through an exotic and violent world and landed back in relative normalcy. Normal, that is, in contrast to the havoc of that week.

//

After our meeting at Aurora Airport, Natalya instructed us to keep silent about what happened. She said the threats to our lives and family would end, and our silence would help her resolve things with the brotherhood. I meekly questioned her ability to prevent retaliation, and she snapped crisply, "Leave it to me!" I was reminded again of how much she sounded like Vasili.

Bo and I left the airport and drove directly to the Lake Oswego police department. We checked ourselves in, and after sitting around for half an hour, we were interviewed separately by a squat detective with a stringy mustache whose name I can't recall because it wasn't memorable, something like Adams, Smith, or Jones.

The detective wanted to know everything about our visit to the Von Baltruschats.

Why were we there?

Because we were searching for Nico and thought perhaps Nico had visited the baron to collect the money he owed to Benito.

How long was the visit?

Almost half the day, including Chinese dinner.

Why so long?

Because the baron was an entertaining guy with many stories to tell.

Did the baron display any unusual anxiety?

No.

Why were we so keen on searching for Nico? Why didn't we call the police?

Because Nico's wife asked us to look for him, and she'd already called them.

Our search for Nico appeared to be quite intense. We even flew to Vegas. Why were we looking so hard?

We're in the middle of raising money, which includes an offer of expensive art. Without Nico, we were stalled.

Did we suspect foul play? The detective didn't say it that way. He said, "Do you think anyone fucked with your friend?"

We had no clue what had happened to Nico.

It went on like that for about an hour. We'd prepped ourselves to tell the truth and exclude certain facts. Bo and I are experts in strategic omission. It's a fundamental requirement in our line of work.

I asked the detective what he thought happened to Nico, and he flipped through some papers and shrugged like he didn't care. Nico lived in Washington State, and the detective's authority stopped at the Columbia River's edge. He called the Vancouver PD, and they told him there'd been no activity on Nico's credit cards or cell phones.

"That's never a good sign," he told me.

The detective was congenial and appeared to accept my explanations without suspicion. It was logical. Bo and I were just two middle-aged entrepreneurs trying to build a business, and we had families, friends, and alibis. There was no reason for the cops to suspect us of anything except poor judgment in selecting a business partner. It helped that the two cases were in separate jurisdictions. Oregon's interest was investigating the death of the Von Baltruschats; the disappearance of Nico Scava was Washington's problem.

The great irony, of course, was that I had killed a Russian psychopath at close range with a Browning bolt-action rifle only three hours earlier, and as far as I knew, two guys, a pilot and co-pilot named Tony and Frank, were still scrubbing his blood off the hangar floor. I've thought about that day and the police interview many times, wondered about my relaxed passivity. How was that possible?

I've convinced myself that I'd sustained a kind of battle fatigue that temporarily suppressed rational fear and braced me with a cool detachment directly after the shooting. I try to revive the feeling whenever I suffer bouts of restless depression.

For a while, Nico's disappearance made headlines: man of mystery, son of a famous artist, local philanthropist, man-about-town, vanished without a trace, D.B. Cooper style. Nico's car was finally found, but nothing else.

Bo and I declined half a dozen interview requests from the local media. The Von Baltruschat home invasion went unsolved. The baron had bragged too often about his many heirlooms, making him a target. The fire destroyed any ability to determine what had been stolen, so few leads were followed. The *Willamette Weekly* wrote several articles about the home invasion, but they were just an excuse to print snarky headlines like "Noble Nightmare," "Highborn Horror," and my personal favorite, "Baron Burning."

The police had a follow-up interview with Bo and me, which a detective from the Vancouver PD attended, but it wasn't much different from our first interview. Eventually, the press lost interest, and the two cases continued to grind along, getting colder each week. Bo and I didn't talk about the investigations much. They were weakening storms, and I suspected that privately, in the dark moments before falling asleep, Bo was comforted with the notion that if push ever came to shove, he'd suffer less than I would.

///////////////////////////////////

Dante and I entered a feeble friendship similar to my relationship with his brother. He never heard from Biker Mike. He did, however, hear from another club member that Beard had gone missing in Mexico. I'd told him that Vasili left with Natalya, which was true, of course, with a strategic omission. The Vancouver police interviewed him about his missing brother, and he told me he claimed ignorance. The police didn't dig deep. After all, he'd been in Vegas when Nico disappeared, and there was no reason to suspect him of anything.

After the interview, I sat with him in Nico's man cave, and he confided that he'd never say a word about his brother's death. For one thing, he considered himself responsible for what had happened and acknowledged he'd committed a crime by not reporting the masterpiece to the authorities, not to mention forging it. He also told me that "spilling his guts *about* Vasili would only get his guts spilled *by* Vasili." I frowned and nodded solemnly. His naive fear of a man he did not realize was dead made me drink another Glenlivet. I pondered the ironies of life, while watching the model train chugging through dusty tunnels in its endless circular journey.

I asked him why he never went for the reward during the many months he'd had it. He said it was always his plan B, but returning the most famous lost painting in history would come with an avalanche of press and publicity. He and Nico had been selling fraudulent art in galleries worldwide, and that kind of scrutiny would kill all chances of collecting any payout.

"I think if I had gone for the reward money, Nico would never have forgiven me. We might have gone to jail, but at least he would still be alive," he concluded, and I agreed.

He told me he'd helped Charley empty the airport hangar and was now teaching her the art business. In turn, she gave him total access to Nico's bar. I noticed he smiled whenever he talked about Charley, and he commented a little too frequently about her natural beauty. Dante had always envied his brother. He'd felt ignored and discounted. I sensed that Dante was about to upgrade his profile.

He also inherited Benito.

Without Nico, Melina left quickly, and Benito's doctor checked him into an assisted living facility, from which he escaped three times. Each time, Benito wandered home, where Dante now lived, churning out sculptures and paintings in his father's name. After Benito's third breakout, Dante accepted his fate and moved his father back home, where he spent his days abusing his son in place of Melina.

Benito convinced himself that Nico was hiding in New Zealand to escape his wrath for stealing from him. Dante did little to persuade him otherwise. The old man's fragile sanity could better manage the idea of a son hiding from him than dying on him.

It was karma, and I smiled when Dante told me the horror stories of "life with father," the latest being that Benito had stopped wearing underwear and refused to flush the toilet because that would wash away his valuable essence.

///////////////////////////////////

Abbie and I spent a few more nights in an uncomfortable truce, and then she packed a suitcase for me and asked me to leave. I was in no condition to put up a fight. She'd borrowed money from her father, which she passed to me to afford a room at the local Residence Inn. She said she was tired of coaxing me off the ledge and wanted time to work through her anger and frustration. She also polished off an old resume and started looking for work.

I often visit the house to talk to the kids and take Boomer for walks. I spent Christmas there. Andrew and Alison are oddly sanguine about my absence. I concluded that they never took it seriously, seeing the separation as a kind of power game between Abbie and me. Throughout their lives, I joked that "mom was the boss," and they now assumed that mom was formalizing her control by banishing me from the kingdom until I accepted her absolute rule. They knew her "rule" required me to get a different job. They are, after all, in their early teens, meaning they know everything and would sooner chew glass than discuss things openly.

///////////////////////////////////

It didn't take long for Paladin to die. All failed entrepreneurs know an essential truth: time spent building a company does not correlate with time spent losing a company. The end of the runway is a cliff, not a meadow, and the crash is immediate and always painful.

Our company coffers had been replenished with Finley's investment. But we'd received the money under the pretense that a Harry

Callahan, now a dead man—not that Finley knew that—made $10 million available for the company. We explained to Fin that Harry Callahan had canceled his commitment, and then we returned most of his investment. We'd already consumed about fifty thousand, for which he kept all the sculptures as payment; a half-million dollars of art from his favorite artist for fifty grand. Fin knew a good deal when it slapped him in the face. We thought it was fair because we knew they were all forgeries.

We tried again to raise capital, but truthfully, we'd run out of momentum. After what happened, our pitch was off. Our enthusiasm had been kneecapped, whacked, and taken for a one-way ride. We killed the sculpture-for-equity program. Angel investors started closing their wallets, especially impulsive ones. Bottom line: even stupid money was hard to find.

Without payroll, our employees took to the exits. Our corporate offices were empty by Christmas, and the "For Lease" sign was up. We still had the glass cage for a few more weeks; the place was a tomb.

///////////////////////////////////////

One day in early January, Alex Danilenko called and informed me that his stepmother, Natalya, would be in town the following Monday and wanted to meet with Bo and me at our office. A chill rolled over me. A festering reality for us was that, although dead, Vasili had never really left. We'd kept his power alive by constantly imagining the tentacles of his lethal clan reaching out for us. We persistently debated how and when Vasili's ghost would exact its revenge. Neither Bo nor I had complete confidence that Natalya could quell the Brotherhood's blood-thirsty need to retaliate. Natalya never communicated with us. Alex was equally obscure. He'd be purposely vague and hesitant whenever I asked if he'd heard anything. I think he wanted me to simmer in worry, to rue the killing of a man he likewise feared and hated but who was still family.

///////////////////////////////////////

Bo and I sat in our office and looked over a muddy plain. That January, Lake Oswego's water level was lowered to allow residents to clean and repair their docks and let the city do sewer maintenance. Four hundred and fifty-five acres of water receded to a puddle surrounded by a bleak vista of mud, muck, boulders, and decaying logs, reminding me of Flanders Fields.

With no reason to visit our office over the past few weeks, Bo and I hadn't seen each other since before the holidays.

"How's Katherine and the girls?" I asked.

"They're OK. Money's tight, and I'm selling stuff." He pulled back his left sleeve to show me his Rolex was gone. "Christmas was hard. Everyone got something handmade; Katherine's great at stuff like that."

I frowned and nodded in agreement. "You think Natalya has good or bad news for us?"

"I don't know the difference anymore, Marty."

"You look tired," I said, and he did.

"It's from too much sleep," he sighed. "I sleep all day, and it's all I want to do. I sit in front of the tube and fall asleep. I watch my girls argue and fall asleep. Sometimes I come here and lie on the couch so no one can see I'm sleeping."

I continued staring out the window, thinking about things I'd already lost. My eyes focused on a distant spot in the sky, and I pointed my finger at it so Bo could follow it. We watched a bald eagle swoop across the lakebed of mushy clay and loam, landing on the pier post attached to the far side of our building. "Look at that," I said, rising and walking to the window.

At the same time, our door opened, and Natalya walked in. "She is a beautiful sight," she said in her firm, throaty voice.

Bo jumped to his feet. "It's the first one we've seen this year; they hang out here in winter and mate."

"Like a winter dacha for eagles," she smiled.

"How do you know it's a she?" I asked.

"She is big. The big ones are girls."

I smiled, a refined ex-Russian mafia art dealer who knew her eagles. I liked her when I first met her and continue to like her now. We shook hands—hers were gloved again—and then spent a few minutes chatting. How were the holidays; why did our lake look like a bowl of sludge; who will win the Superbowl? It felt surreal and aberrant. I had killed her nephew, who she'd sent to terrorize me, but we talked like friendly neighbors.

She'd cut her hair stylishly short. The casual bun was gone. Her black pants were crisply creased, and she wore a cream cashmere sweater and a claret-red silk scarf. Her jacket was a female version of a bomber jacket, not distressed but properly aged from wear. I wondered if her eye for art was as flawless as her eye for fashion.

"Did the buyer finally get the Raphael?" I asked.

"Yes, he did, and he is happy with it."

"The last time you said he didn't know about the fake," said Bo. "Does he know about it now?"

"Yes," she said, looking around for a seat. "I can explain things to you now."

I poured coffee for all of us and then joined Bo on the couch as she sat opposite us.

"All my clients are private. Some are rich...some not so rich. Sometimes secrecy is more important than the product; you understand this, yes?"

Natalya's accent is more soothing than Vasili's or Alex's. She assigns a gentle roll to her R's, and her strong voice is melodic. "Sometimes a buyer wants an item to stay secret from spouse because of divorce. Sometimes the item is for a lover, not the spouse. Sometimes, an item is sold, and the seller wants not to pay taxes, and sometimes an item is not legal. If a purchase is sensitive enough, the buyer will insist the provenance ends with me. No path must lead to them. I provide that service, and I get paid well for it." Her resolute look signaled she was about to share an important secret. "One trick is to ship an item through a freeport. Things can get lost in a freeport if you know what you are doing, you understand?"

"Alex told us about freeports, but I don't know how things can get lost," I said.

Natalya frowned at me, annoyed, and sighed. She walked over to our table, picked up a pad and pen, then sat back down and began drawing boxes on the paper. "A freeport has many storage vaults. Some small, some large." She drew a large square filled with little squares and then lines from one box to another, like a path through a maze. "All items which go into freeport are documented and recorded. I ship everything through Horus Le Coultre, out of Paris. They serve me well. Sometimes crates are not labeled properly, and documents are inaccurate. These are paid-for accidents, you understand?"

We nodded.

"Freeport security is very strong. Many locks, many cameras, like a prison for objects. But like any prison, you can make things happen with money and the right connections, yes?" She shrugged and smiled. "At night, when it is quiet time, and guards, who are not well paid, wander halls, it is possible to move an item from one room to another without notice, you understand? Money can blind people, shift security cameras, open locks, and even rewrite paperwork. Two crates same size can change places like mice trading homes. Afterward, it's impossible to trace where the mice have relocated." She smiled coyly, "What happens inside a freeport stays inside a freeport."

Bo slapped his hands together. "Even if there's a rumor that you bought the Raphael for Chernyschevsky, it can never be proven because the painting evaporates in the freeport. Worst case, if the transaction ever became public, you are the final buyer, you carry all the risk, and the paper trail ends with you."

"I think you must learn not to speak so accurately, yes? I have never told you the name of my client and never will."

"So, who figured out the Raphael was a forgery?"

"Who do you think, Martin? Who can know such a thing?"

"You," I said.

"Yes, of course, me. The Raphael stayed a long time in my storage room because my client wanted to sniff the air and see if anything smelled not right. The whole transaction felt unbalanced. In Portland, Oregon, a stranger tells me he has the most valuable lost treasure in the world. You understand how this is a very odd circumstance, yes? My client is interested but cannot talk to the seller because he is a confidential buyer. Nico Scava was not a trusted source, but I trusted what I saw. I saw the real thing. I felt it in my bones, you understand?"

"So, what happened?"

"My client is a busy and patient man. With an item this big, he was willing to wait and be sure there was no funny business, no ripples in the water, no whispered words in the air, no false sightings. When he was comfortable, he called to say he would make the transfer in a week. I was already in Geneva on business, so I checked my vault. I opened the crate to take another look at such a beautiful masterwork." Her eyebrows arched. "I saw it was fake. Not right away. It was an excellent copy. I admired it until I touched it. It felt different in my fingers, like the difference between a genuine *Russkaya ikona* and a fake *ikona* from a local flea market. I think immediately, Nico, that motherfucker, cheated me."

Bo and I leaned back a little, startled to hear the word "motherfucker" spit from her lips.

"I make mistake then. I didn't think clearly. Anger chewed up my brain. I thought Nico was going for the reward. I think he couldn't go directly to the museum. He needed distance from the transaction. But maybe he found someone who could flip it and share the reward. I called Alex and yelled at him. He told me that Nico had two new business partners. I was desperate and called Vasili. I had to move quickly."

"If your client had found out about the forgery, what would he have done?" asked Bo.

"I don't know, and we will never know. He has never been cheated. You understand to be rich in Russia, you must also be dangerous. To be very rich, you must be very dangerous."

"This whole mess happened because you didn't pick up the phone and call Nico," I said.

"No. This mess happened because Nico's brother switched my masterpiece with a copy," she corrected. "Yes, I made mistake, but not the only mistake."

Bo and I nodded. She was right, of course.

"I felt betrayed and wanted to drink his blood. I wanted Vasili to deliver a message."

She stared into her empty coffee cup and said sadly, "Vasili was never healthy in his head. In Russia, we say, *ne vse doma,* not everyone is home. The same with my sister. She cut open her wrists in a bathtub. Vasili found her on his tenth birthday. He never cried. Instead, he—how you say—threw a temper tantrum. I took him to a doctor one time. He told me Vasili was manic with bipolar disorder. I never understood this. To me, he was just dangerous, and I told people to keep him away from their children and pets.

"When he became *Vor*, I told him not to insult his body like others with so many tattoos, and I told him not to tattoo his visible parts." She smiled. "He did what I told him, and it was funny because my purpose was for him not to disrespect his body, but his purpose was he would not be identified by police as easily."

Bo and I laughed nervously along with her.

"My client, the buyer, knows now. I told him everything, every detail."

She read the concerned expression on our faces. "I don't keep things from him. He has ways of finding things out. It is easier to tell a broken truth after it has been fixed, yes? So, I fixed my mistake and took the action…not you."

"Are you saying what I think you're saying?" asked Bo.

"What is she saying?" I was confused. She practiced what she preached: she didn't speak precisely.

"Yes," she said. "I thought about it on plane back to Miami. Vasili was not in Oregon on brotherhood business. It was my business, and he was making much trouble in it. I know the rules about ending life of a *Vor*. You must have permission. But unlike you, I don't need permission. I am his only blood family. I told them I took my nephew's life because he would hurt more people and destroy the Raphael. The painting belonged to my client, who is more important to '*v Vory avtoritet*' than Vasili, you understand. I made Brody confirm the story."

"They won't come after us," I said, expelling air as if I said, "I'm cured."

"Will they come after you?" asked Bo, looking directly at Natalya.

"No, the Bratva does not interfere in family affairs, and it is good that I have powerful friends to hold up my back. Vasili was my problem, not yours, and I fixed my problem."

I sensed a slight rush as the oppressive spirit of Vasili left me. I felt lighter, buoyant. I began to see a future without him in it. A stillness hung in the air between us.

"Yesterday, I made a deal with Dante Scava," she said, breaking the silence and shifting her weight in the chair. "I will buy his fake masterpieces. I have clients who will pay well for them."

"You want to sell forgeries?" asked Bo.

"No, of course not. In art world, the difference between real and not real is intent. It is illegal to sell a fake painting if you know it is fake. But I have clients who want a fake to hang in their house so they can leave the real one in a bank vault, protected from theft or damage. I have clients who are not rich but want to pretend they are rich. They can pay five figures for an eight-figure painting, hang it in their house, and tell their friends it is original. It is not illegal for the owner to lie; it is only illegal for me to lie." She looked very proud of herself.

"Good old Dante," I said. "He could never attain Benito's brand, but now he'll build his own by becoming the most in-demand forger on the planet."

"Dante told me I must never allow Vasili to work with him. He is very scared of Vasili and doesn't want to see him again." She looked at us without humor. "I told him I could promise him that."

Both Bo and I said nothing, letting the comment hang.

"But I have different offer now for you. It is why I am here. I have important idea. I want to become your partner in business."

Bo and I looked at each other, baffled. "I don't understand," said Bo.

"I want to invest $5 million into your Paladin company and buy part ownership in it," she said in a flat calm voice.

Bo stiffened, and I could see his survival instinct kick in. "You know nothing about us or the business—something's wrong."

"I know a lot about your business," she said confidently. "You explained it to me at the airport. I have since researched you, and your company, and your business model."

"I agree with Bo, Natalya," I said. "Something's not right. Nobody, even an unsophisticated investor, shows up at the door and hands over that kind of money."

"I think you call people like me—*glupyy den'gi*—stupid money," she smiled.

"True," I said but did not smile back.

"You are wrong. I make a smart decision. You make this hard for me, but I will explain so you understand, yes?"

"Please, yes," we both said at the same time.

"My friend, Dmitry Chernyshevsky, the man you insist is the buyer of the Raphael, even though I have never told you that, wants to grow his business in America. Apart from his art interests which are none of your business, he and I want to be your silent partner. Yes, he is a big client, but I also work with him because we are friends, and he trusts me to run his affairs in America. He started a company called Beaumont LLC about a year ago to find opportunities in this country. Last month, I bought into his company with money I took back on plane with me."

"You bought into Dmitry's company with his own money," said Bo smiling.

"I think again you speak with too much precision…but never mind." She waved her empty cup at me, and I refilled it. "After you told me about your company at the airport, I told Dmitry about it, and he liked it very much. The business, and you two men, have attractive features."

"What features?" I said it in her accent, and then I blushed. She laughed.

"Don't be embarrassed. Russian accent has habit of rubbing off on people. I think it is a compliment, yes?" She counted on her fingers as she continued. "Paladin is a national business. It helps out charities and schools. Dmitry is philanthropist in Russia. It is good PR for him if he builds a national business in America, which is helpful to others. He and I agree that the company can grow outside the current idea, buy other businesses, and acquire revenue. My art business cannot grow much more. I have done all that I can. I want to help build something bigger." She sounded like Nico.

"You said we have attractive features." I pointed to Bo and myself.

"You are men who solved a big problem without going to police, which is very attractive to Dmitry and me. A basic code of *Vory* is to never work with police; it is a rule and a sign of courage."

"But you and Dmitry are not part of the *Vory*…correct?"

"It is true. We are not part of Bratva. Never have been, never will be. But that doesn't mean we cannot admire their rules, yes?"

After a while, Bo and I excused ourselves. We needed a few minutes to absorb Natalya's unexpected offer. We walked outside along the lake's perimeter, leaving our guest to watch us through the window. I saw Frank, the copilot, by the building, smoking. I recognized the epaulets on his jacket.

"It's crazy, Bo."

"It's resurrection," he responded.

"There's more to it. She's not telling us everything."

"Even if that's true, why do we care? Every one of our investors has their own agenda. Some want to get richer, and some want to diversify. Some want to manage our business. Some want us to suck up to their insatiable egos. Her reasons don't matter because they've never mattered with anyone else. We don't have to take their advice, instruction, or friendship as long as we keep equity control. We only have to take their money. They vote their shares like everyone else."

"Jesus! Bo! I killed her nephew!"

He looked at the sky, searching its vast greyness for the eagle. "Yeah…OK…better if I'm in charge of Investor Relations." He laughed. "Marty, we've been chasing money for years and never caught this much. It's not just $5 million. Her partner is Chernyshevsky; his pockets are bottomless."

"What if it's dirty money?"

"We're accepting an investment from Natalya. She runs a reputable art gallery. I have no reason to believe the money isn't clean. I have no reason to think Chernyshevsky's money isn't clean. If I buy a candy bar in a grocery store and they give me change, I don't wonder if someone once used that change to buy drugs or pay a ransom. It's just money I received in an honest transaction. If someone committed a crime with it, it was before us, not with us."

I stared at the sodden brown sludge. "Vasili once said to me, 'sometimes the devil taps me on the shoulder and says, I wish I thought of that'…I feel like Vasili is tapping me on the shoulder."

"Look, Marty, refusing Natalya's money doesn't pardon us. If we don't take the money, nothing changes. The police investigations will continue. Nico's body stays unrecovered. The baron's house remains rubble. Beard stays buried in the desert. Biker Mike stays in Mexico, and Vasili stays dead. If we do take her money, none of those things change either. The only thing that changes is our lives get better because we get to build our company. Our skeletons will continue to rattle in the closet either way. I say we go for it."

///////////////////////////////////////

We spent the rest of that day hammering out the details with Natalya. We made notes, which would be formalized into contracts later. She had a strong business sense, and we listened to her. She had complete confidence we would structure things to her liking.

At one point, I stepped outside and called Abbie. I told her we were fully funded and asked her out to dinner. I began to rehearse the speech I hoped would get me back into my house and sleeping next to her again.

Late in the afternoon, Natalya asked her copilot, Frank, to find champagne for us, and he returned with a bottle of Dom Perignon. We pulled out some red plastic beer cups and toasted ourselves.

"This will be exciting," she proclaimed, raising her cup.

"It's certainly unexpected," I responded. "But life is short, so drink up."

She looked directly into my eyes and said, "No, Martin, life is not short. You think it is short only because death is so much longer." She drank her champagne in one long swallow.

After she left, Bo and I sat on the couch where we'd started the day, staring out at the bleak bog that would soon become a grand lake again. It was dusk.

I emptied the remaining drops of champagne into our cups.

"You realize," I said, letting it settle in my mind. "We are partnered now with a Russian billionaire we don't know, for whom shame is worse than death and who could easily have us killed."

Bo gently tapped my cup with his and took a deep breath. "Well then, Marty…we better not fail."

ACKNOWLEDGMENTS

CHASING MONEY IS MY FIRST NOVEL, and it would never have been completed or published without the help and encouragement of many people.

The idea was inspired many years ago by a conversation with my best friend and business partner, Roy Rose, while we were attempting to raise money for a start-up venture. The pressure was so intense I joked that even if someone tried to murder me at gunpoint, I would ask them to invest before pulling the trigger. We laughed, and Roy said, "now, that would make a great story." That got me thinking, and years later became the genesis of this book. The Bo Bishop character is based partly on Roy, and some anecdotes come from our shared adventures. Roy also helped me plot the story arc and answer the constant question, "What happens next?"

The missing masterpiece at the heart of *Chasing Money* is real, as are the details of how it disappeared during World War II. The sources I researched on the painting's history are too numerous to list here but can be found on my website at mbalter.com. You'll also find a list of the sources I used to learn about the techniques used in forging paintings and about the Russian mob.

My 90-year-old mother, Helga Balter, helped with my research for story coherence. She reads German fluently and translated parts of an out-of-print book about the experiences of a German countess during World War II. That inspired me to figure out the journey of the missing painting from Poland to Portland. My mother survived the war as a young girl in Berlin, Germany, and has her own remarkable story to tell. She is a woman of courage and strength, and I'm grateful for her help.

The song lyric quoted on the first page of my book is from "No Such Thing as a Broken Heart" by Old Dominion. The saying, "We age not by years but by stories," is from the poet Pavana Reddy.

I wrote and edited the book over three years, mostly at two coffee shops, JoLa in Portland, Oregon, and Harwood Gold in Charlevoix, Michigan. Thanks very much to Zach at JoLa and Amber at Harwood, who allowed me to occupy a table at their establishments, day after day, for months on end. They are both charming places; please visit them if you're in the neighborhood.

One of my earliest readers was my brother-in-law, Tom Barnes. The fact that he enjoyed my first chapters gave me the impetus to show them to Anne Stanton, and that's when things got serious.

There would not be a book without Anne Stanton's help. She read the early chapters when I was very unsure about my idea or abilities, and her encouragement gave me the confidence to continue. She also connected me with Mission Point Press.

Mission Point Press introduced me to Susanne Dunlap, a great writer (please find her books) and an outstanding book coach. Without her, this book would be much different. Her edits and suggestions were invaluable. She taught me to trim. I lost count of her "this goes on too long" comments, and she was right in every case. I am so very grateful for her help and advice.

Michael and Mary Skinner are dear friends and my two best beta readers. They destroyed all my early drafts with their red pens, and I paid attention. Sometimes it was difficult and ego bruising, but the book is much better for it.

Thanks to my children, Andrew and Ali Balter. Their encouragement and support were fantastic. Ali told me Martin needed to be more complex, and Andrew told me to stop using pretentious words like obsequious.

Thanks also to the many other beta readers who provided

encouragement and advice, including Sierra Mullins, Erica Keaveney, John Griffith, Linda Rose, Nate Raynor, Jason Watson, Valerie Snyder, and my wonderful friend and fellow writer, Andy Anderson. Also, a big thank you to the author Kevin Luby, an excellent writer whose books can be found on Amazon, who took the time to read the finished manuscript and give me some final editorial suggestions.

This book would not be in print without Doug Weaver and the folks at Mission Point Press. I really appreciate your help and support.

And finally, thanks to my lovely wife, Suzanne Balter, who read my manuscript many times and suffered my constant meanderings, discussions, concerns, doubts, and anxieties more than anyone else. She is my harshest critic and my biggest supporter. I take all her input seriously. Thank you, and I love you.

MICHAEL BALTER is an award-winning author and a talented and witty storyteller. Born in Berlin, he grew up in a bombed-out building with bars on the windows and bullet holes in the walls. When the Berlin Wall went up, his family fled to Ottawa and then moved to Detroit at the height of the 1967 riots. During the Vietnam War, Michael served as an air traffic controller at the Udorn Air Force base in Thailand. After graduating college with an aerospace engineering degree, Michael joined Intel Corporation, entering Silicon Valley on the ground floor and building a successful career in sales and marketing. In 1998 Michael was bitten by the entrepreneurial bug and joined a voice recognition start-up that was "this close" to an IPO when they ran out of cash. Over the next twenty years, he became a serial entrepreneur, helping to create and launch new business ventures in Oregon ranging from a toolbox company to a renaissance art firm. One of his business partners was once kidnapped by a Russian mobster, which inspired a portion of the plot of *Chasing Money*, his debut novel. Michael now lives in Charlevoix, Michigan, and is writing the next Marty and Bo thriller. Learn more at mbalter.com